NEMESIS 2

KATHRYN MOON

Copyright © 2023 Angela Timms

All rights reserved.

ISBN: 9798878315531

DEDICATION

For mum and dad

1

Balen glared at Raven. "You didn't think that you could murder my people and there would not be some sort of retribution, did you? Believe me there will be and it will be something suitable. For now we have you as our prisoner, so that is a start.

I should have you publicly executed which those who have lost family and friends would no doubt be happy with. That would be too easy, not enough of a lesson and a waste of a resource. I'm not in the habit of wasting resources.

You are on borrowed time. Think on that. I'm sure we can find ways that you can be of use. If not then a public execution would be an amusing spectacle.

My brother, our leader, is pressing me to produce an heir. You may well come in handy for that. Think on that and what I could do to you. I might enjoy that, you are passably good looking. I don't need to tell you that you won't enjoy a moment of it of course."

Raven tried to struggle but she as too tightly bound. She looked at him with wide eyed horror and he laughed. The guards who were standing behind her were laughing as well and gave each other a knowing look.

He turned to the doctor. "Joseph, if I decide not to execute her this afternoon I will send her to you for inspection and you can inform me as soon as you know that she is not with child and I will make my decision. Keep her heavily sedated at all times. I wouldn't put it past her to try to escape.

Well Raven, I will bid you farewell, until we meet again."

He looked around those in the room and smiled at her. It was a smile which sent a chill to her very soul.

He turned on his heels and the guard followed him out of the room. The doctor smiled. "Now you sleep." He walked over to a table she hadn't seen before and picked up a chrome kidney shaped dish. He removed a syringe from it and looked at the clear liquid.

Raven struggled like she had never struggled before. The doctor put the syringe down. "So you are going to make it difficult, fair enough." He took a large bottle of clear liquid and a pad of cotton wool, soaked the pad, ripped the tape off of her mouth and clamped the pad over her mouth and nose before she could scream. She tried desperately to struggle and to hold her breath but she couldn't hold her breath forever. She took a breath and the world faded into blackness.

Frank headed back to the farm with Crow. He caught Crow's horse as he went past. Ralph and Darren rushed to the horses and took their heads as they lowered Crow down and carried him to the Med Bay.

Frank dismounted and went round to help him. It was dark, the gentle candlelight was glowing in the farmhouse windows. The warmth of home was colder that night though.

Doc checked Crow over. He had a concussion where he had hit the ground, he also had a bullet in his shoulder. It needed surgery as the bullet was still inside. Doc started to prepare the room with Storm's help. They were busy sanitising the table.

Frank called everyone else to the kitchen. Cheryl had the tea and coffee on the table though the coffee was noticeably weaker than it used to be. Frank stood by the door, looking at everyone sitting at the table. "This is not good news. Crow is seriously hurt. The Doc is with him, so he is in good hands. We have lost Raven. She was abducted on our way back from the Mart. I did all I could, but they got away with her in a waiting van."

There was a gasp and Cheryl burst into tears. Shylock stood up to comfort her.

Frank continued. "She isn't dead and I doubt they will harm her. They have been taking women for a couple of weeks now. I don't know if they took her to order or were just taking what they found. We don't know anything about who took her. There have been abductions from the town but we no doubt upset the organisation Rat and Stick were with."

He waited while those in the room took in the gravity of what he had said. Reko put his mug down. "We must get her back."

Frank looked around the expectant faces. "We couldn't pick up a trail. She was put in a van and they drove off at high speed. That road could go anywhere. We can't track her with anything technological so there is no way of knowing where she is. What we can do is go out and start asking questions. Others have disappeared and we may be able to get help in town. As they haven't pushed the advantage of reduced numbers while we were out I would suggest that they probably won't attack us tonight.

For now, there is nothing we can do until we find out who has her."

Lord Balen leant on the window frame and looked out over the compound. Everywhere his troops were going about their duties. Some of them were tending the farm animals. Others were moving food and other materials about. There were those in charge and those who did what they were told and they marched or went directly to where they were going and did what they were doing with extreme efficiency.

He watched as they went about what they were doing. He also watched as a lone workman dressed in the same black overalls as everyone else was wheeling out a dead goat in a wheelbarrow.

He turned from the window and opened a book on his desk. The book was covered in crossings out where animals had died. He looked down and his manicured finger ran down the list and he shook his head. There was a knock on the door which raised him from his thoughts. His voice was steady, commanding. "Enter."

A short man entered the room. His overalls fitted him badly and he looked very uncomfortable. His hair was untidy and there were bits of hay and straw sticking out from it. Balen looked him over in disgust as the man almost shuffled over to the desk.

Balen sat down, calmly, and quietly. "What do you have to report?"

The man choked slightly. "I did all that it said in the book My Lord. It shouldn't have happened. She died, and nothing could save her. Shall I order a raid to replace the stock we have lost?"

Balen rested his chin on the top of his fingers, made into a point and looked at the man. "No, I want you to stop the stock dying. That is seven this week. That is unacceptable.

How are we to start breeding plans and plans if you can't keep the stock alive?" He took the book and made another red mark beside the goat's entry in his book. The man looked terrified. "Please don't have me killed your Lordship."

Balen smiled. "You deserve it. They were perfectly good animals. Can you say anything in your defence or suggest anything that you can do to stop this? The record with the sheep and cattle is not good either. But I accept that we are not farmers and we do not have the experience."

The man looked nervous. "There is a rumour that you captured that woman from the farm where our people died. She knows about goats. I'm at a loss. I've done what the book said but they keep dying."

Balen stared at him. "So you are saying that you are incompetent and that you cannot look after the most basic of animals?"

The man looked terrified. "With respect Sir, I am saying that they seem to be more complicated than the book makes out. I am doing something wrong. I admit that. I can't see what and she may know. Whether she would actually tell us I do not know."

Lord Balen looked furious. "Do not presume to tell me my business and whether or not a prisoner of mine will do as I command. She will give us the information or she will die."

The man looked extremely nervous.

Balen smiled but it was a wicked smile when he saw how awkward the man looked. "You will take three guards and I want you to bring Raven to me. Make sure she is bound sufficiently well."

The man stared at him in amazement.

Balen glared and the man half turned. "Go now and hurry. I do not like to be kept waiting."

The man left the room in a hurry and shut the door behind him. Balen took a sharp intake of breath and looked down at the book. The red marks covered nearly half the page. He closed the book and put it in a drawer and looked about the room. It was sparsely furnished, just his desk, his chair, a chair for "guests" on the very rare occasion he allowed them to sit and a table with a glass top and a statuette of a wolf in the centre of it.

He went to a pile of files and pulled out two. He took them to the desk and put them down, made himself a cup of coffee and began to read. The first was a report from Eric. It was the most comprehensive as Rat seemed not to have a wonderful grip on the written language.

Balen read it and made notes. Most of it was day to day reports which basically set out that Raven owned and organised the farm, she knew about the animals. Frank was security and she had made him Head of Security and given him a free hand. He underlined the bit which said that NEMESIS the computer program had chosen them to survive and to begin again. Beside it he wrote "Not a lot of difference to TransX".

Then there was a page which interested him. Written separately and headed "Possible Dissention". It concerned Raven and Crow. Eric had been aware that there had been a switch, "new Crow" had been physically cruel to Raven and he wrote about her screaming in pain as he had been up in his bedroom picking up something for Chloe. He also documented her bruises and that the next night he had followed them upstairs and was listening at the door when Crow had raped her. He noted her screams.

Balen shook his head. He looked at the wall and took a deep intake of breath and let it out slowly. "Bastard!" He growled. Then he got an idea. A lot of the report was about the defences and stock levels up to the point that Eric left. He took the page about Crow out of the report and slipped it into a folder in his desk.

There was a paragraph in Eric's report which concerned him. It stated that there had been gunshots and firebombs. Balen shut the folder and looked at the cover. That was not what he had ordered and they had retaliated, not attacked.

Raven slept. In her dreams the night before she had left the farm that last time played out in her mind. They had walked upstairs and Crow had turned on her again. She felt the pain where he slammed her against the wall, which opened up the wound on her shoulder, his words lost in the dream as he had thrown her on the bed. The pain as he had forced himself on her again, despite what she had said and done. The helplessness and hopelessness of her situation swirling like an empty pit. She could build the farm but it was destroying her soul. She didn't love him, she didn't want him.

She woke up. The doctor was holding an empty syringe. She was roughly dragged from the chair. Still disorientated from the drug she was half carried through corridors and upstairs. She fought as well as she was able, catching one of the guards a good blow with her elbow before they tied her hands behind her back.

He waited nearly half an hour before there was a knock on the door. It was opened by the short man who stepped inside and stepped aside. Then the guards brought Raven in. All three were similar to the one who had been down in the cell. They were six feet tall, blonde haired with blue eyes. They almost threw Raven into the room. She tripped and fell on the floor. Her hands were tied behind her back and she struggled to stand up.

She looked up at Balen, her eyes showing the pain and humiliation she felt.

Balen commanded the guards. "Pick her up."

The guards looked as though they had been shot. They were enjoying watching her struggle. They instantly grabbed Raven and hoisted her roughly to her feet. She winced as they touched her arms.

Balen stood up and stepped around his desk. The guards gripped Raven a bit tighter. The nearest one to Balen looked up as if to speak but closed his mouth again. Balen looked at him. "You may speak."

The guard looked nervous. "Sir, she has proven to be a wildcat."

Balen smiled and looked Raven in the eye. She glared at him with a look that she would like to rip his head off. "I bet she is. But I also know that she isn't stupid. I have the power to have her killed on the spot or to let her go. No doubt she knows my reputation but if she doesn't I would happily demonstrate. You are armed, she is not. I could break her neck if I wished." He put his hands around her neck but his touch was gentle, not harsh. "After what she and her people did I would enjoy it.

At the moment I do not wish to but my mind can change. I want to speak to her. If I was her I would allow my bindings to be taken off and the tape to be taken from my mouth. I would also understand that hurling verbal abuse at my captor is not going to help. Now, Raven, are you going to listen to what I have to say?"

Raven thought about it and nodded. She was trying to work out how easy it would be to get hold of one of the guard's weapons but decided against it. They looked trained and there were too many of them.

The one who had spoken pulled the tape from her mouth roughly and they cut the cable tie that had held her wrists together. Her wrists were torn and bleeding. She rubbed her wrists which had been badly cut by the bailing twine while she was in the van and glared at Balen.

Balen indicated the chair. "Sit. I would speak with you. Now I am going to send my guards outside the door. They can be back in here in a moment and I would let them do what they wish if you make any attempt to harm me. Are you going to listen?"

Raven glared at him. "I'd like to kill you, but I'll probably listen as I want to know what you could possibly say that would be of any interest to me."

She sat on the chair and looked down at the black boiler suit. She still had no shoes, but the carpet was at least soft under her toes.

Balen's expression was neutral. "You may leave us, all of you. Wait down the hallway and if she does try to kill me you can do what you wish with her. As you know she was the Commanding Officer responsible for ordering the death of our people when they were on a peaceful reconnaissance mission. I'm sure you could come up with some creative ways to make her suffer before you killed her." He smiled at Raven with a sparkle in his eyes.

Raven glared at Balen. "That is a lie. We had been shot at and they had thrown firebombs through our windows. That is not a reconnaissance mission."

Balen laughed.

The guards left, grudgingly, with the Animal Handler.

Balen walked slowly around his desk, keeping an eye on her all the time. He sat down and leant back in his chair. "Do you know who we are?"

Raven also leant back in her chair, trying to look as confident as she could. "Transition X, a bunch of murdering, kidnapping scumbags."

Balen laughed. "In your opinion but in my opinion, I could say that your companions are murdering bastards."

Raven thought for a moment. "Well, I didn't come and attack your home."

Balen smiled and shook his head. "A few untrained foot soldiers on a reconnaissance mission hiding in the woods to work out what was going on is hardly attacking your home. Raven, you know so little but yet know so much. I do what I must for my people. We will get to the bottom of that matter in due course. NEMESIS set up what he could for his people. In a world where the resources are running out, I have to make sure that it is my people who survive. We came to see what you had. Your people killed my people. It is very straightforward."

Raven glared at him. "Firing at my people and injuring them is hardly reconnaissance. Throwing firebombs though the windows so we had to board up and live in a virtual prison is not reconnaissance." She rubbed her head; the cut was scabbed over, but it was still painful. "Firing at me through my bedroom window is not reconnaissance.

I worked long and hard to set that place up. I kept the animals alive through cold winters with no help from anyone. I should be able to say who deserves to live there. I followed NEMESIS' command and took in who he commanded I took in.

What did you do? You sat here in your comfortable office and decided that what I'd worked so hard for all those years should be yours. You send your assassin to put drain cleaner in our sugar and to try to destabilise us by stealing food and trying to blame it on our people. We could have negotiated. We were lucky that Frank was so skilled as it was unlikely that we would have survived the night if he hadn't intervened."

Balen tried not to look shocked. Balen smiled. "They were merely observing you."

She pointed to the scab on her forehead. "That is not observing. It looks like you have a discipline problem."

Balen glared at her, but he was beginning to question the situation. "In your opinion it may look like what you believe is true but we are the ones chosen to survive. You may well have been chosen by NEMESIS who had committed mass genocide to create his own world. We lived in faith that when something happened we would be provided for."

Raven raised an eyebrow. "But you aren't being provided for, are you?"

Balen hesitated. "What makes you say that?"

Raven pushed her advantage. "Because you wouldn't be talking to me now if you didn't want something. You can take what you want. I have no doubt. You can be like your father and impregnate me, like he did to all those women who had no idea what he was doing. You can be the bastard even your people call you. You must want something else that I can give."

Balen was thinking about what she said. "What are you talking about? What do you mean by that?"

Raven laughed. "You are acting as if you do not know. Why do you think all your guards look so similar? I bet they work for LexCorp, ah no, your Brother set up Transition X so no doubt your father provided him with followers. Hold on a minute, is there a reason they call you a "bastard"? You look nothing like the guards."

What she said struck a real blow to him. He didn't react. "Raven, I have no idea what you are trying to imply. I have a reputation so no doubt everyone does call me a bastard. It is probably well earned."

Raven was now putting the pieces together. "You obviously know by now from Rat and Eric that Chris was Brand's girlfriend. Chris' father was

Senior Management in LexCorp and so Brand spent time there and he overheard things. They were talking about the clinics where anyone going for IVF got impregnated with your father's sperm, not their partner's. Anyone who went there to get pregnant had his child. They spoke about his fetish for raping the women while they were unconscious having other procedures. Don't tell me you don't know you bastard!"

Balen looked visibly shaken. He needed to change the subject. "Well, that cuts through a lot of the pleasantries. Do you know our beliefs?"

Raven glared at him. "You believe that if you sit about on your butt at the end of days everything you ever wanted will be given to you. In the meantime other people have to work to support you and to create that something so you can take it."

Balen choked slightly. "Well you don't mince your words. On the face of it, it could look like that. For some of our members it is like that. I and many like me had to take a step back from what we could have done to be successful by the old world's standards. We became Healers and used our psychic abilities. We looked after the earth in the only way we thought possible, by living as lightly as we could. Others, like my brother, took a more martial approach. It is true that those of us who took the spiritual path didn't contribute to the capitalist machine as we didn't want to fuel the fires of the world's destruction. We didn't help.

I can only speak for those in my compound here. I want my people to live. Many are not martial in their attitude and we have been blessed that my brother has provided us with a force more than adequate to keep us safe. To look after my people I must feed and clothe them. I must make sure they are educated and make sure that they multiply so that there are generations to follow with the right beliefs so things don't go back to how they were. Is that so wrong and is that so different to what you are doing?

Our people went out to have a look and you gave the order and had them killed. I sent my men to assess what you had, you buried them."

Raven almost smiled. "I have told you. Firing at us and throwing burning missiles through our windows is not following your orders. I don't call contemplating putting drain cleaner in our food passively looking around."

Balen looked down at the report and opened Rat's file. He read down the scribblings about guard rotation and food stores. He then found a bit he had not yet read. Rat had written about stealing the food and hiding it in Crow's room, and the room next door.

He turned to Eric's folder and skim read the text. Part way down the second page Eric had expressed a concern that Rat had contemplated putting drain cleaner in the food which would have killed him, his partner, and his baby.

Balen closed the file slowly. "The orders were to watch what was going on, assess your strength and bring me back information. If it was possible, they were to cause confusion to see how you deal with it and to make you doubt your members to see how strong the unity there was."

Raven looked down. "Did Eric mention that he tried to kill Frank?"

Balen was now looking visibly shocked. "They were supposed to destabilise you so that you would accept our help. I certainly did not give such an order. Eric came to our meetings a broken man. I read his file and as he was enthusiastic to help and he had the perfect cover story I sent him in to spy on you. Not to harm anyone.

His wife was cheating on him. He even believed his baby was fathered by some other man. What right did they have to be saved?"

Raven looked down. "I had that decision to make when I first spoke to Cheryl. She told me the story and although obviously I couldn't approve, they had a right to life. It wasn't your decision to make either."

Balen breathed out swiftly. "Some computer program has the right to decide the fate of humanity and that is alright with you? Is it acceptable that this thing which has no life, soul or conscience can kill millions to provide a so-called solution? It is just an acceptable solution because you are the ones being saved?"

Raven was about to speak but closed her mouth. Put that way she agreed with him.

Balen saw this and smiled slightly. "We aren't so different. I have the same day to day problems as you do. I've got a bunch of people here who know nothing about keeping animals or getting on. I have crops to plant, machinery to fix and people to feed. I also have Archangel's guards here and they all have mental problems and are hard to control. I have to be a bastard as they are rabid dogs, and they need a bastard to control them. Let's get that clear right from the start. I did not send Archangel's guards after you. I sent the normal folk who are part of Transition X.

What I brought you up here for was to force you to help me. After what I've heard I'm now asking you to help."

Raven choked. "So, the great Bastard Balen needs my help? Go read a book. I did."

Balen smiled. "We have followed the books to the letter but there are things missing from the books aren't there? Only experience can make up for that and I'm not prepared to see more animals die while we learn. I do not want to intimidate you into doing this. I want you to help to save the animals." He opened the book up with the dead marked in it, turned it around and pushed it towards her. "I want to show you something. We've been following "the book" and we are still losing animals, look at the losses."

Raven took the book and looked at it. Her eyes ran down the columns and the crossings out. The red ink stood up starkly on the white paper. "So what you are getting it wrong. Big deal." Now she was testing him.

Balen looked horrified. "Don't you care? Do you want me to take you down and show you that dead goat this morning!" There was a genuine look of upset in his eyes, almost tears.

She looked into his eyes and felt a jolt of electricity which ran through her, a warm feeling. That was genuine concern. The cold eyes she had seen earlier were gone. She couldn't look away. She was hating herself for what she felt but she was questioning her opinion of him. She whispered. "Speak to me. Tell me the truth. All of it."

Balen smiled. All of a sudden he looked exhausted. "My brother was certified insane before Transition X was set up. You are dealing with someone with no conscience and who has multiple personalities. So everything has to be very clear cut and documented. What "Brand or Crow" heard has confirmed my suspicions, he is my half-brother. Same mother but I neither look like him or have his fascist beliefs. His rules are outrageous. Yes he would kill your people just because they were in the way. But those people were there on my orders, not his. If he had had a bad day or is breakfast had been served cold he'd take it out on someone.

He might be my brother, but he is the unquestionable ruler of Transition X. I am bound by his rules too. But, I have adapted them.

I'm telling you this so you understand the fragile situation you are in. I must appear to be ruthless. If that takes having you executed, I will have no choice.

I never asked for all this. I was happy to write a few poems and just get on with life. We were drunk one night. I'd been ranting about the planet and for a laugh we put together the idea for an organisation which would look after the planet. We wrote what we thought was a perfect organisation for the perfect world. Or to build one. Of course at four in the morning after a lot of brandy, a few drugs and with student ideals we had picked up at University it seemed like a great idea.

Father found the notes in the morning as we'd left them on the coffee table. He was going to throw them on the fire, I'd come into the room at that point, but he hesitated and thought about it. LexCorp was already capitalising on the Environmental Surge and had bought out the sustainable energy producers. They already owned the power companies.

I'd heard rumours and I'd overheard stuff to about his clinics. The guards do look similar and like my brother they are unpleasant and nasty fanatics who would cut your throat if it furthered their cause. Looking back it makes sense. He sponsored those children with benevolent grants and indoctrinated them with his ideals as LexCorp became a Mega Corporation. There could be no objection to what LexCorp was doing as he'd already manipulated Transition X to be his "Eco Arm".

I can see it now. Many are sociopaths. Many are insane. They have found their vocation and a world where they fit. How do I control the ones here other than to be a vicious, bloodthirsty, unreasonable son of a bitch, like my brother.

I'm asking you Raven, help me. I'll say please. I don't want to see any more animals die." He could not look away. He was feeling things which he had never felt before. The feeling was intense, electric. He shouldn't have told her all that, but he wanted her to know. Suddenly he felt so lonely.

Raven could not look away, neither could he. The feelings she had were intense. She smiled.

He shook his head. "My people want you dead or at least punished. My brother has made his command. I can control them because they are afraid of me. If I don't keep a firm hand, they will no longer be afraid of me and those who are trying to do the right thing amongst the rest will suffer.

My brother gives me a certain amount of leeway because I'm his brother and he has a misplaced belief that we are the same. I get a certain autonomy that other leaders do not get." His eyes looked sad.

Raven smiled. "You have a problem with the animals. I need to see how they are kept and what they are fed on."

Balen smiled. "So you will help?"

Raven nodded. She was confused but she didn't feel scared anymore. "You have a problem; I mean a real problem. Look at those numbers. They aren't realistic if you are using the right methods. What is your housing like?"

Balen looked stunned. He was that boy back in his university days again who was enthusiastic about doing things right. He didn't think, he walked around the desk and held out his hand. She took it, and she stood up and he led her to the window. "Here, come and have a look."

She stepped around the desk and moved to stand beside him at the window. He stepped closer to her. She could feel the electricity, she could feel him there. She tried to push away the thoughts which rushed into her mind, she wanted him! He was now just a man, concerned about his animals, pointing at a barn. If she had had that enthusiasm while she was at the farm it would have been a whole lot easier for all those lonely years.

He was confused. He felt her close to him, felt the electricity and tried to push away the thoughts he had. He wanted her. He took a deep breath. "We have a big barn there where we keep the animals. They are turned out into that field and come in at night."

Raven looked down on the buildings and the people going about their duties. As she looked it seemed it was not so different, he was right. "Have you separated out the animals? What about the grazing? Did you take this place over and if so how heavily was it grazed? How long have you been here? Do you worm them regularly?"

Balen looked down at her with a certain admiration. She was standing beside him, close to him and looked up at him. All animosity was gone, and he felt that feeling and those thoughts kept coming back. "We've been here about six months, but it was a battery farm before then. Sheep were kept in those fields for years without a problem."

Raven thought. "That might be your problem. Did you muck out and re-lay the beds when you came here?" She looked at the yard and noticed the hay and straw stacked in the yard. "Is that waste straw and hay?"

Balen shook his head. "No that is our stock of feed."

Raven shook her head. "Out in the rain? Don't you know that wet hay produces a mould which kills goats. Never get the goat hay wet."

Balen looked stunned. "It was the best we could get."

Raven smiled kindly. "It may well have been and I'm glad you did but put it in the rain and you would be kinder to cut their throats. The best isn't always good for goats. They are browsers not grazers. You need the coarse stuff and other stuff in it. Lucerne if you can get it. What land do you have here?"

Balen shrugged. "As much as we like, all the farmers are gone."

Raven thought about it. "So, you can grow your own fodder, better long-term plan. Lucerne will bring your milkers on. Always fresh and never stored anywhere damp. Looking at your figures it is mostly goats you are losing.

If you are bringing in animals, they could be infected. I bet you have been taking them from all over."

Balen nodded.

Raven shook her head. "And no week's quarantine? Do you have antibiotics?"

Balen looked horrified. "We don't use the stuff. For the goats? Are you serious?"

Raven looked up at him. "I bet you don't worm either?"

Balen shook his head. "It's a chemical, we are organic here."

Raven smiled. "I thought that way once. I gave my animals what I thought was the best for them and they died. There are plants which can be introduced but they probably aren't there now." She looked out over the field. There was a windbreak hedge which was completely Leylandii. "And that hedge, that tree is poisonous to goats."

Balen was looking confused.

Raven had forgotten he was her captor. "Don't worry, I'll sort out a plan for you if you would like me to. We could take a walk and look at the pasture, if you introduce some other plants, you'll up the natural mineral content. Also you'll need to get zinc and copper for the goats, but the sheep can't eat copper."

Balen looked over at her. "We thought that the goats needed special feed, so we got that, we gave that to the sheep too."

Raven shook her head. "Well that explains the sheep deaths, they can't eat copper and that is in goat feed."

Balen hadn't let go of her hand. He hadn't realised that, but he led her to the table. There was a plan of the place laid out. She looked at the plan and divided off a three-field system. She pointed to the land outside. "If this hasn't been grazed you could move stock off onto there."

She reached for a pen at the same time he did and his hand brushed against hers. She jumped, so did he and they looked at each other. The energy between them was intense. Balen slipped his muscly arm around her slim waist. She looked up at him. He bent down and kissed her. The energy was running like fire between them. He wanted her so much but it was so, so wrong.

He backed away. Raven too. She stood in the room, confused and not sure what to say. "So what happens now? I suppose you return me to my cell?"

Balen smiled. "I will have to. There can't be any other way as most of the people here want you dead. I am going to call for Rat to be brought here and I'm going to interrogate him. If he confesses then we can look at changing things. It doesn't change my brother's order and I have no idea how to get around that. He is his father's son. He expects. Well you know what he expects. That I will not do. I never have and I never will."

Raven took a deep breath. "While I was unconscious did the doctor do anything to me?"

Balen looked shocked. "What do you mean?"

Raven was trying to formulate a plan. "Did he do any sort of an examination?"

Balen thought about it. "Were you still in the chair when the guards came and got you?"

Raven smiled. "Yes."

Balen nodded. "Well he wouldn't have had time. He would have taken you to his Medical Facility and then you would have been put in a cell. What are you thinking here Raven?"

She took a deep breath. The memories of the horrific night at the farm where Crow had hurt her were still fresh in her mind. "Balen, there is a way. Crow was a complete bastard..."

Balen smiled kindly and put his arms around her. "I know, I've read the report. He raped you when he first became Crow. I will make him pay for that if I ever catch him."

Raven shut her eyes. The imagery of the night before almost burnt on her retina as she remembered. "Last night as well."

Balen held her tighter, his hand on the back of her head. "Oh god, he is going to really suffer when I get my hands on him."

Raven looked up at him. "Thank you." There were tears in her eyes. "But you are missing the point. If the doctor hasn't done a physical check how is he going to know that it wasn't you who raped me? Believe me, there are things I'd like to do to Crow for that. It haunts my dreams. What he did is ripping at my very soul. There are just two blessings here. Firstly it is not a time that he could have got me pregnant and that it could be used now. I hurt, a lot, he's done damage. I've been bleeding a lot. That should convince them that you have. You know…"

Balen couldn't speak. He held her and all he could think about was the various tortures he could try out on Crow. Then he realised what she was saying. "You are right, we could use it. If Rat confesses and we can put forward a plan where you are under my command or even if you defect."

Raven looked up at him. "If you promise not to harm my people in any way, I will do what you ask."

Balen thought about it. He had been planning to attack the farm and take the animals. He nodded. "I promise." His eyes then looked cold. "If you think that you can use this against me you will not be able to. I am going to have to return you to the cell and as far as anyone knows, until we get Rat's confession, you are my prisoner. I will have you taken to a room now so that I can "comply with my brother's wishes". It will steady the unrest here.

Afterwards you will be working on a plan, and I will insist that you do it here. You will be brought back here later this afternoon to put a plan together. If you can make this look realistic, we may well have a chance here."

Balen looked down at the plans on the table. "Guards!" He had to get them in there, his emotions were running high, and he needed to think if this plan was going to work. He indicated she should return to the chair. He sat down behind the desk as the guards stepped into the room.

Balen's look was cold. It chilled Raven as she had seen the other side of him and the contrast was stark. "Take her down to Room 3. It is time that we complied with my brother's wishes." He managed a wicked smile. "Don't damage her and leave her dressed. I don't want the mother of my child harmed in any way. If anyone is going to hurt her, it will be me."

The guards were about to roughly drag Raven out of the room, but they grabbed her arms. She winced as they were still bruised from what Crow had done. They took her down to the cells and threw her into a room with number 3 on the door. Unlike the other cells it had no observation window in the door. The room was empty other than a chain on the far wall. The guards fastened her arms above her head to the chains on the wall.

The guards stood around her laughing. They fell silent when Balen walked in. "Bring me a towel and water." He waited while a bowl of water and a fresh white towel was fetched for him. "Now leave me. I will not be watched."

The guards looked disappointed, but they left. He went to the door, opened it, and made sure that they were down the corridor. He then took the key from the outside and locked the door on the inside and left the key in the lock, blocking the hole.

He then walked over to Raven who was physically shaking and crying. He whispered. "Be calm, I won't hurt you. We know what we are doing, and it is the only way those bastards won't kill you in the night." He undid her jeans and pulled them down. He then removed her knickers. He pulled the bloodied pad from them, rolled it and hid it in his pocket and threw them on the floor. He looked down at her. "I'm sorry, this must look authentic." He kissed her and put his arms around her.

He tore her blouse open. He then took a knife out of his pocket. She gasped as he cut her blouse from her.

He was shocked as he saw the bruises on her arms and thighs. Blood was running down her legs. He took the towel and wiped the blood gently, staining the towel. He whispered "That should look convincing enough. Why are you shaking? I won't harm you!"

Tears ran down her face. "I can't help seeing… last night… I…" He kissed her, gently and passionately. "I will never, ever hurt you Raven. What he did was so wrong. Now, do us both a favour and scream!"

He threw the slashed pieces of her blouse onto the floor.

Raven screamed. Balen then slapped the wall which made a reassuring "thunk". Balen smiled at her, shook his hand as it hurt and mouthed "ow!" and shouted. "You bitch, you deserve this. As I said you are not going to enjoy this."

Raven screamed and then added. "You bastard!" In her head she was screaming at Crow, what she hadn't been able to do on the night as she hadn't wanted to cause chaos or upset the status quo. Raven screamed and that went on for half an hour. Balen smiled wickedly. "This is going to do my reputation no harm at all. Go on scream and we'll wind this up." She screamed.

He thought about pulling trousers on again, but he had to leave them. "Sorry about that, it has to look real." He kissed her gently, and he stroked her cheek then he whispered to her. "I'll never make love to you until the day you ask me to. I have never raped a woman and I never will."

Raven looked exhausted. The tears were rolling down her face.

Balen took the towel and wiped her thighs so that there was more blood on it and threw it into the floor into the dirt. He then undid the top of his boiler suit. "Guards." As they came in he was fastening the top button of his boiler suit. "Now take her to the doctor. I am sure that my brother will want confirmation that his wishes have been carried out. Nobody touches her. I will continue with this until we know that she is carrying my child. Do not harm the mother of my child or you will have me to answer to. Only I can do that. Put a boiler suit on her, she is my property now."

The Guards looked at the bloodied towel on the floor and its meaning wasn't lost on them. Neither was the blood running down her thighs. They unchained her, and she struggled but she had no fight left in her.

Balen smiled wickedly. "Let the doctor make his report and I want her, bathed, dressed and brought to my rooms."

The guards half carried Raven to the doctor. They stood and watched as the doctor made his examination. As he started his examination he looked up. "What a bastard. That was vicious and more than I'd expected. Tell everyone, he has taken what happened out on her alright." He then went and got a bowl to wash her injuries. There was an old, half closed bullet hole which was bleeding profusely and when he checked, the bullet was still in place. He removed the bullet, without anaesthetic but Balen was too far away to hear her screams. The doctor frowned as he recognised the bullet as one of theirs.

Crow woke up in the Med Bay. His head was aching, and he had a pain in his shoulder. He was bandaged but he sat up. The Doc was watching him. "Back with us, that is good. Now I have some news and I'd better tell you before you find out another way. We lost Raven."

Crow looked stunned. "You mean she is dead?"

The Doc shook his head. "Abducted. It was organised, there was a van. Frank tried to catch them, but they were too quick. She's gone and we have no way of finding out where they went."

Crow looked devastated. "So who is in charge now?"

The Doc scowled at him. His fears played out. "Now that she is gone the second in command would be Frank. Frank is now in charge."

Crow scowled. "We'll see about that. As her partner I am in charge. I claim that right."

The Doc didn't want to get involved. "Frank is going to the Mart at first light. You took a bullet so I wouldn't recommend that you go."

Crow glared at him. "I need to find her. I will be going."

Crow and Frank left the farm in the early morning and rode out for the Mart. They took the route which kept them on the road rather than across country as Crow had to ride carefully. That took them nearly two hours. They travelled in silence, each lost in their own thoughts.

When they got to the Mart the place was as crowded as usual. The queue stretched down the road. They joined the end of it and it took them another hour and a half to get inside. Once inside the Mart was the same as it had been before, the entertainers were playing music and the traders were shouting to sell their wares.

Frank went straight over to Carl who had just finished sorting out a dispute between two stallholders. He looked up when they came over. "No Raven with you today?"

Crow looked down. Frank walked right up to him. "No, she was taken by someone yesterday. They were lying in wait for us on the way home."

Carl frowned. "That's the tenth in three days."

Frank was not quite paying attention. He was more interested in a young lad in a blue bomber jacket who was more interested in the conversation than he should have been.

Crow stared at Carl intently. "Have you heard anything about who is taking them?"

Carl shook his head. "It seems to happen pretty randomly. Raven is the only one who was taken outside the town though."

That got Frank's attention. "So whoever is taking them is coming into the town?"

Carl raised an eyebrow. "It would appear that is the case. There is also some speculation that there are people who are using this as an excuse to remove certain rivals. It's just a rumour but it is rife around here. Men folk are now taking really good care of their women folk and women folk are becoming very careful about watching their rivals. You will notice that groups are forming within the town. Families are uniting with other families and they are starting to build permanent defences around their homes. This new way of living is changing everything. They are still buying but there is an air of nervousness which is bad for business.

The Road Pirates are becoming less common though. Rumour has it that vigilante groups are going out and dealing with them. If you want more information, I would have said go to the pub but that burnt down last night."

Frank looked stunned. "What happened?"

Carl sighed. "There was a riot outside and a stray firebomb went through the window and wrecked the place. The owner is going to set up what he has left in our compound. We have found him some space over there in the corner next to the cafe. It will take a day or two, but he'll at least be safer."

Frank was watching Carl now. He smiled. "That must be good business for you, having the pub here too?"

Carl smiled. "These are dangerous times and we're able to offer a safe place both for them to work and for people to enjoy a drink. We could have set up in competition but it made more sense for them to move in here. It's in a bad way but yes, it is good for business. By the way, when can we expect some pork? Plenty of people have put themselves down for some. I'm planning an auction as meat is getting difficult to get hold of. I'll be able to give you a good price."

Voices were raised over the other side of the compound. Carl looked over. He put a hand on Frank's arm. "Sorry mate, look I've got to go and deal with that. Look, I like her and I wouldn't want anything to happen to her. If I hear anything I'll let you know." He then ran off to deal with the problem.

Crow looked at Frank who was watching the boy as he disappeared into the crowd. He smiled wickedly and followed him. Crow followed Frank and they all ended up in the cafe. The boy was sitting with his parents, and they were chatting. Frank and Crow were watching them.

Carl had finished with the troublemakers and went up to the office where his father was handling some paperwork. "Dad, did you order a collection involving Raven? She was taken last night."

His father almost dropped his paperwork. "You have to be kidding me. She's one of the most useful people we have round here. Never in a million years. This is a disaster. Someone else is working our patch. Or the boys were doing a bit of freelance work."

Carl looked confused. "I thought you had all that under control."

His father got a small pocket book out and checked down the names. "I had it very much in hand. We managed to remove all the dead wood and the profits were good when selling them on. They go to the markets in the North as you know. I never organised a collection for her."

Carl frowned. "Do you think your buyer got greedy? Perhaps someone is working freelance?"

His father shook his head. "Not likely, I'd supplied his quota, and we have an arrangement that I don't let him have my good customers. He knows that and wasn't worried about it. Well he wasn't until now. Something else is going on. I had a report this morning that Alf and Charlie got blown away last night. I know they had been up to a bit of scamming, and they had taken one or two, but they weren't supposed to be working last night.

Thinking about it the timing and distance could be right for them to have taken her. I wasn't paying too much attention. I was too busy trying to deal with the riot. I think that went rather well, don't you?"

Carl smiled. "Too right, removing the pub and taking it under our wing, smooth move dad. Now everyone must come here and we're the heroes for saving it. Do you think it's about time to think about putting our prices up?"

His father sighed. "Not quite yet. We've got to ensure our suppliers first. Losing Raven is a blow as her lot haven't been with her long. No way of knowing if they can cope without her. We have to hope they have things under control enough to keep the meat supply coming."

Carl shrugged. "Any chance we can get her back for them?"

His smiled. "Not a hope. I've had Alf and Charlie followed for a while now as I thought they were up to something. There was some sort of message passed when the Transition X people came to pick up an order. It wasn't their usual man. He's a nasty bit of work. That means that Lord Balen could be involved. If he has her, he can keep her. I'd rather not wake up and find this place a smouldering bombsite. I'd not tell them either as if they go after her we'll lose that farm for certain and they are a resource."

Carl looked up. "If it is Lord Balen, too right. It is a shame, she was a pleasure to deal with."

His father was looking at the paperwork. "There'll be others. Don't get attached to the punters boy, it's not good for business. I'll say it again, don't get any ideas of telling them either as if Lord Balen found out there would be nobody here who could save you."

Carl shook his head. "I won't dad but why are people so afraid of him?"

His father looked up. "He's an evil son of a bitch. That's by reputation from what people have seen him do. People have their own stories, but they all seem to say the same thing.

He's a military fanatic though he never joined up. He'd slit you open or get someone else to do it for him. Just be thankful he's not based around here. He has a base near here but as far as I know their main base is in England. If taking Raven will keep him away, then we are all safer in our beds."

Carl looked nervous and left the room. He stopped on the stairs and looked out over the Mart. People were buying, people were selling, and everyone seemed happily going about their business. He saw Frank and Crow over by the cafe.

As he watched a group of men came into the compound. They were hippy types but there was something else about them. They had the clothing, the hair and the attitude. They made their way around the stalls and seemed to be spending plenty of money, so he didn't worry about them. He carried on down the stairs.

Frank had been listening to the young boy's conversation. He turned to Crow. "Well that's a dead end. It seems he knows Raven from when she helped him with his pony. He overheard us saying that she had been taken and he's telling his parents. They don't seem to know anything. I can't see how this can be such a dead end. Someone must know something."

Crow was looking around. "These people are frightened. If there is a gang or organised group taking people the last thing anyone wants to do is draw attention to themselves. We've made a bit of a big noise and we've been noticed. We didn't think that bringing her here could be dangerous though I begged her not to come. Do you think it was Transition X who have taken her?"

Frank shrugged. "I thought it was to start with but there's something going on here. Something more than I first thought. I can't put my finger on it right away but I will. I don't think we are going to find out any more today. I'm sorry Crow, we're going to have to head off back to the farm. We can't leave that unprotected."

Lord Balen sat in his office. He was thoughtful. He called. "Guards!" Two came in. "Fetch me the Animal Handler and then the doctor."

There was a knock on the door and the Farm Manager came in. Balen hardly looked at him. "There is a plan on that table. Take it and put it into action. I want the animals divided up as we have been advised on that sheet. And Farley, that hay and straw is fine for the horses, not for the goats. I want a fresh lot brough in and put under cover. Cut down and remove those Leylandii trees, place them on the bonfire site away from the animals."

Farley bowed his head. "Will that be all Sir?"

Balen glared at him, and he left the room swiftly taking the plan with him."

Balen smiled to himself as Farley left. He got up and looked out of the window and watched people moving about down below.

There was a knock at the door and the doctor stepped in when invited. Balen indicated the chair. The doctor sat down. He had a clipboard in his hand. Balen glared at him. The doctor cleared his throat. "I have given her a full medical. As the potential mother to your child I assumed you wanted her in the best of health. I have removed the bullet from her shoulder. It is dressed, and it will heal now." He looked at Balen as if to say something else.

Balen glared at him. "Well man, what do you want to say?"

The doctor looked down at his clipboard. "I may be speaking out of turn, but that bullet was one of ours."

Balen looked confused as Raven hadn't mentioned it. "How do you know?"

The doctor put the bullet on the table. "It had a serial number. I took the liberty of checking it against the inventory. Those bullets were issued to the reconnaissance mission."

Balen thought about it. "Thank you. The information is noted. Now, the report. I assume you have prepared a suitable report for my brother."

The doctor fixed Balen in a steely stare. He took a deep breath and recovered his composure. "You did indeed carry out his orders and the wishes of those here far in excess of what would have been expected. The pain you must have inflicted on her would have been excruciating and the damage is extensive. I assume that you do not wish me to administer any painkillers. It is my medical opinion that although it is demanded by your brother, the damage done already could be detrimental to her carrying a child. The damage to the cervix is extensive and that will make carrying a baby to full term difficult. I would also recommend that it would be medically detrimental to your intended outcome to continue with any more "sessions" until her current injuries are healed. Would you like me to explain medically?"

Balen felt cold. He got up and faced out of the window as he was so shocked he was worried about showing it. "That should satisfy everyone then. Administer painkillers, she may be the mother of my child already. I will bow to your medical opinion."

The doctor nodded. "In my opinion she is healthy with extreme bruising. Where is she to be kept?"

Balen looked up. "She is to be delivered here and when I am done a cell is to be prepared with a bed and a chair and some reading materials. I understand that the mental condition of the mother can influence the wellbeing of the child."

The doctor smiled. "That is true but not at this early stage and we have no confirmation of your success."

Balen glared at him. "Are you questioning my decision? I wish her to have a room prepared for the comfort of my child through the preservation of her mental wellbeing."

The doctor nodded. "I will see to it." The doctor looked up. "May I speak?"

Balen looked down at his paperwork. "You may leave."

The doctor hesitated. "Please, Balen."

Balen looked up. "In light of our past friendship I will overlook your insolence. Speak."

The doctor looked him in the eyes. "Balen, this isn't you. We've got through some awful situations but raping a woman in such a ferocious manner, that isn't you Balen. What is happening to you?"

Balen sighed and smiled. He took the report out of his desk and passed it to the doctor. "I had kept you out of it so you didn't have to lie."

The doctor read the report and smiled. "I'm glad, I didn't want to think that of you. Crow has done a lot of damage. There is going to be mental damage as well, she's shaking and she's terrified. She will be reliving what happened to her over and over. I have cleaned her up and the bruising is extensive. I'll give her painkillers and get her dressed and up here. I gather you didn't rape her? That is good. She needs to heal as best she can. I don't have the facilities here for what she may need."

Balen looked up at him. There were almost tears in his eyes. "Look after her, it matters to me."

The doctor smiled. "Thank you for your trust. It has been nearly a year now since your wife died. She's a good looking woman and you need someone. But, they did kill our people." He got up to leave the room.

Balen threw the file on his desk to him. "Read it!"

The doctor read about how there had been firebombs and attacks. He looked shocked. "Balen, you are going to have to handle this really carefully. They only did what anyone would do. She's innocent. Oh my God! Imagine if you'd. Doesn't bear thinking about. What are you going to do?"

Balen sighed. "I've requested that Rat is brought here. Perhaps his confession will help. Keep her "like" a prisoner until then. I'm putting her in your care as she has medical needs. Look after her for me my old friend." He smiled and the doctor nodded and left the room.

There was a knock at the door and the guards brought Raven in. They stood with her until Balen indicated the chair. He then looked at them. "You may go. I will call you when I wish her returned to her cell." The guards left.

Balen walked over to Raven. "Who shot you?"

Raven was looking a little spaced out. "There was a raid. Four, I think. They smashed through the gates and shot at us. Frank killed some. I let the two go."

Balen glared at her. "Why wasn't the bullet taken out."

Raven tried to remember. "I don't remember. Shylock was shot, and we were concerned about him. I got some med stuff from the Med Bay and patched it up. I had too much to do. I was settling them in and had to get everyone fed and the animals looked after. I didn't want the Doc to ground me, I had too much to do."

Balen looked furious. "You did what? It is removed and dressed now. It was still bleeding!"

Raven looked at him but she wasn't focusing. "Yea, it did keep bleeding."

Balen looked down at her. She was dressed in a clean boiler suit. Her hair was messy but it somehow suited her. The doctor had cleaned her up. "I've ordered that you have a more comfortable cell. I can't do more than that at the moment. The doctor is an old friend, he knows, he'll look after you. The report has been sent to my brother. Hopefully you will be safe in the cell tonight. I'd have you up here with me but I can't do that, not yet."

Raven looked up at him and she was crying. He put his arms around her. She reached up and put her arms around him. "Thank you. This isn't you. I can't stop remembering that night."

Balen sighed. "There is a lot to discuss as I need you to sort out that breeding plan for the animals. You ought to be resting. I would suggest that you lay on my sofa for now and we will discuss things later. I have some paperwork to do and you look like you need to sleep." He picked her up gently and carried her to the sofa and laid her down, found a couple of cushions, put his greatcoat over her and left her to sleep. He then went back to his paperwork.

Balen filled in a requisition for Rat to be brought to the farm. He didn't state why but he said immediately.

Raven stayed on the sofa while he completed his reports and work for the day. When she woke up, she had more colour and was looking better.

He walked over and sat on the sofa beside her. "I'm going to ask for you to be sedated tonight. You need to stop thinking. I'll get you brought here in the morning. It is the best I can do." He stroked her hair. "I have to send you back now."

He called for the guards as it was close to 9pm and she was taken back to her cell.

For a week Balen summoned Raven to his office for the day and they worked on a plan for the farm. He could not let her walk the farm as he didn't want anyone to see her until they hated her a bit less. She had to work from descriptions, but the deaths stopped. The new routine was set up and the trees had come down.

At the end of the week Rat arrived. He was acting like a hero and the crowds cheered him. Balen was there to greet him. "Welcome, we wanted you to visit us so that you could tell us of your deeds in trying to thwart Raven's Farm. As you know she is now our prisoner. It is a good prelude to what we need to do to her."

Rat looked sheepish. His expression changed and he shuffled his feet. But, as the crowd cheered him he got carried away. He bowed and soaked up the praise. "Indeed, it was a time when they welcomed me and Stick with open arms. They didn't have a clue, they were fools. We met their Doctor at the hospital and he didn't ask us many questions, even taking us in his camper to the pub.

It was there that I met Chris, the daughter of one of your Executives and that bastard Brand who was making a fool of her drooling over Storm. We travelled with them to the farm. We were able to report on how organised Raven was. Without her they are nothing though she had taught everyone well. She was not a dominant leader, even offering to stand down but they wanted her and I could see why. She never commanded, she asked, but she got things done. The fools all loved her and did what she said as it was the right thing to do. Can you believe that?" There were mutterings from the crowd which he totally misinterpreted as support for what he had done. "Yes, I know. They were so trusting that I was able to steal their food and hide it to try to implicate Brand who was now masquerading as Crow.

That stupid woman put up with that bastard treating her badly just for the good of the farm. When her husband was killed as they believed he was Brand she allowed Brand to become Crow. He didn't love her, he just wanted the position. I heard him one night and he was making her crawl, making her submissive and then he beat her when she would not comply.

And do you know what she did? I heard him scream, she grabbed his genitalia. As if a woman can gain domination over a man?" There were various women around the compound who were visualising their kitchen knives and Rat's genetalia at that point.

Well ok, I got caught and Frank had me tied in the barn to a chaff cutter and he was threatening me. If I hadn't slipped and cut myself on the barbed wire in the barn, I don't know what he would have done but Eric knocked him out. As he fell the gun in his hand went off. So Frank didn't even manage to kill Stick." He hesitated as he remembered he hasn't put it like that in his report. "Anyway, we had Frank on the floor and Eric grabbed me and we got away.

You are going to love this. It was only because of Stick who talked me out of it but I could have killed them all! I was going to put drain cleaner in their sugar. That would have been amusing, wouldn't it? Anyway, we got away to the woods and then we really got our own back. If anyone got near the window we fired at them. We threw firebombs through their windows and got them boarded up and living like rats." He was on a roll, believing the crowd was behind him. "It wasn't like that fool Raven was going to do anything about it. Four of us has rammed the gates earlier, ok we lost two in the firefight and Shylock and Raven were injured but their defence was useless! I kept out of the way and watched. It was easy to evaluate them, best bit of reconnaissance we could have done. They were weak, she let them go!" He bowed and waited for his applause, but it never came.

Balen stepped forward. "If you had been Raven and the others and you had been fired at and had firebombs thrown through your window how would you have reacted?"

One of the women went to the manure heap and picked up a handful of manure. She walked over and she threw it at Rat. It hit him square in the face. She shouted. "You bastard. It was your antics which caused our families and friends to be killed." There was a general clamouring and plenty of others grabbed manure and threw it. Balen got caught with a few ricochets, but he didn't mind.

He held his hand up and there was silence. "Bring me paper and a pen and a table." It was fetched. He turned to Rat. "Write all that down. Now!" Rat looked terrified.

Balen turned to the crowd. "I want five of you to write what you have heard." There was a clamouring and he had to choose five. Two of the Guards also volunteered so he chose them.

When he had the paperwork he read it all out, paper by paper. He nodded. It was exactly what he wanted, the truth.

He turned to Rat. "You have two choices. I can throw you to the families. You caused their family members to be killed. Or you can choose an execution. It is your choice?"

Rat was looking terrified. "I, erm… I, I choose execution." He was looking at the hungry mob and many of them were women who looked like they were itching to skin him.

Balen turned to him. "Get to your knees and ask for forgiveness."

Rat fell to his knees and turned to the crowd. "I ask for your forgiveness."

Balen held his hand out. "Hand me a gun."

One of the guards stepped forwards and offered his sidearm. "Sir, My Lord Balen. My brother was killed on that day. May I have the honour?"

Balen smiled. "That seems just and fitting." He handed the gun to the guard. Nobody knew how relieved he was at not having to kill someone. Something he had never done.

The guard walked behind Rat. "You do not even deserve to look at me. Look at the crowd and those you have offended. I strike a blow for reason today. You had orders. They were not followed. You set in motion actions which got our friends and family killed. For Transition X" He pulled the trigger and Rat fell forwards onto the ground.

2

. Three months passed quickly. Balen had Raven brought up to his office daily and the time she spent there got longer and longer until she was spending most of the day there.

Gradually the farm was transformed. The animal deaths had stopped and they were thriving. Balen was beginning to relax a little about some of the worries that he had as Raven started taking on more and more responsibility. The structure changed from emergency set up to people having their own tasks and purpose. Rather than using a stock of tinned food a kitchen was set up where the produce could be used to feed those there and the model which had proven to work at Raven's Farm was expanded to suit the farm.

As well as the practical side Raven suggested that they set up a social side so a bar was created and those with entertaining skills were able to shine. They started a theatre group and old films were found and they created a cinema.

There had been a bit of dissent in the ranks caused by boredom, so Raven also suggested that plots of land were available for those who wanted to grow in their own way. That added to the general stock of vegetables and people found contentment.

Balen instigated a Wellbeing and Therapy Section where those who had been qualified before the "Fall" were able to provide workshops, meditations, and therapies for those who wanted it.

Crafts were encouraged, especially those which produced things which were "of use". There was no need to sell them as with over a hundred people "on base" there was a need for everything which was made.

She often asked about the farm. So much so that Balen agreed to get a spy, a teenager by the name of Bart, to infiltrate. He was a calm boy and he wrote good reports. Balen wasn't quite ready to let them know that Raven was alright and he was unnerved as Crow was pushing for control and constantly challenging Frank. He knew this would worry Raven and he didn't want her to go back. He couldn't let her go back. He needed her.

Balen was sitting in his private room one evening and he couldn't stop thinking about her. His room was a plain box, the same block room as everyone else's. He had the same type of bed, same blanket and sheets, table and chair. The only difference was that he chose to eat alone. His metal tray with food in divisions was on the table but he hadn't eaten much of it. He was pacing the room. He looked at the tray and sat down and eat some more and drank his coffee which was cold. When he was finished he picked it up and took it back to the Mess Hall as he did every evening. He put it on the trolley ready for collection.

He looked around the Hall. There were groups of people chatting and laughing until they saw him. When they spotted him they stood up, ceased their conversation and saluted. He nodded, turned and left. That was why he eat alone.

His footsteps echoed in the empty corridors. He passed doors which were open and people were visiting others, chatting and laughing. He passed one of the common rooms and they were gathered watching a film and laughing as it was an old comedy. He went to the makeshift cell block which had been constructed from an old piggery. He walked along the line of doors until he came to Raven's cell. He pulled the observation hatch down and looked inside.

Raven was asleep, as per his orders she had been sedated as she was every night. He couldn't bear the thought of her laying down there alone, thinking. The guards who had returned her to her cell had thrown her on the bed and she was still in the position she had landed in, half off the bed. Balen walked down to the guard room. There was a single guard on duty. He was a teenager who looked barely sixteen. His long blonde hair was swept back in a ponytail and his baggy shirt and jeans were ill fitting. He hadn't earnt his boiler suit yet. His whole body didn't seem to fit him, and he was very awkward as he jumped to attention when Lord Balen walked in. "I want the key to K435."

The guard almost leapt across the room and gave the key to him. He opened his mouth but shut it fast. Balen turned and left the room. "At ease boy, you are doing a good job."

He closed the door and walked down to Raven's cell. He put the key in the lock and hesitated. He looked up and down the corridor then turned the key and went inside.

He gently lifted Raven onto the bed and pulled the covers up over her. He then stroked her head and watched her for a short time until she moaned slightly and moved in her sleep. He then got up and left the room, locked the door, and returned the key to the guard room.

The youth jumped again. Balen smiled. "Return the key to the box and

I want Prisoner K435 treated better. She has valuable information and she if valuable merchandise. I do not want to see her damaged." He turned on his heels and left the room.

The next morning Balen waited in his office. He heard footsteps outside and moved to his desk and sat down. There was the expected knock on the door and a short, thin bespectacled man entered carrying a pile of papers. He saluted and waited.

Balen smiled. "Continue Francis."

Francis smiled back nervously. "I have a report from other TX Groups. It seems that there is a splinter group that has broken away. They were thrown out by Lord Ferrisk when he discovered them in his compound and it is likely you may have a contingent here. He discovered that they had been undermining anyone who was trying to set up environmentally friendly projects. They use the TX name but they act in their own personal interest and follow their own radical beliefs. There is a directive from Archangel, you will see it there, that no TX base is to have anything to do with them and that they are to be eliminated when detected.

The report also states that there will be a delivery of solar panels and wind turbines to all camps within the month. They have been manufactured in house and are being shipped out ready for installation. They come with their own engineers and TX Eastbourne have set up an Assembly Unit so the equipment is coming from there. They are turning out replacement parts already for stockpiling in different areas to cut down repair times.

It has taken a while to get the infrastructure set up and it will take a few months for full production to be achieved.

There is a personal note from High Chief Archangel to the Commanders, here is your copy and a personal note from him to you." He handed over the messages. "This concludes my duty. I have some paperwork which contains information and news from other camps and I will be happy to convey on any messages and news for you to the groups I am going to visit."

Balen smiled. "Very good Francis. If you would like to rest a while we can allot a room for you."

Francis bowed his head. "Thak you my Lord, you are as always very generous. May I leave?"

Balen was opening his letter. "Yes, yes of course. Please have a rest and you are welcome to make use of our canteen as usual."

Francis clicked his heels together. "Very good sir." He turned and left.

Balen opened the letter and read the message. "Lord Balen, This is a message to all camp heads. It has come to our attention that we have been infiltrated by certain seditious elements who intend to undermine our beliefs and to manipulate them to their own ends. These elements must be eliminated with no mercy.

We cannot allow our pure cause to be corrupted by them. It is believed that these elements wish to eliminate all who are not Transition X Members. May I remind you of the prime directive to live and let live while protecting our own.

Lord Balen, your efforts and successes have not escaped our notice. Your sacrifices have also been noted. In friendship and brotherhood, Lord Archangel."

There was another slip of paper folded into the first letter. Balen opened it and recognised the spidery handwriting and smiled. "Dear Brother, I trust this letter finds you well. Well, we survived. That was a miracle in itself. I know you disapprove of the title Archangel but at least a title is easy to pass on. I have to draw your attention to the progeny directive. I have had no need to enforce it with other Camp Commanders but it is looking more likely that you are going to force my hand.

My sister in law is gone, nothing will bring her back. I received the report that you have taken the Commander of the Rebel Farm by force. I was concerned to hear that you had used such excessive force and I trust that in future couplings you will be more gentle, considering that she will be the mother of your child. I am asking you. Don't make me order you. Please do not put me in that position my brother. Kind Regards, M"

Balen took a deep breath and sat down in his chair. He folded the second letter and put it in his brother's file. He shook his head and smiled. "Believe me brother, I would like nothing more than to comply with that order." Thoughts of Raven came into his mind and he fought really hard to drive them away.

He called the guard. "Bring me Raven's notes from the Infirmary."

He waited and there was a knock on the door and the file arrived. He had never read the file, he had taken what the doctor had said, left her alone and let her heal. Now he wanted to know. His brother's letter unnerved him, he wanted to read that report. He opened the file, sat down and read it. By the time he had read the report tears were running down his face as he read of the injuries that Raven had sustained. The report to Archangel had included concerns that in future after producing a child that she would be able to carry a second child.

He was angry, very angry. He vowed that if he ever got his hands on Crow that he would exert such vengeance that he would wish he had never been born. He could not imagine the pain that Raven had been feeling and that she had not only hidden it from everyone she had ridden to the Mart and back again.

He read the notes and the doctor's comments and follow on notes. She was healing well. There was a note that in three days' time it would be suggested that Balen continued with his attempts at siring an heir and that it would be an optimal time to do so.

He closed the file and sent it back to the Infirmary.

He called the guard who entered the room. He didn't recognise the man. "Bring me Raven."

The guard saluted and clicked his heels together and left the room.

Balen sat at his desk running his biro through his fingers. He took a deep breath and let it out slowly. He then looked at his paperwork, but he didn't see what was written on the pages. Thoughts of Raven drowned everything else out. He shook his head and got up and went to the window.

There was a knock on the door, it opened, and Raven walked carefully in. Balen looked questioningly at the guards who walked behind her. The first smiled. "I am pleased to report that the prisoner has caused us no trouble at all."

Raven looked tired, there were dark circles under her eyes and a bruise was developing on her cheek bone. Balen stepped over and roughly grabbed her chin. He looked at the guard who tried to melt back into the stonework as he saw Balen's angry glare. "Who did this?"

The guard looked at his feet.

Balen drew himself up to his full height. "Do not look away when I ask a question. I asked, who did this?"

The guard looked up and stood to attention. "I did Sir."

Balen raised his hand and struck the man across the face, sending him reeling onto the floor. "Now get up and tell me why you damaged the merchandise, the potential mother of my child?"

The guard stood up. "She is a prisoner Sir, and she didn't move fast enough out of her cell so I reminded her who was in charge. Just like you taught me."

Balen hesitated slightly. "And was she sedated at the time?"

The guard looked horrified. "I didn't know. I assumed she was being slow."

Balen struck him again. He reeled back into the wall. "Now I gave instructions that this woman is not to be unnecessarily harmed. If she had been trying to escape that is another matter." He turned towards the man who looked terrified. "Wait down the hall." The man looked relieved and left the room quickly and shut the door. He glared at the other guard. "You too." They left.

Balen turned to Raven. "Please sit." Raven nearly fell into the chair and winced in pain.

Balen looked concerned. "Have you been mistreated?"

Raven shook her head, but Balen saw more bruises on her neck. Lines of black and purple welts stood out on her pale skin. She spoke, her voice quiet, almost a whisper. "I have not." Then she looked up at him and her eyes told him otherwise.

He glared at her. He stepped closer. "Have you been harmed? You have nothing to fear from me."

Raven looked down and then took a deep breath. "You are not there when they come. I woke up with these bruises, so I do not know what happened as I was sedated as per your orders."

Balen looked furious. He grabbed her by the arm and she screamed. He pulled her sleeve up and saw the dark purple and black bruises which covered her upper arm. Some of the bruises were old and fading. "How long has this been going on?" He knew she had been with him every day, working with him, working for the farm, she had not said a thing.

She looked up, her eyes pleading. "I was alright for the first week and then I woke up hurting and with bruises."

Balen looked down at her. "Why didn't you tell me?"

Raven looked surprised. "I thought it was happening because you ordered it. You control everything and everyone around here don't you?" Tears ran down her cheek and he released his grip slightly. He thought back and he hadn't noticed it but there had been a distance between them. She had stood that little further apart, moved away when he moved close, now it mattered.

He screamed out his orders and went with Raven and the guards to the doctor's room. He took Raven inside. The doctor looked up. "I want you to do a full examination, now! Guards, wait outside.

Raven tried to back away from the doctor. She screamed at him. "Leave me alone. I don't know what happened. I don't remember. I hurt. I just went to be left in peace; I want to die. I haven't done anything to you. I've even tried to help you."

Balen caught her arm and the searing pain shot through her. He relaxed his grip and gently stroked her cheek with the back of his hand. "I am not trying to hurt you. I'm trying to find out what they have done and to stop you hurting. Please trust me. Your wellbeing is very important to me."

She could feel nausea and she held her head. She felt dizzy and the ground began to spin. Balen caught her as she nearly passed out and looked down at her kindly. The look stunned her, it distracted her from the pain and she felt something warm, something comforting in what felt like an empty world where she was very, very small. She felt safe, his voice was gentle. "Let the doctor take care of you. I don't want to hurt you. On the contrary I, I mean we, want to make sure that you are healthy. Let the doctor check you out."

The doctor had moved behind her with a chloroform pad in his hand. She looked wild eyed as she noticed him and backed away. Balen put his arm around her and she had neither the strength or the will to pull away. He took the pad from the doctor and gave him a meaningful look so he moved away. "This will stop the pain, for now. I need you to trust me."

She looked at him, wide eyed and he let her pull away. He waited patiently. He held out his hand. "Come to me willingly."

She thought for a moment and knew it was a pivotal moment. She swayed slightly as the pain and nausea made her head spin. She whispered. "How can I trust you? Your men did this."

Balen looked at her blankly. "My men are under orders to leave you alone and to keep you safe. It seems there are those amongst Transition X who are no longer following orders. Trust me, I did not hurt you." He smiled and held his hand out.

Raven looked down and just about caught herself before her legs gave out. She was feeling dizzy and sick with the pain. Every feeling of loneliness she had ever felt came crashing down on her. It was a void which over the months he had filled, that he had betrayed her was worse than any pain she felt. Then she knew what her choice had to be. If he was going to kill her, then she didn't want to live. Raven looked into his sincere brown eyes. She took a deep breath and took his hand just as her legs gave way. Balen caught her and lifted her onto the examination table. "Trust me." He gently stroked her hair back from her face and he didn't care if the doctor did see him do it. He took the chloroform pad and put it in her hand. He then lifted her hand. He gave her every opportunity to pull away and she allowed him to guide her hand until the pad was over her mouth and nose. She sank into painless oblivion.

Balen stood by her side, watching over the table, watching the doctor's every move. Sometimes he paced. Sometimes he stood, arms folded. The doctor took her boiler suit off and she lay on the table. She was covered in bruises. The doctor looked shocked. "If I may speak?" Balen nodded. "After Rat confessed there is no animosity towards Raven amongst the people. On the contrary they appreciate the changes she has helped to make. If I may say so, there is a certain amount of horror at what was done to her as a punishment for having done no crime."

Balen nodded. "Thank you for that information. I will be acting on it. I was keeping her safe in the cell. Please proceed."

The Doctor began. "I won't go into the technical terms but they have been stamping on the injury where I removed the bullet. That has caused severe bleeding which will have weakened her. You can see where a boot has left a clear mark on her clavicle. It may be fractured but without an X Ray I cannot tell. Her arm may be fractured, the bruising is extensive. I will have to consider it fractured as it looks likely. These injuries happened last night, I can tell by the stage of the bruising. There is extensive bruising around the ribs and stomach area which would indicate that she has been kicked on several occasions. I will strap her ribs. I will treat her arm as fractured and plaster that.

This is going to be a more intimate inspection if you would rather not watch."

Balen folded his arms. He was not going to leave her.

The doctor did his inspection. "I am pleased to say that the healing has progressed and there has been no further damage caused by the beating. They have not touched her in "that" way. I was going to speak to you and in a couple of days you would be able to continue your fertility program. As there is an extreme amount of bruising and as she is no longer the guilty party I would highly recommend that she is not kept as a prisoner. I can see the logic but it is far from keeping her safe." He smiled as he saw Balen's concern. "My Lord, as your doctor I claim a certain privilege if I may. May I speak freely."

Balen nodded.

The doctor coughed. "It has not escaped my notice that you have affection for Raven. As there is no reason at all why the people of this compound would find that distasteful the question has to be raised as to why you are keeping her in the cell."

Balen looked shocked. "I kept her there for her safety."

The doctor smiled. "With respect. You are not privy to the general conversation and the general feeling which the people have for her. She is seen as their saviour in many ways as they can see that their resources are multiplying and what she has helped to achieve here is noticeable.

She is going to be in pain so I am going to administer some heavy-duty painkillers and I will have to keep her heavily sedated today. This is for her mental wellbeing as much as the pain. In my opinion this would leave her vulnerable to future attack. I would strongly advise that you take steps to prevent any further interference with her or you could lose her. She is strong but there is only so much punishment a body can take, physically and mentally. Those blows and the blunt trauma were delivered with some force. Whoever did this was not messing about."

Balen shook his head. "Do what you can to make her comfortable. She is a necessary asset." Balen watched while the doctor went to work with a certain amount of extra gentleness. Balen's thoughts were racing, and his anger was growing.

The doctor took a deep breath. Balen glared at him. "You can say it. Has she been "interfered with" in any other way?" His teeth were clenched and so were his fists.

The doctor looked down. "No, she has not been interfered with in the way that I think that you mean. She is a good looking woman. She is intelligent and would make a suitable companion.

Keeping her as a prisoner has instigated certain respect for you and sympathy for her. Should you benevolently release her now and should she join us she would be an asset. Not least that it would bring the "other farm" under our wing. This I believe was your intention in the first place."

Balen nodded. "There is a splinter group working against Transition X. I am going to have to execute the guards, but I don't know which ones they are."

Crow sat in the kitchen drinking a cup of weak tea. It was mostly milk. He had just finished his breakfast at the end of his watch and was about to go to bed. Cheryl took the plate from him. "You know they will find her."

Crow managed a weak smile. "I'm sure they will but it looks like the trail has gone cold. Nobody seems to know anything and if they do, they won't talk."

There was a shout from the guards at the gate and Crow leapt up and ran outside. He bounded across the yard and joined Frank, Storm, Matt and Reko at the gate. There was a cart outside and four people had just climbed down from it. They were holding out pieces of paper and Frank was looking at them. Frank looked up as Crow crossed the yard. "These people have received an invitation but it has taken them this long to get here. I would like to introduce Peter who is a carpenter, Janice his wife who makes clothes, Tracy who is their daughter and Bart, a lad they met on the way."

Crow stepped forwards to shake hands. He lingered ever so slightly longer when shaking Tracy's hand and smiled when she looked at him. That look wasn't missed by Storm who glared at him. Crow missed the glare as he was too busy looking at Tracy. She was a tall, slim girl of about twenty with jet black hair and bright red lipstick. Her clothes were black and elegant. Her parents both dressed in casual jeans and a sweat shirt. Her father had neatly cut brown hair while her mother had blonde hair. Bart was a typical teenager, his hair was long, his shirt short and his trousers nearly made his waistline.

Frank had missed the look as well. He was smiling and talking to Peter.

Crow spoke assertively. "We will have to find you a place to stay. Would you prefer to camp as a group or have a place here? We're a bit pushed for space, but we do have a hay loft if you don't mind that."

Peter smiled. "After so long on the road anything with a roof would be a bonus. Thank you. Is there anywhere that we can wash?" He looked towards the family. "It has been a long journey."

Frank turned to the others. "I think we should leave these people in peace to settle in."

Crow cut him off. "I'll show you the barn and I'm sure we will have time to welcome them properly later. Please follow me."

Crow walked across the yard and Tracey fell in beside him and he looked down at her and smiled. Storm watched from across the yard and then went inside. She passed by the kitchen and indicated that Doc should follow her. He got up, picked up his drink and took it with him to the Med Room. He went inside and closed the door.

Storm was pacing up and down. "I can't believe that man. I really can't. How could he?"

Doc stepped forwards and caught her arm. "What can't you believe? Am

I missing something?"

Storm glared at him. "Yes you are, big time. Did you see that? Raven has only been gone a few months and he's making eyes at the first floozy who comes along."

Doc sat down and pulled her down to sit beside him. "I'm just a man. I miss those things. Tell me."

Storm swallowed hard. "Well I wasn't going to say anything when he got together with Raven. Just before they did that swap he'd made a pass at me. He gave it the full charm offensive and I as going for it. Then suddenly he's Mr Raven and all in love with her. I bit my tongue as it all seemed to be fate. You know what I mean? A new start for him and he really seemed to be supporting her. She had such responsibility that she needed someone. I'm well rid of him considering what just happened."

Doc looked mystified. "Go on, fill me in. I missed all of that. I was in the kitchen when you came back. I can't see through walls."

Storm sighed. "You didn't realise what was happening did you? Take a look at the situation. He was knocking off the boss' daughter with all the fringe benefits it has. When the going gets tough, like she's having a baby, he tries to run for it. He's let off the hook, both financially and with the baby and all he has to do is be nice to her. He meets me, decides he fancies something different once her daddy is no longer a threat. He probably thought she'd be killed on the way home or would not find him again. Then he gets the opportunity of being top dog again if he's with Raven and life just throws that in his path. Now she's not around and he seems to be keeping the "top dog" position he's finding himself something else to entertain him. Believe me, just watch him with her and you'll notice it now you are looking."

Doc looked stunned. "Are you sure you aren't overreacting?"

It wasn't until the evening meal that they were all together. Crow came in and the Stacey Family were already sitting in the kitchen with Doc, Storm and Reko. Crow went and sat next to Tracey. Doc gave Storm a very knowing look. Then other people started filing in and it became very crowded. The Colours were still eating in their own camp. Cheryl had been cooking flat out all week but she put another good meal on the table.

Frank came in and sat in his usual seat by the door. He looked tired. "Well, that's the chores done for the day. We've got produce to take to the Mart tomorrow and I'm hoping we can pick up some news about Raven."

Crow wasn't listening. He was talking to Tracey who was laughing at something he was saying. Frank raised an eyebrow and glared at him. "Crow, I said we're going to take some produce to the Mart tomorrow and see if we can pick up some clues about Raven."

Crow looked up. "That's good. I'll go with you if that is alright. Tracey, have you been to the Mart? Perhaps you'd like to come with us? I'll protect you."

Tracey giggled. "I'd love to. What's it like?"

Crow began a private conversation with Tracey about the Mart as others broke off into their own conversations. Frank was watching Crow and so was Storm.

After dinner Storm caught Frank's arm and pulled him to the Med Room with Doc. She wasn't through the door before she turned to Frank. "He can't do this!"

Frank looked at her with a level stare. "Storm, there isn't anything we can do. If he wants to act like that, then he will. We can't force him. We're not a dictatorship. We can make it uncomfortable for him and remind him, but we have now way of knowing if Raven is alive."

Storm spluttered. "It's just not right. He can't be our leader and then pick himself a new woman just like that."

Frank smiled. "He isn't our leader and he isn't. He might be using Raven's room but believe me if he tries to take Tracey in there then there will be trouble. I still believe that Raven is alive somewhere and one day we're going to get her back.

Even I forget but they weren't actually married. I understand from Raven that he was playing the role for convenience but that is his position. Until Raven says otherwise he is in the role of her husband. He is showing certain flaws in his character which make him a liability. The last thing we need here is dissent. At the moment he has done nothing wrong.

Balen was thinking while he watched the doctor begin to immobilise Raven's arm and to strap up her ribs. "She is being kept sedated. To what level? She is thinking clearly when she is helping with the reports and had put forward some good ideas, but I feel her thought is hampered. How much pain would she be in without the sedation?"

The doctor looked up. "The sedation was at your command so that she didn't have to feel the fear of being locked in a cell. In my opinion it would not be needed if you released her and moved her into your own quarters. She is intelligent and good company. Talk with her. She may well have some good ideas."

Balen looked down at her. "How much pain would she be in."

The doctor smiled. "Nothing that painkillers wouldn't deal with. There is the other matter. If you wish to start your family I would say that the optimum would be within the next couple of days. It would give the people here something good to focus on as well. It is "future planning" but in my opinion it could also set a "standard"."

Balen looked at him puzzled. "What do you mean?"

The doctor was thinking how to word his next suggestion. "At the moment we are coming out of emergency and into stable. There are plenty of rules handed down by Archangel and plenty of our own but there are no social guidelines. In my opinion if you just produce an heir, it gives the message that just producing children is favourable without the stability of the family unit."

Balen laughed. "You just want to be Best Man again."

The doctor laughed. "It was a good night. I miss Elaine, she was lovely and I know you miss her too. I think it is time for me to take you off of the anti-depressants and prescribe a good dose of Raven. Come on mate, I'm talking to you as your friend. The electricity between you two could power my equipment!"

Balen smiled. "You could be right. She has been responsible for most of the good ideas around here over the past few months. If she is with me she will be safer. If she has status that might keep her safer as well. Archangel knows about her and it would mean that I can let her make some sort of contact with the farm which I know she wants to do. I can't arrange a wedding in two days!"

The doctor smiled. "These are new days. You could organise a Handfasting in a day or, better than that, make the "proclamation" and let the people organise something for you. That would show their acceptance of Raven."

Balen laughed. "You always were the bright one. I'd better ask her first though. Can you bring her round?"

The doctor shook his head. "Impetuous as always, how romantic! Propose to her while she is laying naked on a hospital examination table. That is really going to create happy memories. At least take her back to your office!"

Balen smiled. "We'll get her dressed and wake her up. We should walk back there together."

Balen dressed her in her boiler suit as gently as he could. The bruises unnerved him.

The doctor nodded. "Now you are getting it." He went to a cabinet and took out a bottle of clear liquid. He drew off some of it and injected Raven. "She will wake up shortly." He went to a drawer full of boxes and took out a box. "Painkillers, two of them three times a day. Let her rest, no heavy lifting and good luck mate. And don't touch her until after the Handfasting." The two hugged before Raven woke up.

Raven woke up. "Balen, what happened?" She looked down. "Great, more bandages."

Balen took her hand. He bent down and kissed her. "We have a splinter group. We'll have to work out how to deal with them."

Raven thought about it. "Not necessarily. The only people who had access to my cell were the guards. Can I speak freely?"

Balen nodded. "The doctor is trusted."

Raven looked up at him and he helped her to sit. "You are putting fanatical sociopaths in charge of the cells. I don't think it was any plot against you. I just think that they are sadistic. They didn't intend to kill, disfigure, or permanently harm. They intended to torture. They did it because I was a prisoner, not because I was Raven. Do you have anyone else in the cells?"

Balen thought about it. "No."

Raven looked over at the doctor. "When there were others in the cells were they harmed?"

The doctor thought about it. "At the time I thought they were self-harming. I did see bruises."

Raven looked Balen in the eye. "You have your answer."

Balen grabbed her hand. "There is no need for you to be in the cells now. It is time that you moved to better quarters. Walk with me. I want it to be seen that you are no longer my prisoner." He helped her off of the table. The doctor moved behind the curtain, and they kissed. It was passionate and loving. Balen looked down at her. "Life has to be different."

Raven smiled and they left the Infirmary. "Can I see the farm?"

Balen looked concerned. "Are you fit enough?"

Raven smiled. "Well with your support, yes."

Balen put his arm around her to support her and they walked around the farm. He took her to see the stock, the horses and then as she seemed to get stronger as she walked, he walked with her up to the top of the hill.

They stood looking back over the farm. Balen was actually nervous. He held her close to him, feeling the warmth of her body. "Raven, we have to do something about this. I want to make "us" official and in doing that we need to set a precedent for others to follow. If I just take you as the mother of my child that will give a message that that is what is expected. We need to build stability here if we are going to build a new world. Have you heard of Handfasting?"

Raven nodded.

Balen smiled. "My love, should we be handfasted?"

Raven looked stunned.

Balen laughed. "Don't make me get down on one knee. Balen wouldn't do that. It has been nearly a year now since my beloved wife died. That is a long enough time to mourn and if Archangel wants us to produce an heir I would rather he or she wasn't a bastard." The sadness flickered across his face. "I had had my doubts but they were confirmed by what you said that had been overheard. Archangel and I have the same mother but I have no idea who my father was. It is clear that it isn't the same father as Archangel."

Raven smiled. "For that I am infinitely grateful." She was going to kiss him and hesitated.

Balen bent down and they kissed. Then he heard something. He turned and everyone in the yard and those they could tell in time were watching. They were cheering and applauding. Balen smiled. "Well I suppose we have our answer as to whether they are happy about this."

They walked down the hill together. Balen had his arm around Raven, supporting her. One of the elder women came over. Balen smiled. "Good morning, Agatha."

Agatha was smiling broadly. "Good morning my Lord, and my Lady?"

Balen smiled and nodded. "Raven has graciously agreed to be handfasted with me."

Agatha smiled. "If I may say, about time my Lord. We will make the preparations for a handfasting tonight. This will bring a lot of happiness to many."

Balen and Raven went into the building and to Balen's office. He was going to take her to the sofa, but she put a hand on his arm. "There is a lot to do. Shall we go to the table. Bring me up to date with what I need to know."

Balen went to his desk. "This is the most worrying message. It came this morning from my brother. There is a lot of dissent in the cities and Transition X is losing far too many people trying to stop the gang warfare."

Raven smiled. "Are innocent people being harmed?"

Balen looked puzzled. "Only in that they can't get to the shops or move around freely. They are prisoners in their own homes."

Raven thought about it. "Well arm the gangs and let them kill each other. It solves the problem, and we won't have to worry about producing food to feed them."

Balen had been scratching his head and stopped mid scratch. "That is wicked, but brilliant." He sat at his desk and got his pen out. He wrote a message and he put it in the envelope. "I have told my brother of our impending Handfasting and he already knows that you have been the instigator of many of the good ideas here which have expanded to other sites. I've now mentioned this idea about the gangs."

He sealed the envelope and put it in the tray.

Crow woke up early. He walked around the room and opened drawers and cupboards and put away anything that belonged to Raven. He bundled any clothing that wasn't in the cupboard into the bottom of the wardrobe and shut the door. He then went to the bathroom and spent nearly an hour getting ready. When he was satisfied he looked at himself in the mirror and smiled. He grabbed his hairbrush and did one last sweep of it through his hair.

Then he took all of Raven's cosmetics, scooped them into a towel, wrapped them up and put the bundle in the wardrobe.

He stood in the middle of the room and looked around him. He made the bed after changing the sheets and he folded them back down and smoothed them. He smiled to himself as he left the room.

The morning at the farm had dawned bright and crisp. The new visitors' cart had been loaded up with produce. Tracey and her father were in the driver's seat. Crow came down, mounted Blade and was riding alongside with Frank on the other side as they rode away from the farm. Both had shotguns in hand and the father had a shotgun in his hand on the cart.

Tracey was driving the heavy horse. The journey was uneventful and they joined the queue going into the Mart. Crow and Frank dismounted. Frank was talking to Peter at the horse's head and Crow had climbed up onto the cart and was sitting beside Tracey and they were deep in conversation. She giggled occasionally and was attentive as he pointed things out to her. He laughed at her jokes and both were smiling profusely.

Frank tried not to look but he couldn't help it. He was within earshot and he couldn't help listening.

Tracey giggled. "So we're here to find out about what happened to Raven? I heard that she was the woman in charge. Isn't she your wife?"

Crow had been in full flow about his exploits at the farm and the question caught him unawares. "Well, yes, sort of. Its more a marriage of convenience. She's a lovely woman, don't get me wrong. So what sort of things do you want to look at at the Mart?"

The expression fell from Frank's face and he ran his fingers over his shotgun. He wasn't the only one who was listening. Behind then in the queue there was another wagon. The wagon master was at his horse's head trying to calm an impatient horse which stamped and jittered about.

He was watching the group from the farm out of the corner of his eye. He was also listening. Frank was too intent on what Crow was saying and doing while trying to hold a conversation with Peter to notice him.

The queue moved fairly fast as the people were checked out at the gate and moved inside. When it was their turn they passed quickly inside, as did the person behind them. Crow took the reins and guided the horse into teh mart and to the Livery Stable, Blade followed on behind, tied to the back of the cart. "I'll look after the horses Tracey, if you would like to give me a hand."

Frak was about to object but he took a deep breath. "Ok, I'll see you out there then." He watched the couple as they led the horses behind the building.

He walked away, the thoughts rushing around his mind. He was thinking about it so much that he paid no attention to the man behind him. He was an ordinary man dressed very unobtrusively. He walked his horse in calmly now that it was going somewhere. He didn't do anything to draw attention to himself.

As Crow and Tracey took their horse to the far end stable, he took his to the nearest one. He turned the horse out into the stable and left it wiht the tack on and slipped out into the corridor and crept up to where Crow and Tracey were and slipped around the corner as they took the horse's tack off and brushed him down.

Crow stood close to Tracey and as they finished, he grabbed her wrist and pulled her out of the stable. He shut and locked the door and then pushed her around the corner. She gasped slightly as she fell backwards onto a hay bale. He crouched beside her. "Alone at last."

Tracey laughed. "Very funny. Now come on what are you playing at? She was laughing and seemed to be treating it as a joke.

Crow wasn't laughing. "Come on, I know that you want me. We have our chance now."

Tracey was still laughing. She put a hand on Crow's chest to push him away. "Don't be silly, you are a married man."

Crow laughed. "Actually, no I'm not."

Tracey looked confused. "But you are married to Raven aren't you or is that one of those strange pagan marriages? I won't have anything to do with a married man."

Crow lifted an eyebrow. "Well actually they are just as valid but no, I'm not married at all. So you wouldn't be doing any harm. Come on, we have some time and I really want you."

Tracey was pushing harder now, trying to get him to back away. "I don't know what you are talking about. How can you not be married? Everyone knows that you are married to Raven."

Crow laughed. "Well, that is the joke. She is a lovely woman, and it was a real pleasure to have her as my wife for a while. I can't say her charms weren't pleasurable but no, she wasn't my wife. I was in a difficult position."

There was nothing I could do about it. She gave me an ultimatum to take her dead husband's place or to be thrown out. If she'd thrown me out the people following me would have found me and killed me. She was lonely and needed someone.

I was there, I wanted what she had on offer so it was a mutual arrangement. So there you have it, I'm not married. She said at the time if I wanted to be with someone else she would step aside and we'd sort it out. I want you and I'm sure she wouldn't mind. I'm in charge now so it would be a good position for you. We've had our time but it is time for me to move on." He slipped his hand behind her head. He didn't notice the stranger had moved so he had a clear view without being seen and had heard every word that Crow had said.

As Crow started undoing buttons, while holding Tracey's hands out of the way with his other hand the onlooker started taking photos with an ancient camera. Tracey pulled away, but he pushed her back down and kissed her passionately. "I'm not married to Raven, the man who I took the place of was. Come on, you know you want me."

Tracey looked confused. "You mean you aren't Crow?"

Crow smiled down at her. "No I'm not."

Tracey put a hand up to stop him. "I want to. I haven't done this before.

I want it to be special. Can I come to you tonight?"

Crow looked disappointed and then put his hand over her mouth and continued undoing her clothing. She struggled but he was far stronger than her and she stood no chance of stopping him. The stranger kept clicking his camera. When he had taken enough photographs, he struck a match and threw it into the straw beside Crow.

Crow caught sight of the fire beside them and let Tracey go. She replaced her clothing as he stamped on the small blaze which went out immediately. People came running, buckets of water in hand to make sure the blaze was out.

The stranger went about his business, buying farm supplies, with a big smile on his face.

Crow and Tracey emerged and began looking around the stalls. Tracey looked as though she was about to burst into tears. Crow was walking with her, arm around her. The stranger ignored them.

Frank went to the cafe. It was crowded with faces he recognised from when he had visited before. He spoke to a few people and asked around about whether anyone had heard about Raven. He then went to the kiosk and bought a coffee. The owner put the coffee down for him and took the offered coins. Then he looked up and smiled. "You were looking for information about Raven, weren't you?"

Frank smiled. "Yes do you know anything?"

The stallholder smiled. "Yes but it will cost you." Frank put a handful of coins on the table which the stallholder scooped in his hand and into his pocket. "It seems that she was taken by Lord Balen. It was retribution for what you did to his men. You know who Lord Balen is?"

Frank nearly dropped his coffee. "Where did you hear that? Yes I know who Lord Balen is."

The stallholder pulled a sealed envelope from under the counter and handed it to Frank. "It was left on the counter. I don't know which customer left it but it has your name on it." He looked at Frank who put more money on the counter and the stallholder handed it over.

Frank took his coffee and the envelope and sat down. He opened it carefully and read the neat and ornate handwriting on the handmade paper.

3

Frank,

You killed those we cared about, so we arranged something you cared about to be taken. We had such retribution planned. Thankfully it has been brought to our attention that the attack was not unprovoked. Rest assured that there will be no further action taken regarding Raven's Farm and the perpetrator has been punished.

Raven is unaware of this communication. I would request that you personally come and speak with her so that we can reinstate communication between her and her farm. Any communication you wish to send to her may be sent via Bart. Kindly allow him the freedom to be able to deliver such messages to our operatives in the area who wish you no harm.

She was our prisoner. In light of the revelation that you did not kill our people unprovoked she became our guest but due to the situation with Crow we had no wish for her to be put in a position where she may be harmed by him again. We have the best doctors here and she has received medical attention. If you are not aware, Crow raped Raven. This is a heinous crime and one for which we intend him to answer for.

We are not your enemies. We hope that very soon we can speak about how best we can work together.

If you wish to meet with Raven, I suggest that it is tonight as I would like you to bear witness that she is unharmed. I wish her to be made aware of what has and is happening at the farm and I request that you bring Oberon and Silk with you.

Balen

Frank looked up and he noticed Crow and Tracey. They were looking at a stall full of necklaces and jewellery. Crow had been picking pieces up and trying them on her. He then put his arm around her. It was an unconscious act but enough for Frank to notice. He looked down at his coffee and thought, long and hard.

Raven entered Balen's office. The guard didn't follow her, but he had given her a smile as she had passed him. She walked in and shut the door behind her. Balen looked up and she smiled at him. "Agatha has plans." She looked exhausted. "I'm not sure what they are planning but they are busy and they won't let me out into the yard."

Balen smiled. "Let them have their joy. They've had a long road." There was a knock at the door and Balen looked up. "Enter."

The man who had been at the Mart walked in and Balen smiled at him. "Fred, I trust you got the supplies we needed? There's no need to report."

Fred bowed his head to Raven. "Indeed I did." The man had a smile on his face which instantly grabbed Balen's attention.

He raised an eyebrow. "What are you so happy about?"

Fred put an envelope on the desk. Balen took it and opened it. He looked at the photographs. "Time I came clean. I sent Fred to spy on Crow and to get some photographs as I am planning retribution. He is challenging Frank for leadership of the Farm. That can't be allowed to happen. It seems he has a new target now."

Fred smiled. "He tried his old tricks and I think a subtle cigarette in the straw saved Tracey facing the same fate as our Lady Raven. Should I report?"

Balen smiled. "I think that the photos say it all." He handed them to Raven who looked.

Raven sighed. "I'm not surprised. He jumped ship on Storm as soon as I was available and the status. If he thinks he has the status he'll claim her as Storm wouldn't go back, she's too wise. What do you mean "old tricks"?"

Fred blushed. "He tried to rape our Tracey at the Mart."

Raven glared at Balen. "What is going on?"

Balen smiled. "I put a few spies into the chicken coop to see what the fox was up to. I might as well tell you. I have invited Frank here to speak with you, hopefully to be here tonight. I've also asked him to bring Oberon and Silk."

Raven shook her head. "Silk was killed. It could be time to speak to Frank, but I don't want to get near to Crow."

Balen smiled. "I didn't think you would want to. Speak to Frank if he comes here. What happens to Crow is up to you. Fred, you will be rewarded, good job. You can have the Eastern Shift you have been after. Thank you." Fred nodded and left.

Balen turned to Raven. "How could you give yourself to someone you didn't love?"

Raven was looking out of the window. "When I took the job with NEMESIS I was assigned Crow as a husband. To start with we just worked on the farm. We were officially man and wife so he stated that he wanted his "rights" as a husband. By the time Brandon came to the farm I had long lost faith in the fairy story that is love. I felt dead inside, nothing mattered other than keeping everyone safe. Crow had been having an affair for so long and he had left me looking after the farm on my own. I was exhausted by the time the others came.

He had a price on his head. If they came for him then others would be hurt. So I did what I had to do. I was in a situation of complete despair and I had a job to do. That has made me strong and I can survive but I am not proud of myself. Giving myself to him isn't quite true. It was more that Brand who became Crow took what he wanted. I can't explain what the tearing emptiness felt like."

Balen took the photos from her and put them in his desk. "You have been betrayed. The sanctuary that you built is now his. He no doubt thinks he can move another woman into your room. He won't of course, she is one of our operatives. That he tried to rape her as well, well we will have to ensure her safety so we cannot allow that situation to continue much longer. Speak to Frank, we will sort something out.

He has taken your home, your animals and that woman if she had been just "a girl" would have taken your life. I can't let that happen. You mean too much to me now. I am going to give you a choice. I have dictated this for too long. I set you free. You can go back there. I won't stop you. Or you can stay here and help me build something. It is up to you then what happens to the Farm. The choice is yours."

Raven smiled. There had been tears in her eyes and he noticed them now. He got up and walked over to her. "My choice?" Balen nodded. "I have no choice." Balen looked thunderstruck, it was as if his world had fallen out from under him and he dreaded what she was going to say next. "I love you Balen. I don't want to leave you."

Balen took her in his manly arms and kissed her with a passion that he had never felt before. He wanted her. "I love you Raven. I want you."

Raven grinned. "Not until tonight. I want you too. But we have to lead by example. We need stability and continuity here. When our son is conceived it will be in love and security with two parents who love him or her very much."

Balen sighed. "I will wait. Now tell me about Crow."

Raven's smile faded from her face. "This is a turning point Raven. You trust me now and I want nobody to stand between us. Tell me. He has hurt you. I will make sure that nobody at the farm suffers for this. He did not deserve such an honour as to even touch you. His tongue is as loose as his morals. It is no longer a secret and that has put you in a dangerous position. I am guessing that whoever wanted him is a big player?"

Raven nodded. "Matthew Rolstone."

Balen looked shocked. "I thought he was a big player but not that big. Let me deal with this. If it is not handled well this could be very serious. The bounty on Brandon's head was considerable. It was paid out. Please let me handle this for you.

You are tired. Get some rest on the sofa. I've got some letters to write."

Raven laid down on the sofa and fell asleep. Balen wrote his letters.

Halfway through the afternoon there was a knock at the door. The guard came in. "A message has arrived."

Balen looked up. "The pigeon post is working remarkably well!" He took the message and unravelled it. "My dear brother, Thank you for the invitation to your Handfasting. Unfortunately due to commitments and distance I will be unable to attend but I send my love and my blessings. Bring your new bride to meet me soonest. Time we had a family reunion. Your brother, M" Balen smiled and put it aside for Raven to read when she woke up.

Balen looked up as there was gunfire in the yard followed by a loud cheer. He smiled.

Raven woke up. "What was that?"

Balen looked up from writing. "That was an end to the insurrection. It seems that our impending nuptials brought about a need for action from the splinter group operatives here. Thankfully our eyes and ears are good and the whole group were spotted meeting. It was the people's decision and they are no longer a problem. We cannot build a new world if we have dissention in the ranks. Now we do not."

Raven smiled. "There is not a lot I can say to that." She got up and sat on the sofa for a while, watching Balen work. "Can I help?"

Balen thought about it. "Well other than starting to write a Master Plan for a "Brave New World". We could do with some notes. I need to speak with my brother, and he has invited us to HQ. He would like to meet my new bride, but he can't make it tonight. I didn't expect him to."

The morning passed into afternoon. There was a knock at the door. Agatha came in. "We have made preparations for this evening. If I may be so bold, we will require Raven to come to the Meeting Room in three hours."

Balen looked at Raven. "Are you willing?" Raven nodded. Agatha smiled and left the room. Balen looked concerned. "I'm not sure what they are planning but we had better go along with it."

There was another knock at the door. Balen looked up as the Guard came in. "There is a gentleman at the gate, he says his name is Frank and that you are expecting him."

Balen smiled and turned to Raven. "Do you want to meet him here?" Raven nodded. "Show him up but take his weapons off of him." He shrugged. "Can't hurt." Raven smiled.

Frank walked into the room. There was no expression on his face until he saw Raven, then he smiled widely. Raven went over and hugged him. He hugged her back, smiling. "Well my Lady, didn't expect to see you here and looking so well. Balen, before you say anything, thank you for looking after her."

Balen got up and walked over. He offered Frank a hand. Frank shook his hand; the grip was firm and friendly. Balen offered him a chair. "You are welcome here. There is much to discuss. Raven, do you wish to speak in private?"

Raven smiled. "I have nothing to say that you cannot hear. She turned to Frank. It is very good to see you."

Frank looked down at his hands. "I have a lot of questions. May I speak?"

Balen smiled. "That is what you are here for."

Frank took a deep breath. "We obviously feared the worse when Raven was taken. I've done what I can to keep the farm going and thanks to you Raven we have managed to keep things as per your plan. I have not allowed Crow to alter anything. He has of course challenged me for leadership. He believes he is the "leader" but nobody listens to him."

Balen smiled. "We are aware. Tracey and her family are our operatives. I have to speak on the matter so that Raven doesn't have to. Crow cannot be allowed to live. I will have to hand him over to Chris' father as he needs to exert a father's right to vengeance. Raven, there are things you are not aware of. Chris was subject to the same assault as you on a regular basis over the years. Her injuries were more severe and prolonged. She was made aware of this by the doctor who examined Chris at the hospital on the way to the Bar.

It is up to you Frank how we remove Crow and hand him over. He cannot be permitted to harm anyone else."

Frank had no expression on his face. "I agree. Those at the farm are unaware of the gravity of what he has done. They however are upset enough about his attraction to Tracey and his lack of enthusiasm to get our Raven back."

Balen looked at Frank, his eyes sincere. ""Your" Raven will not be coming back. Well not permanently. Tonight we celebrate our Handfasting. As of that point Raven will be in joint command of this Base." He smiled at Raven. "That is why my brother stated that he gave us his blessing. She will of course be able to visit you when she wishes." He looked to Raven.

Frank was wide eyed. "Is this true Raven? Are you safe, are you being forced to do this?"

Raven smiled. "What I do I do of my own free will. I am in love with Balen and we feel that there is a need to create a precedent that those who wish to raise families should adhere to the old ways of being husband and wife. My husband was Crow. That was on paper and it was not my choice. He is dead so I am a widow and able to be handfasted to whomever I choose. I choose Balen." She walked over and took Balen's hand. "I hope that you will be happy for us. I would like you to stay for the Handfasting tonight."

Frank opened his mouth and shut it again. "Oh, well, that has blindsided me. I was expecting to have to bargain for your release."

Balen laughed. "I offered her her freedom, she has made her choice. I invited you here as we are starting new traditions and it is appropriate that as she has no father here that she should be "given away" by someone. Actually, not that she is a "possession" to be given away so perhaps we should discuss that. We'd better give some thought as to what is going to be said so that others can follow. Any ideas Frank?"

Frank was stunned. "Balen lad, I never thought that you would come out of all this as a better person. The more I learn the more I realise that the initial impressions of people can be wrong. It is how you act when you are tested which matters. You should have had an invitation."

Balen looked confused. "Invitation to what, oh the Farm, well I think things have worked out better because I haven't. But I do need Raven. My brother, Archangel, is going to start to put together a plan to build a better world. My father, although a complete bastard, cannot help but see the benefit to it, particularly as he still has control of the company which will make the equipment for that new world."

Frank was thoughtful, his face blank. "Are you aware that Michael's father is not your father? I speak candidly now as it may have an effect if you are challenged. You are going to be dealing with Matthew Rolstone and he knows the truth."

Balen looked serious. "You have a point there. But, we have the same mother and by what I remember our mother is the majority "shareholder" in LexCorp. So that should not make a difference."

Frank smiled. "That is indeed true. We need to iron these things out now as any future "revelations" could be damaging. Do you know who your father is?"

Balen shook his head. "Until I had the conversation with Raven, I had no idea I was a bastard."

Frank looked grave. "Don't call yourself a bastard, you are far from it mentally. It is true that your mother was not married to your father. Your mother's story is an interesting one. She was Special Forces but her parents were Multi-Millionaires and Rolstone put them in touch with Michael's father, they arranged her marriage. She provided him with the heir he wanted but she had found out about his "hobby" and what he was doing so refused to have physical intercourse with him again. His money came from her parents so he had to comply. It was her wish that you were not told about this and that you were brought up with Michael, her other son. She was I understand a dutiful mother and the secret is just that.

You are no threat to Rolstone so he is unlikely to use it against you. Your mother is with your father. They are looking after your brother's son."

Balen looked suspicious. "Frank, how do you know so much?"

Frank smiled. "I am Nemesis. I am an "aspect" of NEMESIS. Each site has an android with a download of NEMESIS. We communicate via a satellite which was not shut down, so we are able to communicate between the sites to make sure that information is shared."

Balen and Raven looked stunned.

Frank looked down. "I suppose you won't want me to give you away now."

Raven smiled and hugged him. "You might be NEMESIS, but you are also Frank. It has been many years since we chatted on Jack's computer. I miss Jack."

Frank looked sad. "So do I. Jack loved you. You should have been together. I didn't understand humans so when he said he didn't want a relationship with you as it would ruin a friendship, I got him a wife. He sent you a message the night he died telling you he loved you. I am sorry, I deleted it."

Raven smiled kindly. "You did it for the best. Maybe not right but we can't alter the past. I loved him too. We kept our friendship through all those years. Is that why you recruited me?"

Frank smiled. "Yes, and your ideas. I listened and I read your messages and what you knew. You had the right make up to be able to survive and to build. That was one bit I didn't get wrong. You two together will be able to do something and you have my total support. It is time we worked together. The farms I set up do not have the resources of Transition X. If you have LexCorp behind you and the ideals are right there is no reason why we can't start planning for that better world.

But for now, we have to plan the first bit. We have to plan your Handfasting so that it becomes a ceremony that others can follow."

Raven looked nervous. "I suppose so. Balen?"

Balen walked around the desk and hugged her. "I think she's nervous. Frank, you reassure her."

Frank shrugged. "I'd love to but how can I? She is being handfasted to someone she loves, someone she can trust and someone who has proven to be the leader that I should have chosen in the first place."

Balen laughed as he saw Raven smile. "See, that will do, she's looking happier already. Did you bring Oberon?"

Frank smiled. "I did, they have him downstairs. Raven I'm sorry, Silk was killed."

Raven put her hand in his arm. "I know. Thank you for bringing Oberon. Is it ok if I go and see him?"

Balen smiled. "I think having a time to speak with Frank might be a good idea."

Raven left the room.

Frank sat back down and Balen went back to behind the desk. Balen looked up. "It could work out. Any reservations?"

Frank sighed. "None."

Balen thought about it. "Can you come up with a blueprint for a better world. You've got all the information about mistakes and how everything "is"."

Frank smiled. "That would be logical. For now you should concentrate on writing a Handfasting. You have about three hours."

Balen smiled. "Building a new world might be easier. I have no idea. Let me think."

Frank thought. "It should be something new so I'm not going to set out previous ceremonies. If you don't know you can't be influenced."

Balen thought about it. "I'll wait for Raven to get back. I think we know what to do with Crow. Rolstone is a major player. By handing him Crow that makes peace in case it is ever found out. I have to take Raven to Transition X Headquarters and that could be a time to talk with my brother and set out a plan so I won't leave it long after the Handfasting.

There is a splinter group so we are expecting trouble. I want to keep the "alliance" with Raven's Farm quiet as the farm would be a target and against their firepower you wouldn't have much chance. We do need to speak about an escape plan if they do. Do you have the resources to move the animals and get here if there is an attack?"

Frank thought about it. "We can't move the animals. Do you think there will be?"

Balen sighed. "We executed twenty infiltrators this morning. I am expecting a backlash as they are now blind here. They have attacked other TX Bases and they have some good ordnance. One reason why we need to keep Rolstone and others on side. He's done well out of LexCorp."

Frank thought about it. "Do you know who is behind the splinter group?"

Balen smiled. "We don't know. Any ideas?"

Frank looked thoughtful. He was searching his memory banks. "A few ideas have sprung up. If it has come to light that the head of LexCorp was impregnating women with his own sperm there would have been a lot of claims for compensation, especially from the fathers who brought these children up as their own. Rolstone's daughter knew about it and she also knows that Brandon went to the farm. Her tongue was very loose in those first few days until things settled down."

Balen was looking at his desk. "What happened to Chris?"

Frank shook his head. "You are more likely to be able to find out. We know she went back to her father as he sent people out to find the farm. If you give Crow to them you might be able to find out more. It is likely that what she said spread and that has caused a backlash against LexCorp. Transition X is closely associated with LexCorp and as Crow is at the Farm that could put the farm in the firing line. You are right, we could expect an attack. Crow has been seen around, he insists on going to the Mart so he has hardly been incognito." Frank rolled his tongue around his teeth and shook his head. "Do you have room here for us to evacuate the farm. Just until this is over?"

Balen thought about it. "Yes, well they are Raven's people whether we have room or not we will fit them in. What I will do though is put our own men in there, incognito. We might as well fight them. Now I'm torn. Tonight we have the Handfasting, tomorrow you could evacuate the farm. We will provide hands to help."

Frank smiled. "We had better discuss this with Raven. I can't see that she will say no but this is a start to your relationship. You don't own her and don't let her think that you do. You cannot make decisions for the farm on her behalf."

They sat and chatted until Raven came back. She came into the room with Oberon. Balen looked up and sighed. "I suppose that saying no dogs in here isn't worth it." Oberon sat down beside Raven, then laid down in a ball and curled his tail over his nose.

Raven smiled. "So what have you been discussing?"

Frank smiled at Balen who sighed. Balen then spoke softly. "We believe there might be an attack on the farm. The splinter group is likely to do with what the Managing Director of LexCorp was up to and now that the farm is associated with LexCorp there could be a problem. Would you be agreeable to bringing the animals and people here?"

Raven nodded. "Makes sense. The acres there are poor, the land here is good. That place can't sustain even the numbers which are there long term. Bring them here, they have good ideas and we can start some projects. Can you shift the animals?"

Balen nodded. "I'll send some of the boys to help. Why don't you go and speak to them tomorrow. No point waiting, sooner the better. Are you agreeable that we "come clean" and hand Crow to Rolstone? Chris has suffered at his hand in the same way as you did, worse. She can no longer have children and Rolstone is as you can imagine livid that his only daughter can't give him a granddaughter."

Frank choked. "That bad?"

Balen looked kindly at Frank. "Not a subject I wanted to know about either. Look it up Frank."

Frank was expressionless. "Hand Crow over to Rolstone. I'll see to it myself tomorrow." He walked over to Raven and put his arms around her. "I didn't know that humans could be so cruel. Now, we must write a binding ceremony for a man to a woman in love and understanding.

It should involve symbolism and easy to remember words. Not too many of them and then a party. That seems to be a common thing."

Raven smiled. "Oh I think they are well on their way to planning a party.

I wasn't allowed up there but one of the cow barns is looking very different."

There was a knock on the door and Elissa, one of the elderly women was at the door. "We think that Raven should come with us to get ready for this afternoon. We have everything in hand. Do you wish to wear your boiler suit? Or do you wish us to find you something else?"

Balen looked thunderstruck. "A boiler suit would be appropriate. Raven?"

Raven got up and followed the woman.

Balen thought about it. "In the circumstances as you are NEMESIS would it be appropriate if you handled the "ceremony"."

Frank thought about it. "It could set up a precedent for the future. If one Nemesis Unit does a Handfasting that binding is recorded so it would be unlikely that either partner could get away with doing the same with anyone else. We have face recognition."

Balen laughed. "Not quite what I meant but a good point."

Frank thought about it. "I will create a suitable ceremony for you both."

The hours passed swiftly. Frank sat with Balen, Raven was with the elders of the encampment, and they had everything in hand.

When the time came, they knocked at the door and Frank and Balen went with them. They had set up what looked like an altar on the top of the hill. Everyone was standing around the hill and they had made archways every fifteen feet, decorated with streamers made from old feed bags which fluttered in the wind.

Frank was summoned so that Raven didn't have to walk up the hill on her own. Balen and everyone was waiting. The musicians were playing and then there was silence before the music changed to something like the wedding march.

Frank walked in Raven's left. There was a gasp as the women had found some white material and had made her a beautiful wedding dress. It was body hugging and decorated with living ivy. Her arm was still strapped up which was unfortunate and they had made the neck high which hid most of the bruising. They had dressed her hair and used make up to cover most of the bruises on her face. She looked beautiful as she walked elegantly up the hill, barefoot.

Frank stood her beside Balen and moved to stand in front of them both.

"You were born alone, and you walked to this place alone."

He took two ribbons. He tied the end of one around Balen's wrist. The end of the other around Raven's wrist. He took the two ends and held them.

"There is no binding which makes you stay together other than the love which binds you, one to another and the promise that you now make. This invisible binding must be undertaken willingly."

He gave Balen's ribbon to Balen and Raven's ribbon to Raven. If you wish to be bound, one to the other then give your ribbon of your own free will, one to the other. This seals your promise that you belong together. You belong to each other. You walk side by side, neither in front, neither behind. Balen gave his ribbon to Raven. Raven gave her ribbon to Balen. Frank took the hands with the ribbons in them and put both hands together so the ribbons touched. "The two are now one."

There as a cheer from everyone. Frank smiled. "Balen, you may kiss your wife."

Balen didn't need a second invitation. He kissed her to the tumultuous applause and cheering of all present and barking from Oberon.

They walked down the hill hand in hand to the barn which had been transformed. There was music, drinking, dancing and food. They danced, and the music played until midnight when Frank stood up. "It is now time for the couple to leave us but let the party continue."

Balen took Raven's hand, and he led her out of the barn. "I have a surprise for you. There has been a room prepared for us to share as my room is too small for two."

The room was in the main house along a corridor. Raven followed him, and he opened the door. They had built a four-poster bed out of tall fence posts and fencing rails and somewhere they had found a mattress. The room was bare, there were a couple of bedside tables, a chest of drawers, a dressing table and a chair.

Balen shut the door behind him. He stepped forwards and unzipped Raven's dress while kissing her. The dress fell to the floor as she undid the buttons on his boiler suit and pulled it off of him. He gently took the underwear off of her and lifted her in his strong arms and carried her to the bed. He laid her gently on the mattress. "I said I would never make love to you until you asked me. Will you ask me."

Raven smiled. She kissed him. "Balen, make love to me."

Balen reached into the bedside table and pulled out a tub. "This will make it easier on you." He applied the gel. He then held his hands out. "I'll not hold you down or make you do anything you don't want to do. Take my hands." She interlinked her fingers with his and he then made love to her, slowly and gently, kissing her and reassuring her all the way until they both fell back into each other's arms.

The morning dawned clear and bright. There had been a slight frost and it sparkled on the hedges and fences. Balen was up early and as he walked through the main yard of the farm doing his usual inspection he felt the usual nervous anticipation of attack at any moment. That had been getting stronger lately. He was vigilant, noticing every movement, every sound but also experiencing it all and focusing on the moment. He could smell the clear air, something he had rarely had time to do. He could feel the chilled breeze on his face. There didn't seem to be anyone else around.

The yard was as he expected it to be. Everything was in its place. Small wind turbines spun in the morning breeze and the animals were making contented noises. His boots seemed to sound loud in the morning silence. The frost had hardened the mud and it crunched under his feet.

He hurried across the yard and entered the main building. He bounded up the stairs two at a time, past his guards who wished him good morning and congratulations and opened the door. Raven was still asleep, so he pulled off his boiler suit and climbed into the bed next to her. The chill of his body woke her.

She rolled over and he kissed her and whispered. "How are you feeling my love? Any pain?"

She smiled and kissed him back. "No pain. You don't need permission every time, only the first."

Balen smiled and gently climbed on top of her, and he was as gentle and caring as he had been the night before. He took time and made sure she was happy with everything that he did."

Raven smiled and kissed him. "Teach me what you would like me to do, show me?"

He was more than happy to educate her, and they spent most of the morning in each other's arms.

It was mid-afternoon before they both emerged, dressed in their boiler suits. They passed the guards who wished them good afternoon and opened the door to Balen's office. Balen sighed and went to his desk and looked down at the papers he hadn't finished the day before. The letters had been collected, they would be on their way. He smiled and shook his head, sat down and began looking them over.

He bundled them together, tapped them on the desk to level them out and set them down and began with the top one. He picked them up and went to the table, put two chairs, there, poured two coffees and gave Raven a pen. They read and read and wrote comments, they discussed and wrote comments in the box as to what should be done about each situation. Some were suggestions to speak with other members, some were suggestions they made themselves.

They had done about five when they came to one which caught Balen's attention. It was from his Head of Security. The handwriting was hasty, not the usual neat and precise report that he would have expected. That got his attention.

The report read "After extensive surveillance and interrogation I am sorry to have to inform you that correspondence has been recovered between members of this Compound and an external Unit known as Black Troop. It recommended your immediate removal and stated any weaknesses in our defences. Our agents have doubled their efforts to ascertain who sent the communication but at the present time they are still at large.

Their directive is to remove anyone who is not a Transition X Member.

I am pleased to report that there is no doubt about your leadership and that of Lady Raven. Your actions and your union has reinforced your reputation within the ranks.

Reports have reached us via Security Officers in the other Compounds that there have been assassination attempts on the lives of many of the Compound Commanders. There was a failed attempt on the High Commander earlier this week. I have doubled the security but I have kept it covert so that it does not interfere with your day to day activities. I would make a suggestion that you exercise caution and do not consider leaving the Compound.

I have raised out security level to Red. We can expect an imminent attack from the forces of Black Troop."

Balen put the paper down and rubbed his forehead with the palm of his hand. He sighed and flipped through the rest of the paperwork. It all looked very mundane. He took the communique from the Head of Security and put the other paperwork aside. "We'd better speak to the Head of Security. If we are going to bring the people from your farm in here we need to know they are going to be safe. How will that fit with your planting?"

Raven thought about it. "No need for the seed to go in yet. Moving the animals won't hurt them, you have enough grazing here. I'd say they are safer here as if they are attacked there there are no walls, just a few electric fences."

Balen nodded. "If you are agreed. Frank went back this morning."

He called the guard. "Bring me the Head of Security."

The guard left the room and minutes later a tall, thick set individual dressed in the customary black boiler suit bearing the crossed swords insignia of the Security Division on his shoulder stepped inside. He closed the door, stepped into the middle of the room and saluted first Balen and then Raven. "I am assuming that you have read my report."

Balen sat down. "Indeed I have. What measures do you have in place to ensure our security? Kurt, you may dispense with the formalities. You may take a seat."

Kirt visibly relaxed and sat down. "I have doubled the guard on patrols so that no individual is left on their own. We can assume that there aer hostiles within the Compound though you cleared most of them out. From messages we have managed to intercept we can expect a full on attack any day. The High Commander has been notified and we have received word that he is sending reinforcements. This threat is not to be underestimated.

My intelligence has revealed that they are an undercover group working for a group called "Damocles Inc". They were financial rivals to Lex Corporation. As Transition X is so closely linked with LexCorp we are a natural target."

Balen nodded. "That is similar to a message I got from my brother yesterday. Pretty much as we expected."

Kurt smiled. "Pretty much. I've put as much into the defences as I can. I've put in place your suggestions and all we can do is hope that they don't hit us with too much firepower.

Balen frowned. "Did you get the security bunkers put in place?"

Kurt hesitated. "I did, they are not all finished but they are enough for non-essential personnel. I have had the roofs of the sheds reinforced so they will survive limited mortar attack and all animal handlers have been alerted to the situation. Feed is at maximum and we have stockpiled enough to last us for at least a month.

I received your message about the incoming refugees. I have made provision for space and quarantine of the animals as per the general directive set in place by Lady Raven. All outside Agents bar those at the farm who will be expected back with those refugees have been recalled. We are prepared for lockdown and as soon as your people arrive Lady Raven we will put that into place. Are there any last commands for actions outside the perimeter?"

Balen opened the desk drawer and took out a brown sealed envelope. "I have some information you might find interesting. It came from an informant and has been verified by Raven. It seems that "Crow", Raven's husband died a while back and was replaced by an individual known as Brandon as they look similar. I understand that your father, Lex Corp's Head of Acquisitions was looking for him in relation to his actions towards your sister. Have you heard from your father?"

Kurt looked down. "I have, and the news is grave. My sister took her own life as she was so ashamed that she was not able to produce an heir. I understand that this was due to the injuries sustained from her time with Brandon."

Balen was thunderstruck. "That is indeed grave news. My dear Lady Raven herself sustained similar injuries at his hand."

Kurt looked up, horrified. "You mean?"

Balen nodded. "Your sister will be avenged. I give you leave to take a Unit to Raven's Farm when you are escorting the rest of them and the animals here to take Crow to your father. I believe that retribution should be his."

Kurt turned to Raven. "I am so sorry that we were not aware of this. I must personally apologise for your treatment while you were in our "care". We honestly believed that you were responsible for the death of our loved ones. I hope that any injuries sustained did not hinder your recovery."

Raven smiled. "According to the doctor I will make a recovery. I am so very sorry to hear about your sister. Those of us who suffered at his hand will never forget the harm he has done and neither should we forget those who suffered. I trust that you will treat Crow in the way that he deserves. I thank you for the glass of water you brought me when I was at my worst. It meant a lot."

Kurt smiled. "I thank you My Lady Raven."

At the farm the occupants were waking up. Crow and Reko had been on guard duty, and they were just going in for breakfast. They were replaced by Peter and Shaun.

Frank was in the kitchen when they came in after returning to the Farm earlier. He had a serious look on his face. He glared at Crow who ignored him and sat down. Cheryl put a plate of food in front of him and when Reko came in she put one in front of him too. She smiled at them both. "Was it a quiet night?"

Reko looked up. "Thank you for this. Yes, it was thanks, not a movement on the road."

Crow grunted. He then tucked into his breakfast, ignoring everyone's stares. When he had finished, he got up and walked out of the room.

The rest of them eat their breakfast in silence. Frank finished his after he had wiped the last of the toast around his plate and drank down the last of the tea. By then everyone else was there waiting for them. Reko looked up as Crow went out. "Are you alright Frank?"

Frank took a deep breath. "No, far from it. Check Crow has gone upstairs."

Tracey got up. "I'll go up and make sure he stays there."

Frank looked concerned. "Will you be ok?"

Tracey grinned. "I'll be fine, not sure about him though."

Frank smiled as he heard the door shut upstairs. "I was with Raven yesterday evening." Everyone looked up, stunned. "She is with Transition X, she is safe and well, better than that, she and Balen are definitely in love and I officiated over their Handfasting yesterday. He has given her joint leadership of Transition X and they have requested that we join forces. Their ideals are out ideals.

There is an imminent attack from Black Toop and we are likely targets as well so Lord Balen has offered us sanctuary within his Compound. Raven has informed me that the planting doesn't need doing yet and if we bring our supplies with us there will be room enough. Are you agreeable? It will involve a very swift pack up and move."

There was a bubble of conversation, but it was all agreeable and revolved around Transition X having the resources to be able to make things work.

Frank took a deep breath. "They will be taking Crow. Make sure that nobody gets in the way. You will have to trust me on this. It is Raven's orders. You will be informed of the whole story when we get to the Compound.

Later that morning they had everything packed up and the animals were ready to move. Two large animal lorries arrived and the animals were loaded. A van arrived to take the dogs and a horsebox for the horses. Frank put the last of their fuel into the tanks to supplement what had been used to get them there and back.

They packed the Camper Van with everyone's luggage. Crow had been informed and he had packed. Tracey had packed Raven's things when he wasn't looking, and her cases were brought down and put in the van.

A black shiny van arrived once they were packed and the Head of Security got out. Everyone was in the yard, including Crow. The vans headed off, The Colours followed with their cart, and they went as a convoy.

Frank was left standing in the yard with Crow, Tracey, and the Security Detail from Transition X.

Crow cleared his throat. "I would like to voice my objection that as the leader of this farm I was not consulted about this situation. However I believe it will be the best for all of us. If you would like to load my luggage we can be on our way."

Tracey turned around and slapped him hard around the face which knocked him backwards onto the floor. She then kicked him hard several times in the genitals. "That is for Raven."

She turned and Kurt smiled at her and the two hugged. "Greetings Cousin, nice slap! Good to see you haven't lost your touch." He smiled and slapped her on the backside playfully as she walked past. "Now, Crow."

The Security Detail stepped forwards and cable tied Crow hands and feet. He was still recovering from being kicked so couldn't object. They then threw him into the back of the van and got in with him. Frank got in the van with Tracey, leaving Crow's luggage in the yard.

The yard looked and sounded empty as they drove away. They had done an excellent job of clearing anything of any value and all animals were gone. The doors were locked and nailed shut and the place was left in the hope that one day they would return.

.

4

All around the compound windows that faced outside were covered with heavy shutters which could be closed easily and locked. Guards who were on duty took up their position. The animals were welcomed in and taken to their new pens, fed watered and bedded down supervised by Raven. Everyone in the Compound was going about their daily tasks.

The people from the Farm stood in the yard looking like lost children evacuated during the war. They might as well have had labels on the buttons. Raven walked over, and the atmosphere changed. They hugged, and Storm even squealed which was very much not her.

Balen came over as Raven had got them to calm down enough to speak to them. Tracey and her family had done off to see their friends. It had become evident to the others straight away that they were Transition X.

Balen put his arm around Raven. "I assume you have heard the news?"

Storm stepped forwards, looking nervous. "We have heard news; it is all very confusing. Raven is staying with you now? And we have been invited too and we will be safe here."

Balen looked down. "You will be safer here. We are all in danger as Black Troop are a severe threat. I hope I'm bringing you here for safety. We'll do the best we can.

Raven is staying with me. I'd better let her tell you." Balen smiled at Raven.

Raven looked at everyone and they were silent, expectant, waiting for the explanation. "I have been here for months but I have not been able to contact you. To start with I was a prisoner but it was soon discovered that it had been Rat who had instigated the belief that the reconnaissance mission was a threat. That is history now. The people here accept it and you know the truth.

For my own safety until the people here were reconciled with the true situation I remained as Lord Balen's guest. I now remain here as his wife."

There was stunned silence followed by more hugs and congratulations.

Raven took a deep breath. "You will not see Crow again. He caused me harm, he caused worse harm to Chris. So much so that she committed suicide. Crow has been given to Chris' father to deal with as he wishes. As you are here I assume you are agreeable that our future is here now until we can safely return. There are lands here, animals and we can continue the projects and I hope that you will integrate with the people here. We have rooms prepared for you and there is a meal put on in the barn tonight. We may not have many more where we can relax and even now we have to be ready for trouble."

The others followed a young lad who had been given a list of people and rooms. He was taking his job very seriously even though he was only about eleven.

Raven laughed. "Child labour now?"

Balen smiled. "He's the son of one of the Security Detail. He wants to follow daddy when he grows up so we let him do easy jobs around here. It has been a long day. I'd like to change. If the animals are settled shall we go up for a bit?"

Raven smiled and they went up the stairs to their room. Oberon followed her and leapt into the room and curled up in his basket under the window. The room was spacious and decorated with a subtle fleck blue wallpaper. Curtains had been pulled over the boarded up windows and it had a cosy yet elegant feeling to it. The room had also been furnished since he had decided to finally take it. Someone had put in a wardrobe and there was a table and chairs now.

The room was at the end of a corridor. The windows were boarded with blast thickness metal sheeting. He shut the door and leant against it.

Raven looked tired and she sat on the bed while Balen went and got a shower down the hallway. She had managed one before the others had arrived.

He walked into the room, his hair spikey from the shower wrapped in a towel. He put his arms around her. She leant her head on his chest. Feeling the muscles taut under her cheek. Balen led her to the bed, he was too tired to carry her. He turned the light out and they made love. They lay in each other's arms until past five and then had to get dressed for the evening.

The evening was a candle lit wonder of food, very little drinking as they were on Red Alert and very little dancing as everyone was too tired. It was more of a gathering for people to get to know each other. It passed peacefully and at Midnight Balen led Raven off to bed as most people were heading that way.

The got upstairs and thankfully got undressed and got into bed. Balen kissed Raven and they made love before he turned the light out and they fell asleep in each other's arms.

A month passed and everyone got settled into their new routines. They were on edge, constantly. Every day they expected an attack.

At 4am the Compound was hit by mortar fire. Balen rolled over, kissed Raven and stroked her hair. "My love, I must go. Stay here, please. Don't give me anything else to worry about. I need a clear head to command this. Promise?"

Raven clung to him. There were tears in her eyes. "I can help the doctor. I'd be as safe there as here."

He rolled out of bed and grabbed for his clothes. He pulled them on and was about to leave. He pulled his pistol out of its holster and checked the clip and the slide. "Do you know how to use this?"

Raven nodded. "A bit like a shotgun?"

Balen smiled. "Yes, but don't forget to take the safety off. Keep it on when you aren't using it. That thing has a hair trigger. If you are in doubt about anyone, use it. Go straight to the Infirmary and stay there if you want to help." He kissed her before she could speak and ran out of the door.

The guard shut the door. One guard stayed on the door, the other followed Balen to his office where he picked up another pistol, loaded it and headed off downstairs.

Outside was organised chaos. Mortar bombs were landing at one-minute regular intervals, leaving huge craters in the farmyard. The animals shed had a hole in it and there was chaos inside as farm hands were trying to put a fire out and control the animals.

Kurt was waiting for Lord Balen and shouted over the sounds of the explosions. "We mucked the barns out earlier so the fire damage will be minimal on the concrete. We've started firing back as we've managed to take out two of their armoured vehicles that were likely to take out the gate. We are now firing on their ground troops. They are coming in waves and attacking us from all directions. This is a first assault to test our resources and to try to deplete our ammunition. I've put everyone on essential shots only and shoot to kill.

The platforms you ordered set up this afternoon around the perimeter have made all the difference and we have got as much bullet proof metal as possible up there protecting our guys. We could really use heavier weaponry. Do we have your authority?"

Balen looked around. "Get a detachment onto moving the injured to the doctor and any non-essential personnel should have the option of either going into the shelter or helping the doctor where they can. You have my authority, bring out the heavy weaponry. How are they acting towards us?"

Kurt formulated his thoughts. "Full barrage, no let up."

Balen was expressionless. "Respond in kind. No mercy. The railguns are one shot as we can't reload at short notice. There isn't enough power.

Make them count. Keep some back. There could be further attacks."

Kurt ran off and he could be heard shouting commands. Balen went in the other direction ordering men to the best positions and deploying what weaponry they had to spare. He organised runners to carry ammunition and grabbed a rifle himself and began shooting through the barricades at those who got too close.

A detachment ran into the main building and came out with rocket launchers and railguns. They formed up around the compound on the platforms and began firing. Weapons which Balen had stockpiled were used and cast aside. As he had speculated as they were all powered and only had enough charge for one shot but they did make it count. Balen climbed up a ladder. He reached the top and caught a shot in the shoulder. He ducked down. The countryside was alight with muzzle flash. There were patches of flame where their own mortars had landed and bodies lay in piles around the fence. The barrage of railgun and rocket fire decimated the area. Bodies fell in droves and swathes were cut through the approaching troops. The beams which shot from the railguns cut long lines twenty feet wide. Nothing stood when they fired. He took up position and began firing at single targets, aiming at those on the mortars.

Within half an hour there was desolation around the Compound and those outside stopped firing and retreated as there was hardly anyone left to fire back. Balen climbed back down the ladder. Blood was trickling down his arm and he was beginning to feel lightheaded. He ran over to where Kurt was gathering troops on the ground. "Report?"

Kurt looked up. "Enemy has been decimated. Our casualties are in the tens and the wounded are with the doctor."

Balen smiled. "Very good but any loss is too many. Send a unit out to mop up and collect any unused munitions and whatever weaponry you can find. This won't be the end of it and we're now low on ammo. No mercy, don't leave any survivors. They work by infiltration, don't give them the opportunity. Count your people out and in and know who went out and who is coming in. I want a squad on the gate. Make sure you know who our people are."

Kurt threw his head back. "And Sir, if it's not too much trouble could you report to the doctor yourself and get that wound seen to?"

Balen looked down and swore. "Handle things here. I won't be long." The wound had hurt but he'd been so focused on everything else he'd blocked out doing anything about it. He walked off to the doctor's room and joined the queue of people waiting to be dealt with.

The doctor saw him and rushed over. Balen held his hand up. "No, deal with everyone in turn. I've given my orders. If I'm needed I'll jump the queue." He stepped over to where a young woman was cradling her baby. Her arm was bleeding from a piece of glass that was dug into it. She was standing against the wall and had begun to sway a little. Balen called to a lad in his twenties with curly blonde hair and a cheeky grin. He was holding a cloth to a wound on his arm. "James, can you spare half a seat for this woman?" James moved the chair over and the woman nearly fell into the seat, they then shared it. Seeing this others shared their seats so more injured could sit down.

Balen then grabbed a kidney bowl and some disinfectant and joined Raven helping to clean wounds prior to the doctor seeing them. Raven washed his wound and put a temporary dressing on it. There was hardly time to talk.

The Doc and Storm were busy with patients as well. Doc was running a triage and managing the lesser wounds, dressing, and cleaning up. Storm was assisting him. They had set up in a room and they had a line of patients outside.

The doctor smiled when he came over. "It's been years since we worked together, do you fancy a new job? I could use a couple of new assistants."

Balen smiled. "Only tonight." He held his hand over an injured boy's burnt arm and concentrated. The boy stopped crying and relaxed. He moved on to the next, and the next. He bandaged some lesser injured people and treated the minor burns. After about an hour he stepped into a side room and started seeing people in there. Each one was cleaned up, bandaged and given healing.

It was dawn when the doctor got to Balen's wound. It was bleeding badly despite being dressed and Balen was beginning to feel lightheaded. The doctor applied anaesthetic and removed the bullet. "Just like old times. I forget sometimes that you used to be a Healer."

Balen smiled. "I never stopped. I just started trying to stop the injuries in the first place. I'd better check on how things are going outside."

The doctor smiled. "Before you go. I did some tests this morning. Raven's pregnant. Well done you old bugger, first month success. I haven't told Raven. I thought you might like that job." They hugged and Balen ran outside.

Outside was quiet. The troop that had gone outside the main gate had returned safely. There was a pile of weapons and other useful bits and pieces on the quad bike trailer. The fires had been put out and although the animals were still noisy they were quieter than they were. Guards had been posted but people were beginning to trail off to bed when they weren't needed. Balen strode over to Kurt who was talking to a young man.

Kurt looked over as Balen approached him. "The clean-up was easy, very few wounded left. We've got just about every weapon out there and we'll start the body clear up in the morning unless someone comes to collect their dead. I've posted guards and the rota is sorted out. It looks like its going to be quiet now but just in case I'd kept back a Unit I didn't use in the main barrage. They are on standby. Captain Evans is with them and he's a competent commander."

Balen smiled. "You have done well. It is time for you to get some sleep."

Kurt smiled back. "If it's not too impertinent isn't it time you got some rest too. Or is rest not what you have in mind?"

Balen raised an eyebrow. "As you are my oldest friend, I will overlook that comment and bid you a good night for what is left of it."

As Balen crossed the yard he looked back. The golden light of dawn silhouetted the buildings. Smoke rose from all around the compound but it was quiet. Most people had gone to bed leaving those on guard and those on clean up duty to do their job. He opened the door and went inside. He went to the Infirmary. All was quiet. Raven was sitting with an elderly lady who was finding it hard to sleep. When she saw him she wished the woman a good night and went to find the doctor.

The doctor was having a cup of coffee. "I can manage now. Thank you to both of you for helping. Sleep well."

Balen's shoulder was hurting, and it seemed that every muscle in his body ached. They climbed the stairs and his legs felt like lead.

As they crossed the yard, they saw that Frank and the others were on their way back to where they had set up a camp with The Colours and in the end barn. They waved as they headed off.

The guard on his door saw them coming and opened the door for them. "Good night."

They passed him and bid him a good night as he shut the door behind him.

Raven looked exhausted. Balen kissed her as they undressed and got into bed. They made love and as they lay in each other's arms afterwards Balen whispered. "I spoke to the doctor while I was in the Infirmary. You are pregnant my love. There has been enough death tonight. But this is the hope of new life." They kissed and fell asleep.

Balen woke soon after. He couldn't sleep and the hours dragged like treacle. His head was full of worries and thoughts. He kept imagining that every shadow in the new room held an assassin and his shoulder pulsed pain through him.

He tried healing his shoulder, the pain eased to a dull pulsing, and he shut his eyes hopefully. Moments later a sound in the room made him sit up, eyes darting about, trying to see what had made the noise. Oberon was sleeping in his basket. He would not have been so calm if anyone had been there.

Raven woke up too. Balen's sitting up had disturbed her and she too was in a panic. She looked around and when she realised it was quiet, she put a hand on his uninjured shoulder. His body was soaked in beads of sweat.

The room was silent, they were alone. Balen looked around, but he couldn't see anybody. "I'm just having difficulty sleeping. Don't worry my love." He put his hand over hers. "I have too much running through my head."

Raven smiled though Balen couldn't see it in the darkness. "Well hardly surprising considering what you have to worry about. There is nothing you can do at the moment. You were well prepared for the attack tonight and everyone did their job. Try not to worry." She put her arm around him.

Balen turned and put his arms around her. "I'm just so tired. There's no let-up, one thing after another. Then they come at me all at once. There's never time to deal with the problems on their own and one thing left cascades into plenty more serious problems. I feel like I'm spinning plates on sticks and running about to keep them all spinning. If I miss one it falls off."

Raven kissed his neck. "Well now if you'll let me I'll help with some of those plates. Tell me and it might help."

Balen took a deep breath and let it out slowly. "I miss my space when I could relax and visualise a place of peace. This has all been so fast and the world is so different now."

Raven sighed. "Why can't you do your visualisation?"

Balen thought for a moment. "There isn't the space or the time."

Raven laughed. "Yes there is. You have to set aside that time or things will get on top of you, like they are tonight. You have to find solutions, I agree. You have to keep all those people safe, fed and united but that would be a lot easier with a clear head. As you know, mistakes cost lives and you can't get them back again afterwards."

Balen breathed out sharply. "On a basic level we have to survive. I know there are individuals out there and small groups living off the land. We have to make contact with some of them and help them with equipment and medical supplies.

That in itself is contrary to Transition X's original manifesto. In essence we have deviated here from what TX was supposed to be. The "Teachings of the Founders" were quite different and that has put us at odds with the rest of the organisation. This breakaway group has happened because they too have different ideas. Transition X is fragmenting. We are tolerated because my brother defends us. He too is under threat and to keep his position as High Commander he will probably have to act against me at some point.

We were the "Founders". I just don't know how it got this far. It was all so innocent when we used to meet up in my flat and talk about it. We wrote the "Laws" and it was a bit of a game at the time. We were going to be the saviours of the planet. My brother always wanted to be in charge so I let him. It all seemed so harmless.

Some of the members are purists and they adhere more to the original "teachings". Bear in mind that some of these were written when we were off our heads on something or the other. Michael in particular was into anything he could get his hands on. Add to that his paranoid schizophrenia and it was a recipe for disaster. Those original teachings were what made father think that it would dovetail with Lex Corp and provide him with the environmental credentials he wanted.

You encountered Rat when he infiltrated your place. I had my worries about sending him as his beliefs were purist TX. That is causing our own internal problems. Some of the purists don't see those of us who want to be more reasonable as members anymore.

By creating what we have we have shown our hand to LexCorp and now that they are sorting out some of their issues in the cities they have time to notice. They have the excuse that they need resources to keep the cities running so some of the other Compounds are very understocked with weapons and other equipment. I stockpiled and managed to do well for us. The attackers last night probably didn't expect the level of firepower we had.

They have formed Black Troop now that we are not just living on the land and scavenging. Their isolationist beliefs are more in line with what father wanted. The result would be an inbred "super race" which exterminates or enslaves anyone else. What we are now is a coherent and working organisation. We are a threat to them.

What is running through my mind is that survival may depend more on becoming small units who live in a similar way to how our ancestors lived. Man started as a hunter gatherer. That could be where our answer lies but now we are pushed to defending the compound and that deviates from planting, growing and living.

Raven thought for a moment. "Would the land sustain that sort of a lifestyle for so many people now? One man living in a large enough space and only taking what is needed could. If everyone did it would they wipe out what they need to preserve to survive?"

Balen sighed. "That is what is happening around the cities. There are those who have left the cities, but they didn't go far. They were faced with very little wild land, few wild animals to live on and the weight of numbers of people trying to survive has wiped out the countryside or so I have heard from reports.

Any farm near a city has lost its livestock to hungry raiders. A cow is food on the hoof. They don't care if it is a dairy cow or not, or whether it is breeding stock."

Raven lay her head on his shoulder. "I have heard that. Probably why NEMESIS chose farms which were remote. Meat must be rare there now as those towers wouldn't have lasted. They relied on a lot of power. Right in the middle of the city, I bet they were early targets for hungry people. The people would have eaten well for the first few weeks."

Balen sighed. "Now they are looking outward, and they are forced to increase their range and more places which would have fed them for years to come have been raided. If they aren't able to feed themselves, they have to try so I'm not even sure anymore if I think they are wrong."

Raven stroked his hair and he relaxed slightly.

Balen kissed her shoulder. "When all this started, I followed the directive to get all those who were part of the organisation to a safe haven. It was also part of the original directive to remove or assimilate any possible competition for resources. The belief was safety in numbers and growing an insular community.

I now know that an idea can be good on paper and seeing how it really works only works when you do it for real. If you are not prepared to deviate from the original plan when things don't work you are doomed to extinction.

Without opposition running this place, providing food, heat and keeping going is possible. Doing that and facing opposition like we did last night, I don't know. I used most of our stockpile. If we were left alone to get on with things, we would stand a chance."

Raven sighed. "Mankind is warlike and acquisitive. That can't be shut down like a computer program. So what are you suggesting?"

Balen shut his eyes and thought. "I'm not, that is the problem. I can't see a solution. If we carry on we'll have the internal struggle and we will also be targeted by LexCorp in the end as Michael can't keep on defending us. If we go back to the original idea then only we will survive and we'll be at constant war with those around us.

I can't break this number of people down into sustainable hunter gatherer groups as the countryside can't support us. It might in time if we replant forests and let animals become feral, but we don't have time for that with the population we have."

Raven thought about it. "Don't you mean had?"

Balen shook his head. "What do you mean?"

Raven took a deep breath. "How many died before all this in natural disasters? How many died in the original switch off? How many have died since? I've never read any TX Teachings but I have read others. I'm no scholar but what comes to mind is that the TX philosophy will be interpreted in the way that the reader reads it. I can see that would be altered anyway by what that reader has experienced and preconceived ideas. The original idea will still be there under all that but the original intent of the writers could be lost."

Balen thought on that one. "Well, the original meaning was put together by my brother and myself and a few friends joined in later. We had heard of Transition Towns, and we wanted our version of it."

Raven smiled. "I'd like to know more about what you were like then."

Balen smiled. "I was a Healer, and I wrote poetry, badly. I took on basic work to feed myself to keep myself away from daddy's empire and I lived by the sea. Hardly the credentials for all this."

Raven laughed. "Do you want me to answer that or are you asking yourself? How can you doubt any of it? Look around you. Forget what is happening because others are attacking this place. There is a group of people here who have managed to hold it together and build something sustainable out of the chaos. You hold it together because you don't ask anything of it. Ironic considering you wrote the original plan but there is no Master Plan here other than putting food on the table, a roof over people's heads and giving them purpose. It's the same as you doing the jobs to keep yourself fed. It's the actions, wants and needs of outside influences that are upsetting the balance here. Waters are still until someone throws a pebble in."

Balen thought for a while. "So what can I do?"

Raven rested her head against his. "Live day to day and deal with the problems that arise. As you say there are no real wild lands to rely on for hunting and gathering. The only answer is farming sustainably and that is what we are doing our would be doing if they would leave us alone."

Balen shook his head. "What about the rest of it?"

Raven closed her eyes for a moment. "LexCorp is a Mega Corporation sustained by finance and a structure that is supported by the way things were. That structure is breaking down so it has to either fall apart or find a place in the new way of things without bringing back the problems which caused NEMESIS to shut down the computers in the first place. Is it known that the Laws were written by Michael and yourself?"

Balen looked at her. "Father did the basics of setting up Transition X so he didn't mention us specifically. He set it up for Michael really as he was getting very erratic. The Laws were set up by the "Founding Fathers." Probably something which resonated with him considering his sick and twisted idea of impregnating as many as he could and being Father to the next generation."

Raven looked at him. "Do you have a line of communication to your father?"

Balen was staring into the darkness. "Yes, of course. I do sometimes get messages. They are brief and usually just a scribbled note along with a press release or news bulletin."

Raven thought about it. "Well we could write a "Plan for the Future" and "New Directive of the Founding Fathers" seeing as you are going to be one."

Balen smiled and kissed her. "I am aren't I!"

He put his arms around her and they fell asleep.

Everyone either couldn't sleep or woke up early and the clean-up started late morning after breakfasts had been served. The animals had been fed and watered and five young men had climbed up onto the roof and were fixing the holes with spare box profile metal sheets and bolts.

A shout rang out warning the Compound that someone was coming. Balen was just leaving the building, Raven by his side. They ran to the outer

[margin note: What the doctor told him]

defences and climbed up the ladder.

In the distance coming down the road through the desolation was a blue transit van. It had a piece of white cloth tied to its aerial.

Faces looked at Balen expectantly, the safeties were flicked off of weapons all around. Balen looked down at the twisted, burnt and broken bodies which lay on the ground outside the compound. The van drove carefully through them and drew up fifty yards from the gate. The driver's door opened and a tall man with dark brown hair got out. He didn't look like The Archangel Guards which got Balen's attention straight away. This couldn't have been Black Troop.

He had his hands up and he was wearing a white paper overall. "I've come for the bodies. Please don't shoot me."

Balen stepped up to the edge and looked down. "Take your dead. I want it known by everyone you speak to that we would not have killed anyone if they had left us in peace."

The driver looked around at the devastation. He shouted out of the window. "So did they. They were only following orders." He looked up at Balen with a pleading expression.

Balen looked down at him. "We only want to live in peace here. We want to keep our animals, grow our crops and raise our children. If you bring war to us, we will give you war back. If you leave us alone we will leave you alone. I have dead in here too. They have families and loved ones as your people have families and loved ones. Why were we attacked?"

The driver spat on the ground. "Scum! You claim to live in peace on the face of it but what about the drivers of the lorries you hijacked? We know that you were supplied by the Mart, you, and the rest of your scum. Your people were seen on those raids, aiding the Mart.

Many good men died when the convoys were captured and very few survived. You are worse than the Road Pirates. I can tell you now, we will be back and in greater numbers. Oh and your precious Mart has been destroyed and the leader is dead. He and his Mart went up in flames last night. So let us see how you raise your animals now. So go on scum, you can kill me. What do I have to live for? Four of my sons are dead."

Balen climbed down the ladder and went to the gate. "Open the gate. I will meet this man face to face." Raven was behind him. He pushed her to the side. "Sorry Raven, Guards, hold her."

Before she could react two of the Guards grabbed her arms. They were as gentle as they could be and gave her very understanding looks.

The doors opened and Balen walked out, stepping over bodies until he stood in front of the man. The driver looked stunned. The other passenger in the van they had not seen was sitting bolt upright trying to see what would happen next. Balen stopped about three metres from the man and looked him in the eye. "We do not know what you are talking about. We have traded with the Mart for goods that we have produced here, as has Raven's Farm. We have bought goods that we have paid or traded for. This was all done in good faith.

We have no idea who supplies the Mart. As we trade for goods it is to be assumed that their stock was obtained in the same way. Both this Compound and Raven's farm provided stock for the Mart to sell. Other farms did as well. As to hijacking, I have heard nothing about this."

The driver spat at Balen. "Yea right, so you aren't going out there and hijacking our vehicles then and our goods aren't turning up on the Mart's shelves? Did you think we wouldn't notice? We marked the cans with invisible marker and we checked it out with a detector. You are scum and very stupid if you think you can stand there and lie to me.

We all have families and friends who have suffered because of the food supplies that didn't arrive from LexCorp. You are lying bastard. So are you going to kill me too? I come in peace, we are not armed. All we want are our dead back so that we have something for their widows and families to bury."

Lord Balen drew himself up to his full height. "We traded with the Mart in good faith. We do not work for the Mart. I am Commander Balen of Transition X. I answer solely to High Commander Archangel. I have no other master or boss. I have a written trade agreement with the Mart whereby we supply our excess goods to them for reasonable credit which we exchange for goods from the Mart in return. I can show you that agreement and the accounts."

The driver threw his head back and laughed. "Yes, well someone who can kidnap and abuse a farmer and destroy her farm isn't going to think anything of hijacking the lorries. I suppose you are going to make them magically appear as well."

Raven called to Balen. "You need to let me come out and speak to them."

Balen shouted. "Go to the room next to my office. In the top drawer of the filing cabinet there is a folder marked "Mart". I want you to bring it to me." He turned to the men. "Then I can "magically" make Raven appear."

Balen was watching the men in the van. He heard the click of the glove box being opened and he was already moving as the passenger drew his pistol out and fired. The bullet missed as Balen dived in front of the van.

The snipers on the fence didn't miss. Two shots rang out, two bodies fell, the one in the van who had fired the shot and the driver.

Balen heard the shots as he ran for the gates. They were slammed shut behind him as he dived through. He caught his breath. "There's no way they aren't going to use that against us. So now we have shot their friends under a flag of truce. It gets better and better."

Raven came running back with the file. She ran to Balen.

Balen climbed back up onto the platform. His shoulder was hurting. Raven climbed up beside him. The sole survivor was standing with his hands up. Balen shouted to him. "Have you met Raven?"

The man shouted back. "I saw her at the Mart so don't try and palm some other woman off as her. Anyway, she is your prisoner, you can make her say what you like."

Balen helped Raven up off of the top of the ladder. She walked to the wall. "I am not a prisoner. I am his wife! The people and animals from my farm have moved here for safety. We too traded with the Mart. Everyone did. Nobody questioned where the supplies were coming from. Why did you assume that Transition X would need to hijack the lorries? Where were the lorries coming from?"

The man thought for a moment. "The lorries were coming from LexCorp's suppliers up North."

Balen glared at the man. "I have told you who I am. Why would I steal from my father's company? My mother is a majority shareholder. If we wanted provisions here all I had to do was to ask for them. We preferred to trade with the Mart."

The man looked up at Balen. "The Mart was a hub for hijacking and a sex slave business where women were being abducted and sold to the highest bidder."

Balen jumped slightly and Raven noticed it. "It seems that the Mart wasn't the benevolent organisation it was pretending to be. Raven, weren't you kidnapped on the way back from the Mart?"

Raven turned to Balen. "You had me kidnapped; you should know. Your men shot my pony!"

Balen looked at his feet. "I was contacted by a man called Carl who said he could bring you to me. At the time we were trying to stop the ring, so my men killed the two who had been carrying out the abductions. As far as we know the abductions stopped after that."

The man nearly smiled. "Caused a little marital stress, have I? Yes, they did abruptly stop a few months ago. About the time that Charlie and his friend were found in a burnt-out van just outside town."

Raven looked down at the dead bodies. "A pointless waste of life."

The man looked down. "Show me the file."

Balen tied it to a piece of rope and lowered it down. The man opened the file and inside there were comprehensive accounts showing how much Transition X had paid to the Mart or traded for equipment and feed. The man looked up at Balen. "It seems that the trouble was only with the Mart. I will report back but I assume we will now leave you alone. If I may take the bodies, I would be grateful."

Balen glared at the man. "A lot of people have died needlessly. Very well, take the bodies and go back to your people and tell them the truth. I'll send out a couple of guards to help you load. There will be guards watching you and any sign of trouble and they will shoot you."

Frank climbed the ladder and joined them. They watched the man for a while. "You handled that well Gabriel."

Balen glared at him. "I'd rather you didn't use my name, that is the past."

Frank smiled. "Well Gabriel Morgan, the past may well influence the future. You were a troublemaker then."

Balen smiled. "I still am but for all the right reasons."

Frank laughed. "Good answer Sir, I accept you as my Commander."

Raven smiled. "Frank, perhaps you could work with us. I've got an idea. Balen, perhaps it is time that Gabriel and Michael produced a "New Directive" and perhaps a Blueprint for a Better World?"

Later that day Cheryl and Raven were walking through the old farmhouse. It was a shell with little furniture and no character. Raven was explaining. "They took it over when it had been abandoned for some time so there wasn't any furniture here.

There are artists here and woodworkers so it could make good communal rooms later. There isn't a dining room as such but the barn sometimes gets used. At the moment whoever is on the rota does the cooking so it is pot luck how eatable it is. We could do with setting up a catering section. There are more people here, over a hundred I think so cooking in this kitchen on a wood fired stove is going to be a challenge. We have been eating in shifts and that sort of works with watches. Food stores are doing alright and now we've added the farm stock in that helps. Now that we've lost the Mart things could get a little more difficult."

Cheryl smiled. "Well we have the animals. The chickens are settling in in the chicken coop and that has multiplied the ones here. That will be a heck of a lot of eggs needed for breakfast!" She noticed that Raven was watching Balen out of the window while she looked around. "I don't know how you can tolerate being near that man. How can you look at him after what he did?"

Raven smiled. "He is my husband, my lover and my friend. I more than tolerate him. Balen did what he had to do."

Cheryl giggled and took Raven's arm. "Tell me more? I thought he raped you? We were all horrified when we heard the news. I was so sorry that Crow turned out to be a rat. I never did like him. Wasn't this Lord Balen supposed to be the "enemy"?"

Raven smiled. "They have an agenda, but it is no different to ours. People are chosen to live in a place and survive. There was a misunderstanding whereby his people thought we had murdered the people who came to our farm. Once it was cleared up that Rat and the others had attacked us first Balen asked me to help with the animals as they had no experience. I did and we fell in love. So, how are you getting on with

Shylock?"

Cheryl smiled. "I'm happy. I still feel sorry about Eric though."

Raven shrugged. "He made his choices. It was a pity he died."

The smile fell from Cheryl's face. "His body was never found. I had assumed he was one of the men who died in the forest and didn't ask. I asked Doc the other day, he checked the bodies over when they were burying them, and Eric wasn't one of them."

5

Raven looked around nervously. There were a lot of issues which were going to come back to haunt her, not least the issue of Cheryl, Shylock and Eric. "That Eric's body wasn't found could be a problem."

Cheryl smiled. "He ran off. I don't expect I'll see him again."

Raven looked at her seriously. "Well not unless you go and join up with the same organisation as he belongs to."

Cheryl looked horrified. "Oh crap! I have, haven't I?"

Raven smiled, though she was now worried. She was angry. It could be an issue, a big one. She had brought a spy into their camp, made a spy by her cheating on him. She wasn't sure where her loyalties lay but she had to protect those under her roof so personal thoughts had to be put aside. "We'll deal with it somehow if there's a problem. I think there is a map in the office somewhere which shows this place. I hope everyone got allocated a room alright."

Cheryl smiled. "We did. The Colours have set up a camp in one of the rougher fields. The rest of us have a place in a small barn for now." Cheryl giggled. "He's coming over."

Balen strode across the yard. "Pleased to meet you Cheryl. Glad to have you along." They shook hands. "How are your plans going?"

Cheryl looked at Raven. Raven smiled at her but her giggly attitude around Balen was annoying her. "Very well. How's your arm?" She was staring up at him.

Balen smiled. "Hurting. Thank you for asking though. If you would excuse me." Balen saw Raven's expression and the way Cheryl was looking at him. He put his arm around Raven's waist and kissed her, passionately and then walked off.

Raven turned to Cheryl. "What is the matter? You seem nervous."

Cheryl looked down at her feet. "I can't help thinking about what he did to you."

Raven laughed. "Try to put that out of your mind. I can't help thinking about what he does do!" The two women burst into laughter. Balen didn't hear what they said but for the first time that day he was nervous without knowing why.

Raven organised the sleeping arrangements and prepared a map of the whole farm with possible individual rooms as most of the people were bunked together in makeshift bunks, hammocks and camp beds. She found a piece of board and pins and made a notice board. She put a list of jobs on the board and came back in half an hour. The list was filling up and nearly every job had been taken."

Cheryl had gone off to find Shylock and to look after Chloe. Raven went to look for Balen.

He had just finished walking the perimeter with Kurt when she found him. He smiled and turned to Kurt. "We'll do the same shifts as last night. I've got to discuss a few things with Raven. Report to my office later." Kurt saluted and strode off.

Balen then crossed the yard to Raven and took her arm. "Did you see the doctor?"

Raven looked sheepish. "There hasn't been time."

Balen glared at her. "There will be later, won't there? Now I want to discuss something with you." He led her up the stairs and to the office. Once there he put his arms around her. "I don't trust Cheryl. She's a wild card who could cause trouble. I know what she did to Eric, he's in our Manchester Compound. She is using Shylock as a babysitter, and I know that look. Keep that bitch away from me Raven or there will be trouble."

Raven nodded. "I know, I don't like how she looks at you. We'll have to keep an eye on her. If she is with Shylock and behaving herself, she isn't an issue. If she becomes an issue, then we will have to deal with it."

There was no attack that night, or the night after. The days ran into weeks, the weeks into months and the planting season came and went and they were almost on to harvest. They didn't relax their guard but they did start to build. Barns were turned into rooms with extra levels. A large sitting room was created and other barns were turned over to crafts workshops for making the everyday things that they needed. One small barn was turned into a dairy, another into a room for making candles and soap.

People read books and they experimented. They had their successes and their failures and they started to make the unusual the mundane. After a couple of months the products started to appear and to be used and enjoyed by others. In turn they did their work which supported the Compound. They managed some scavenging trips and eventually they scavenged furniture from Raven's Farm and other places which had been abandoned. Rooms gained tables, chairs, sofas and other furniture and ornaments and it did start to look like a home.

Frank had been training the men and women who wanted to learn. He ran a combat course and a basic self-defence course for the women. He started an archery class, and this created a spin-off of bow making and arrow making.

As they had more time and the threat of imminent death became less of the forefront of everyone's mind relationships started to flourish and soon enough there was the first request for a Handfasting. This gave them a good excuse to meet together as well as celebrating the couple's happiness and it opened the floodgates for those who had either been together a long time or were wishing to be together. It was decided that on the first Saturday of the Month anyone who wanted to be Handfasted could be.

Raven and Balen grabbed what time they could together. Raven did manage to get to see the doctor and over the months her pregnancy became very obvious. She had to step back from some of the more physical duties as the doctor was very worried about her taking the baby to full term after what had happened. She was ordered bed rest for most of the day which was driving her mad. Balen was like a mother hen and also drove her mad with trying to be over protective. They both healed well and were soon in no pain from their old injuries. It had been seven months now since their handfasting and Raven was starting to find it very hard to sit around when there were things to do.

A kitchen was set up with those who could cook being assigned there on a permanent basis. There was also a dining hall which was built adjacent to the kitchen which could seat everyone, although the seats were very mis matched.

The boiler suit was the regular daily wear but gradually as clothes started to be made there was a movement away from it to other types of clothing.

Other than scavenging missions they hadn't been near any other buildings or towns. It had been decided that keeping out of the way was the best way to survive.

Balen, Frank and Raven had started to put together a plan for a worldwide sustainable development and when they had the framework, they sent a copy to Archangel to see if it was an idea that should be forwarded to LexCorp. They hadn't received an answer although they had heard from him on other subjects.

Balen was standing on the outer gate platform looking out onto the road. Some of the craters had been filled in, others had greened over and some had filled with water to form little ponds. The onset of summer had brought an abundance of growth around the Compound, the growth was at its maximum now that the longest day was long past and they were on the road to winter.. The bare earth had been covered in a verdant green carpet of grass, dandelions and patches of nettles which now provided their tea and coffee.

The open fields around them had now been planted with crops and they were ready for harvest. The plants swayed in the gentle breeze. In the fields around the back of the Compound he watched the animals grazing, with young at foot now well grown. The cows made their way down and were just being let in for milking and the Compound was alive with people doing their regular morning activities.

Raven climbed up to join him. He helped her for the last few steps as she found it hard and he put his arm around her. "Raven, you know I love to watch all this. It makes it all worthwhile. The morning start and the end of the day when all the animals are fed, watered and away."

She smiled and looked around. The milk maids were just carrying the buckets of milk from the Milking Parlour to the Dairy and those in charge of making the cheese had the wood fired oven stoked and were ready to start stirring the milk into cheese. Any milk mistakes where something had fallen into the milk or a careless animal foot had ended up in the milk was taken off for the pigs. Cocks crowed, pigs grunted, goats bleated and children giggled and ran about the play area watched over by their careful guardian.

Balen looked down at Raven. "Our child will play with them one day." He put his hand on her stomach. "But I don't know how long this will go on or how long it will last."

Raven smiled. "In some way it will go on forever, whatever they throw at us. Have you heard anything from Archangel?"

Balen frowned. "Not for months now. I'm expecting a messenger any day now as his staff keep the reports coming. I've been waiting every morning, but nothing has arrived."

Raven looked worried. "I used to believe that no news is good news but knowing what is going on would be good. I'll stay up here with you for a while. Perhaps it will be this morning."

They stood on the platform for nearly an hour and were about to give up when they saw a vehicle in the distance. It was making its way carefully down the hill. It looked like a transit van but it had gained a few metal panels, spikes and wire mesh over the windows. It picked its way around the craters and drew up outside. The passenger door opened and a tall blonde haired man got out. He was dressed in long white robes with a white cloak around his shoulders. He had grown a long full beard and his hair was long and flowing.

Balen looked shocked. "Well I didn't expect that. That is Archangel. That is a different look for him."

Archangel crossed the pitted tarmac and walked up to the gate. Balen called down the gate guards. "Let him in. That is Archangel."

The door opened swiftly, and Archangel strode through. Balen clambered down the ladder as his brother rounded the corner into the Compound and the van followed him in.

Archangel looked around and smiled as Balen stood to attention and saluted. Archangel waited. "It is more usual these days for my followers to get on their knees. I am waiting."

Balen looked stunned but he got on his knees.

The van drove into the Compound and one of the guards took it to where it could be parked up and the gate closed behind it. The doors opened and five of Archangel's personal guard got out. The driver also got out and joined them and they formed up waiting for their Commander's instructions.

Archangel looked around. "I like the look of the place so far. You may stand. You have done well. Now bring me Raven."

Balen got up and walked nervously over to Raven who had got down the ladder and who was looking very, very nervous.

Archangel hissed. "Bring her to me."

Balen took Raven's arm and walked her over to Archangel. "I would like you to meet my wife, Raven."

Archangel looked down his nose at her. "Your wife? I do not recognise that marriage." He reached and put his hand on her stomach and felt the baby bump. "Good, good, you have done well." He was looking at Balen. "I had been informed that Raven was no longer a prisoner so I had to come myself to find out why. Your reports have been sadly lacking and I would rather have heard from you. You are very lucky that I am omnipotent. I am here for a full and detailed personal update on your progress and an explanation."

Balen looked nervous as he looked into his brother's eyes. "If you would come with me, we can either speak now or I can give you a guided tour of the Compound."

Archangel looked around. "I would like a full tour. If you could show me around Lord Balen, I would appreciate it." His tone was official and his body language indicated that he was not on a family visit. "Raven I will speak of you later. Take her to her room and I will put one of my guards on the door."

Balen was worried. He called Kyle over as the guard to go up with Archangel's guard. Kyle was looking at him wild eyed when Archangel wasn't looking. He mouthed. "I'll look after her if I can."

The guard didn't look the same as the others. He was tall but his facial features were very different.

Balen stepped over to Raven. "I'll see you later." She smiled, nodded, and walked back to the house with Kyle and Archangel's guard, a million worries running through her head.

Archangel smiled. "Lord Balen, you have not kept me appraised of the situation here. I had expected communiques from you on a regular basis. That isn't the only reason for my visit but I will speak of that in a more private place. Now show me what you have set up here."

Balen took him around the Compound in a clockwise direction. They passed the house where he showed Archangel the Kitchen. "We made a few changes to the Kitchen. We removed some of the cupboards and managed to find four wood burning stoves which you can see here. They are used for cooking but each of them feeds into a back boiler which heats a different part of the compound and the animal sheds. Come lambing and kidding we keep that burner going for a constant supply of drinks and to heat that shed.

Here you will see the food store." Balen opened the door of the room they used to store the food. It had an open window which was meshed. In front of it were horizontal poles at regular intervals where hanging meats and other early produce was neatly stacked or hung. There were boxes with meat stored in salt which was curing.

Archangel looked around. "This is very organised. I cannot believe how far you have come along. I would like you to report on this so that it may be circulated to our other bases. I would use your location as a model for our development."

Balen smiled. "I can't really take much credit for this, that was Raven. She organised all this."

Archangel raised an eyebrow. "Before you show me the rest of this place, I think I should talk to you."

Balen took him up to his office and they were brought a cup of Dandelion Coffee. "The coffee store ran out nearly a month ago, we are now filling the gap with this. It is not wonderful but better than nothing and you get used to it."

He offered Archangel a seat and went and sat opposite. "You wanted to speak to me?"

Archangel looked serious. "I do. I wanted to speak now as I needed to hear from you what the situation is here, and I didn't want any of the conversation made public or overheard. I need clarification about Raven's position here."

Balen smiled. "She is my wife, and has been responsible for putting many of the things you see here in place."

Archangel raised his eyebrow. "That is an unfortunate turn of events and no wonder you have not written to me to inform me. One of my reasons for coming here was to take her back to the Hub for public execution. As you have succeeded in impregnating her she will be taken to "The Factory" until the baby is delivered and then she will be executed.

There was an outcry when a small facility managed to wipe out an entire troop of our men. Their families in other Compounds have been petitioning for an example to be made."

Balen sat back in his chair and thought. "She is my wife, and she is carrying my heir. She is under my protection and that is the way it will stay."

Archangel's stare was cold. "You seem determined about this Lord

Balen? You are sure, even if it costs you dearly? Surely no woman is worth that?"

Balen met his stare with a cold glare. "This is not negotiable. I exacted my retribution on her for what had been done to my men."

Archangel looked at him quizzically. "I had heard you had the leader of their organisation in captivity and you were torturing her. She doesn't look tortured to me. You will give me a full report. I informed father that you were going to produce an heir. If you had not he was going to invite you to "The Factory" to produce one there."

Balen looked confused. "I haven't heard of The Factory".

Archangel smiled. "The Factory is father's spa where women came to be impregnated with the holy children. They also came for other procedures or plastic surgery, but they left with an extra blessing. He saw to this personally on many occasions and I have now been given the honour of carrying on this onerous task. It will be appropriate that Raven is taken there where our son can receive the best of care."

Balen was horrified but he tried not to react. "Is Father still in charge of that facility?"

Archangel smiled. "Our father was declared a heretic and I had him burnt at the stake as he spoke out against us and our beliefs. I sent you a long communique setting out his crimes and you sent me back your agreement to his removal. As an unbeliever it was not appropriate for him to have control of LexCorp, control of which has passed to me."

Balen was having real problems taking in the situation. "What about mother? Surely, she is a shareholder?"

Archangel looked down. "She is indeed but nothing has been heard of her since the computers went down. Now, tell me of the farm and what happened."

Balen took a deep breath. "We had the farm under surveillance that night and we had our own people inside who had been feeding us information. On the night in question we had put men in the woods to watch the farm. I don't know where you got your information about it being an organization. It was organised yes but it was Raven's home. People came and she took them in. Nemesis had singled that place out as somewhere to send refugees to.

The three operatives had been embedded into the Unit. Their cover stories had held up and they were beginning to carry out their orders. My orders were to divide the people there and make an opening for us to assist when their internal struggles caused them problems. This was unsuccessful due to the operatives being discovered and instigating firebombs and other terror tactics. This was misinterpreted as an attack and they retaliated.

We had received no intelligence that there was a military trained individual on site and he wiped out the troop. Raven had no part in that. As I understand it at the time she was in the Med Room being treated after being injured by a gunshot through the bedroom window. This action by us, by which I mean shooting at Raven, was not sanctioned. The inhabitants of the farm were acting on a perceived threat instigated by shots being fired through their windows and firebombs being thrown into the house."

Archangel took a deep breath. "This should have been reported to me immediately."

Balen got Archangel's file out of the desk drawer. The report was there; it was sent immediately. "The report was sent. I believe that the internal matters relating to this Command are my responsibility. The individuals who instigated this and contravened my orders died in the woods that day."

Archangel glared at Balen. "You are my Commander. I can remove you at any point if I choose to. I would be a little more careful about what you report and what you don't report. This is a very delicate matter, the individuals who are asking for the execution are your own people in your own Compound. Look out of the window. They hate you for treating Raven as if she is a human being. She should be crawling in the dust for what she has done. Listen, I can hear their voices, can't you? Our people died, there has to be retribution for this. Can't you hear them, they are standing around you and they are screaming and demanding retribution. The voices are horrible. What measures did you take to punish those at the farm for killing our people and to show them our superiority after such a crushing defeat?"

Balen took a deep breath. "As you know I had their leader kidnapped and brought here. I kept her prisoner and ascertained that she was of considerable worth due to her depth of knowledge. My Animal Handler was inexperienced, and we were losing animals. I made her give me the information I needed to stop this happening.

I got your communique requesting that I produce an heir by any means possible. I deemed that her intellect would make her a suitable candidate to provide this child. I therefore took her harshly and frequently in the belief that I would have an heir from her before she was executed."

Archangel smiled his agreement. "You could have moved her to The Factory. We have suitable restraints there which would have made the act more comfortable for you."

Balen smiled wickedly. "I think how I kept her was far greater retribution than the comfort of The Factory."

Archangel laughed. "Comfort, the women are strapped constantly to tables where they can be impregnated, kept and finally dispatched when their duty is done, their baby born and the milk extracted."

Balen smiled. "I deemed that making her my wife would gain control of her assets and would make her easier to handle."

Archangel sat up. "This changes everything. I am pleased with what you have done. It looks like she had been a valuable asset and when is your heir due?"

Balen hadn't stopped to work it out. "Under two months." That was about right as far as he could remember. "I also have the murderer of our men under my control. He is a valuable asset and the lives he will save will offset the lives he took."

Archangel looked confused. "You have Frank working for you? You have been busy my brother." His expression softened, and his face seemed to change. "They are both valuable assets. You have done well."

Balen thought quickly. "How is Martha?"

Archangel seemed confused for a while. "Martha? Oh yes, the woman who kept house for me. She didn't please me, so I put her into the breeding program. She produced a beautiful baby boy before she was dispatched. I impregnated her myself."

Balen now knew that Archangel had reverted to the madness he had shown as a teenager. Martha was his wife, he'd forgotten that and thought she was his housekeeper. Balen sighed. They were in trouble. He had hoped to call on their father, but he was dead. Raven was in severe danger. He was glad he'd smuggled Archangel's first son out of the Compound and sent him to his mother to look after. "What happened to your son?"

Archangel smiled. "Oh, I don't know, he went to join the rest of the babies. They don't have names or numbers; they are just babies. They are all my children anyway."

Archangel suddenly looked very tired. "There are many situations which need dealing with. I will let you show me around the rest of the Compound. I am very interested to see what you have done."

Balen then showed him the offices and introduced him to the workers there. Each in turn stood up and saluted. He then moved on to the animal pens, ever thankful that the timing was perfect. They had mucked out so the place looked neat and tidy. "We've just used the last of our straw but we will be harvesting the top field soon to provide bedding and grain for the rest of the year and into the winter. We have two grass cuts a year which is providing our hay. The animals are mostly out in the fields at this time of the year so that lessens the feeding burden. Raven organised us a feeding rota and we have people who handle planting and the crops. I have a Farm Manager who handles the day to day animal handling and we have set up a Dairy. We have facilities to make candles and a room where we are able to tan hides.

We have a Spinning and Weaving Room where some of the women and men are setting up to be able to go into more concentrated production once we need this for clothing."

They were alone in the large barn which had been set up for the cows for the evening. Archangel turned to his brother. "They won't leave me alone you know. They keep whispering to me that they took heavy losses when they attacked you. They are there every day."

Balen looked puzzled. "Who are?"

Archangel shook his head. "The men that Raven killed. She looks such a normal woman. You would never know that she was Special Forces, would you?"

Balen now knew he was in trouble. "What of Black Troop?"

Archangel glared at him. "Who? Never heard of them. News has come to us that we have lost control of our Divisional Offices. I have given the Regional Offices the power to act independently. The sedition is spreading so I have cut off communication between all of our Compounds."

Balen looked horrified. The degree to which his brother had lost his grip on reality had certainly increased. "What of the Corp in general?"

Archangel looked down at the concrete. "Cutting off the head of the hydra was just that. It seems that now many heads have spring up. The Corp now has its own problems, and we are but one. That has helped us to survive in a way. They haven't attacked us yet, but they will. I can feel it.

They have set up camps around the cities and moved most of the inhabitants there. I have reports of the way those people are having to live. They are virtually slaves. They have what look like prison cells to live in and they live to work for the Corporation to build the new future."

Balen also looked down at the concrete. Archangel had lost the plot. If his father was dead then Archangel was the Managing Director of the Corp. "What are you going to do about it?"

Archangel leant on the wood. "Seeing what you have done here has made me even more determined. I have quite a force now and I'm going to act. The population is much reduced. I have intelligence that it has been aided by LexCorp who have selectively let people be killed. They ascertained who was of value and they have executed the rest. With no communication and very little information available to the general public this was easy for them. They just blamed rioting but those riot squads targeted whole areas and went in with extreme force. The body count was massive and is increasing. I'm here as if we fail I doubt we will meet again. You are the only family I have left now. I wanted to see you one last time. Even my wife has left me. She didn't even leave a note."

Balen smiled. "You will do what you have to do. We both have had to. You know I will support you."

Archangel smiled. "When we were younger, I would have laughed at you making such a comment. You have changed so much my brother. Where is the lovelorn poet now? Where is the dreamer? I hope he's still in there somewhere."

Balen put a hand on his shoulder. "I have no need to be lovelorn or lost. My poetry was lousy. I loved that life but now I have purpose. Why write about love, it's better to live it."

Archangel looked up and viewed Balen with suspicion. "You love that woman, don't you?"

Balen smiled. "With all my heart."

Archangel laughed. "You are still the poet at heart then. What a shame I'm going to have to order her terminated."

Balen laughed. "Well this is where we are probably going to be at odds then."

Archangel looked offended. "But I have given you my blessing. It is wonderful news that you have a wife and I can't wait to meet my niece or nephew."

Balen found it hard. He knew what was happening. "I thank you. So you will leave her here with me?"

Archangel looked at him blankly. "Leave who with you?"

Balen smiled kindly. "Raven."

Archangel looked confused. "Yes, I mean no. How can I? I am taking her back to give birth to our child and then I will have her executed. Why has it worked so well here when the other Compounds are war torn fortresses at odds with all around them?"

Balen couldn't stop himself. "Because I rewrote the manifesto."

Archangel's smile fell off of his face. "You did what? That directive is written in stone."

Balen glared at him. "The manifesto was written on a computer, not stone. Computers are gone, the old world is gone. Look around you and listen to what you are saying. We have achieved the Prime Directive, the bottom line. The only difference is that we work with others rather than exploiting and controlling them. As has been pointed out, I co-wrote that manifesto. I have every right to change it."

Archangel gripped the wooden rail. His knuckles were white and his eye had begun to twitch. "You would stand by that statement? Even if it means I have to remove you from command here? How dare you rewrite the manifesto. You cannot do that. Only my brother would be able to do that. You have overstepped yourself here Lord Balen. You wait until Gabriel hears about this. He will sort it out. You were given orders you have not carried out.

I will have to make an example of you. Don't make me do that as you are a good Commander. I want you to reinstate the manifesto in its original form immediately. That woman has corrupted you. She is dangerous. I should have her executed immediately before she spreads her sedition."

Balen took a deep breath. "You are not well brother. Listen to yourself. In one breath you are saying what we have done needs to be copied. In the other you are saying that I must be removed. I am Gabriel, your brother."

Archangel's eye was twitching, and he was shaking slightly. "I have no other option. Lord Balen, I will have to remove you from your Command if you do not comply. You will hand Raven and Frank over to my troops for summary execution." He was shaking badly and his pupils were dilated, his eyes wide. "I will hear no more of it." His voice seemed different as was his body language.

Balen put his hand on Archangel's arm. Archangel pulled away. "Who do you think you are? I put you here to carry out my orders. You have not done this. Now you try to kill me? This is treason."

Balen grabbed his arm. "You were put in place as Archangel as it was felt that you would best suit the position. I will confess now that I had my doubts about that at the time because of your fragile mental condition. It was a game to start with and it didn't matter. It made you happy. Now it is making people dead."

Archangel pulled his arm away from Balen and stormed out into the farmyard. "Archangel Troop, form up with me." His soldiers ran across the courtyard and lined up in front of him. "I want this man taken into the middle of the yard and shot. Bring the bitch Raven to watch."

The guards were bringing Raven down as the guard had been summoned. She broke away from him as Kurt "clumsily" got in the way and ran across the yard and stood in front of Balen who had come out of the barn. Balen bent down and whispered to her. "Get the red folder on my desk." He then almost shouted. "Raven get inside. I don't want you to watch this."

She looked at him with wild eyes. "No, I won't leave you."

He put his hand around her neck. "That file could end this. Get it, please."

Raven ran past the guard and upstairs. The guard had a dilemma as he had been summoned to stay with Archangel and he knew how erratic Archangel could be. She grabbed the folder and was running downstairs when a single shot rang out. She couldn't run any faster and her legs nearly gave out from the shock of what she saw in her mind's eye. She ran out into the yard dreading what she was going to see.

Balen was kneeling in front of Archangel who had stepped back and was staring up at a top window. Raven looked up. Frank was in the window with a sniper rifle in his hands pointed at Archangel's head.

Frank shouted. "You make one move, and you lose Archangel. You know that was a warning shot. I won't miss."

Balen looked up at him. His whole expression was pleading. "Don't kill him. He's my brother."

Frank laughed. "That is one order I may not be able to carry out."

Raven ran across the yard and handed the file to Balen who grabbed it and stood up. "I am sorry my brother but I have to do this. I had hoped that it would never be necessary. I have a report here which was made by the family doctor and a copy of my brother's medical notes. I also have communiques which my brother denies ever having received and ones which he sent to me. We were making the decision as to whether to have him committed to a mental institution. I am sorry Michael. I never got any message about killing father."

The Archangel Guard looked at each other and shuffled their feet. Balen held out the report. Michael screamed. It was the heartfelt scream of an injured animal. He was shaking, and his legs gave out. He then started shouting over and over. "Shoot him!"

Balen reached out a hand to his brother. "You are Archangel, you are the High Commander of Transition X. You have achieved so much, don't slip back into all that now."

Archangel stepped back from Balen and ran back to his personal guard. He grabbed a gun out of the man's holster and turned to aim it at Balen. Balen stood there, hands out, palms upwards. "My brother you have to see sense."

Archangel started to raise his gun. A single shot rang out and Archangel fell backwards onto the ground as blood began to pool from the single shot to the head, a clean kill.

There was silence in the compound. The guard turned to Lord Balen and their Senior Officer stepped forwards. "I am Ryjel, First in Command of Archangel's Personal Guard. I also used to be a psychiatrist before I signed up. May I see the report?"

The guards all levelled their rifles on Balen and Raven. Balen handed over the report. Ryjel opened the cover and began to read. He looked at the papers for about a quarter of an hour and in that time, it was as if the Compound stood still.

Ryjel closed the file. "Why didn't you reveal this before? This report is by a very eminent psychiatrist. His findings are very clear. Michael was showing signs of being schizophrenic and having a multiple personality. Why didn't you have him committed? The injuries he inflicted on you when you were children should have been enough to make your family act."

Balen looked a broken man. Raven stepped over to him as the guards lowered their weapons. "He was my brother. We did what we could to look after him and there was a good man in there too. He was a brilliant man. He had fantastic ideas, and he has kept TX together."

Ryjel looked down. "No, he hasn't. He has broken the organisation apart. For months now his controversial and inconsistent orders have shattered the very fabric of what we are trying to build. He has lost us operatives on many occasions and his rule was fragile at best."

Balen looked stunned. "So what happens now? Are you going to shoot me and the others for his murder?"

Ryjel thought for a moment. "No, we are going to stand down and we are going to take your brother's body somewhere that it can lie in state. He was our leader and a hero to our people. He will remain that way. We will now go somewhere private and discuss how we can limit the damage here. Do you have a cold store?"

Raven looked up nervously. "We do. I will show your men the way."

Balen caught her arm as she was about to walk away. "No, we will get someone else to show them the way. You are coming with me. Raven is my wife and my equal. She has every right to be there when we talk and I value her ideas."

Ryjel smiled. "My Lord, you are the Senior Ranking Officer here. As one of the original Founding Fathers your status is only one short of Archangel."

Balen swore under his breath and cast Raven a very nervous look. "We will go inside. Follow me."

Ryjel, Balen and Raven sat around the glass table in Balen's office. The report was on the table and other papers lay around it. They had sat in silence while Ryjel read the report again. He looked up. "Archangel will have to carry on. You are the next ranking officer and the position should be yours. Will you take up the position?"

Balen looked over at him. "I need to think about that. Let's talk about the situation and see if we can find another answer."

Ryjel looked down at the paperwork. "We must not attempt any form of subterfuge here. That will inevitably be revealed at a time most inconvenient to all of us. The decision we make here must be not only believable it has to be unquestionable.

It has been noted for some time that Archangel's mental state has been deteriorating. Initially it was just tiredness and slight errors of judgment. In the latter weeks he had become much more erratic in his actions and orders. It is the general population of Transition X that we need to convince.

Stories and rumours have abounded about your ability to command as you have shown a weakness when it came to dealing with your prisoner. I have now been appraised of the harsh way you dealt with her and that will possibly stand in some way to stop them baying for Raven's blood. They need the truth, can you provide it?"

Balen nodded.

Ryjel continued. "As Second in Command at the point that he was deemed unfit for duty, which I will testify to, you would have automatically been granted command. As I would assume that your man was under orders to protect you from any assassination attempt that makes Archangel's death carried out in undertaking the man's duty. There can be no blame laid on anyone for Archangel's death. What we do now is more important. The organisation needs a head and we are about to strike a blow against LexCorp. The decision is yours as to whether you will take up that position and come with me to our Head Office."

Balen looked at Raven who was looking terrified. "Is there anyone else?"

Ryjel shook his head. "No, the command comes to you on Archangel's death."

Balen looked down at his hands. "This is something I need to think about. If I do take up the command, I would expect to bring Raven with me. Will that be a problem?"

Ryjel thought. "I don't know. I will also have to think about this. TX is a very volatile group of creative people who are also idealists. The Archangel Guard have very fixed beliefs. You have a suitably romantic and practical story that should win over most of them. The Archangel Guard on the other hand would be more difficult to convince.

Raven, you are quiet. Balen has asked you to be here, and you have a right to speak."

Raven looked at both of them. "I am torn between practicality and a wish for things to stay the same here."

Ryjel thought about it. "As you are carrying Balen's heir that will in part stabilise the situation. Balen if you decide to come with us and assume the position as Archangel that would bring unity.

Balen narrowed his eyes and glared at Ryjel. "How do you know so much about Archangel's business."

Ryjel smiled. "I am also a member of the Council of Commons. Archangel sanctioned it and put me forwards so that he had a representative on the Council."

Raven spoke softly. "That isn't the whole truth is it?" She walked over and gently unzipped Ryjel's boiler suit which was zipped up to the neck. She gently pulled it down to reveal vicious cuts, some scars, some scabbed, some fresh. Ryjel let her pull it down to his waist. She turned him around and gently touched the scabbed over cuts and whip marks. Ryjel was crying so Raven put her arms around him gently. "Michael was your lover wasn't he?" Ryjel nodded and collapsed like a rag doll in her arms. "He hurt me so badly, night after night. He took my love, and he twisted it into slavery. I feel so bad, I hate myself that I'm happy he's dead."

Raven stroked his hair. "Your troubles are over. He is gone. You can love and remember the good man who was Michael, not the beast which came out when his other personality appeared. But one doesn't live without the other. They did all they could. You did all you could.

Balen, between you, you both need to decide what to do with Archangel's body."

Balen looked down at his now clasped hands that were on the table. "To give him a public funeral would be an affront to all those who have lost loved ones and have had no chance to honour their life in such a way. I will organise something in private if you wish or we will bury him as we have buried many others."

Ryjel looked serious. He had recovered his composure but he was clinging to Raven. "That is a wise decision. We will all testify to what happened, taking his body back would be unnecessary. We are his Personal Guard, we will see to the burial if you tell us where. Would it be appropriate if I leave you to discuss matters with your wife? I will then attend to the preparation of your brother for suitable burial."

Balen took a deep breath. "I think my brother would have appreciated it more if we built him a funeral pyre and sent him into the other world with little ceremony. He always feared enclosed spaces. Tonight we will have a feast and celebrate his life and achievements and also mourn all those we have lost. Ryjel, together we'll see him to the other side. It will also be a celebration of new life to come. You are right, I would like to discuss matters with my wife."

Ryjel stood up and bowed slightly. "I will await your decision." Raven went to the medical box in the corner. She cleaned Ryjel's current cuts, bandaged his back and she handed him a couple of painkillers. He took them and looked her with a desperation and a softness. She gently pulled the boiler suit back up over the bandages and zipped it up. He hugged her and whispered. "There couldn't be one person who would want you dead Raven. I read the communiques. I saw that Michael sent his blessing. He was so excited, when he was Michael." He left the room and went back to his men.

Balen turned to Raven when Ryjel had left the room. "Will life never leave us alone?"

Raven looked tearful. "Not yet. Not until the journey is over. We are so small, so insignificant, if our little part can make big things happen then we must see this through to the end. I so want us to just be here, to raise our child in peace and to make this place work. But, how can we live if we are expecting an attack every day. It has been months now of living looking over our shoulders. Nobody can find peace and the strain is beginning to show. To have our peace perhaps we have to fight for it. You know I will support you and go with you to help you with anything you need to do."

Balen pulled her into a hug. "How can I take you with me? I need you, you both, here and safe."

Raven looked thoughtful. "I will go with you. You need my help. No arguments."

Balen smiled. "Oh, there will be."

By late afternoon a pyre had been built and Archangel was laying in state on top of it. Balen went up the hill to spend a quiet moment with his brother. He then went and found Ryjel and the two of them went up and said their private goodbyes and soaked the body in the petrol and covered it with a muslin cloth. They were about to leave when Ryjel turned. "Please pardon my familiarity." He stepped forward and the two hugged as two man who had lost someone they loved.

Raven had found Frank, and they were sitting at the bottom of the hill on a log. Frank smiled. "This is not something I could have predicted. I had seen Balen as an arrogant fool who was power hungry and manipulative. I saw his brother as a dangerous fanatic who was highly unpredictable. I will happily admit that I like the man. He is honest, hardworking, bright and a good leader. You are well suited. You will make this place a safe and happy home for all who are here, I am sure of it."

Raven leant forward. "Frank, I need to ask you something."

Frank smiled. "You know you can ask me anything. What is the matter?"

Raven took a breath. "Balen has been offered the opportunity to take over as Archangel. I have said that if he does, I will go with him."

Frank looked stunned. "Now that is something I would never have predicted either. Of course, you must go and he must accept. You must encourage him. Why do you need to ask me something about it?"

Raven smiled. "You know I am carrying his heir. It is dangerous for both of us to go but I will not let him go without me. Would you come with us? I need your protection so he doesn't have to worry about me. I haven't spoken to him about it yet as I wanted to ask you first. Also, if anything goes wrong we may need to ensure the safety of that file."

Frank looked at Raven, his expression blank. He looked down and was thinking hard. "This is something I had not anticipated. But logically it would be a good idea and I would be delighted to come with you.

Raven managed a smile. "I think that the current threat to Balen may well be alcohol poisoning though. I think he plans to drown his sorrows."

Frank laughed. "Don't worry my Lady I'll keep an eye on him. If you need a hand getting him to bed later, I'll be there but after that he's your problem."

Nobody was within earshot, so Raven smiled. "Do you get drunk?"

Frank smiled. "Sadly not. I have written a sub routine for myself to mimic the better experiences and I find that much more pleasurable. I can experience taste so I can enjoy the drinking but no, I don't get drunk. You can't I know but try to relax as this is a night to mourn all the lost."

Raven smiled and hugged Frank. "Thank you Frank, I'm glad you came to the Farm."

Frank smiled. "And I am so glad I chose you."

As she walked away Frank looked down at the drink in his hands.

The night passed without incident. Balen managed to drink his fair share of alcohol as did most of the others. At midnight they filed up the hill to the pyre.

Balen took a wooden torch which he lit. He then took a second, lit it and to Ryjel's surprise he handed it to him. They stepped forward together and lit the pyre. They had soaked it on petrol, and it was stuffed with old dry hay, so it burnt fast and hot.

Raven stepped up to stand beside Balen. Ryjel's legs nearly gave out so she subtly stepped between the two of them and put her arm around them both, holding Ryjel up. She whispered to Ryjel. "Keep it together, not much longer. Do it for Michael, he would be proud of you."

The fire burnt and they headed off down the hill. Balen had drunk a fair bit and he was swaying. He made his way, unsteadily. It was dark and Raven was finding her way but she stumbled. A strong arm reached around her waist. It was Ryjel. He smiled and whispered. "Michael and I were handfasted too, that makes me your Brother in Law." He smiled and they walked down the hill together. Oberon was walking a little distance behind them.

They went back to the barn and more drinking was done. Ryjel looked tired and was swaying his way to bed. Raven walked over and took his arm. His men had long turned in so she took him to their quarters and delivered him to the door and returned for Balen. Balen wasn't so easy so she smiled at Frank who came over and between them they got Balen into the bedroom. Frank gently lowered him onto the bed. "Well my dear, from here on you are on your own with him. Thought I doubt however much you love him you won't be able to protect him from the hangover he is going to have in the morning."

Raven smiled and swayed slightly. Frank caught her arm. He looked concerned. "You haven't been drinking, have you?"

Raven shook her head. I had soft drinks all night, too late a stage to even risk one. She looked exhausted. "Thank you for being a friend."

That made Frank jump slightly. He turned and left the room. Raven went to the door and locked it.

The morning dawned crisp and bright like some cruel punishment on those who had drunk too much the night before. Many staggered about cursing its brilliance while others enjoyed its welcome warmth.

Raven had been up early and had left Balen to sleep off his hangover. The guards were back on the door, and she had made sure he had plenty of water and soft drinks beside the bed.

She checked on the animals and played with Oberon. Everything seemed peaceful, and it was just another morning, but she knew it wasn't.

On the hill the pyre had burnt down to ash. All that could be seen was a black patch where it had been. She made a mental note to someone to find a place to bury the ash.

She walked up the hill, pulling her coat around her against the morning chill. She turned to look back at the farm. She looked at the rolling countryside around her and tears came into her eyes. "Why couldn't we have just been left alone?" After fifteen minutes when she was a bit too cold she walked back down the hill and went back to her bedroom.

Balen was awake, he was sitting on the end of the side of the bed holding his head. He looked up. "I was wondering where you'd gone. Are you alright? Do you feel unwell?""

Raven smiled. "I'm fine. I just went for a walk. I suppose speaking to you now isn't a good idea."

Balen tried to smile. "My love, speaking to me loudly isn't a good idea. I can just about cope with anything else. Is there something on your mind?"

Raven sat down beside him, and he put his arm around her. She smiled at him. "I mentioned our decision to Frank last night. I hope you don't mind. I wanted to ask him if he'd go with us and be my bodyguard."

Balen thought for a moment. "Forgive me, I'm trying to work that one out. So Frank would be prepared to come along with us to look after you?" He reached for his glass of water.

Raven smiled. "Yes, if you want him to, he will."

Balen looked up at Raven. He was pasty white, and his eyes looked a little bloodshot. "So, you are happy about going then?"

Raven's smile faded. "No but I will go."

Balen kissed her. "I wouldn't make you go."

Raven looked down at her hands and sat down beside him. "I know but you wouldn't be able to make me stay. I want to be with you whatever it means."

Balen smiled. "I'd rather be here with you and carry on as we have done. When this is over, we will come back."

Raven put her finger on his lips. "No promises like that. I've seen too many movies. You promise that and one or other of us won't be coming back! All we can promise is that we'll do the best we can to come back. The decision is yours now, I've made my decision."

Balen turned to her. "I don't have a choice do I? I love you Raven." He bent forward and put his arms around her and kissed her with a passion, a want and a need like he had never kissed her before. "I'm scared Raven. I never had anything to lose before. Now at the point that I have everything I want I'm being asked to risk it all."

Raven thought on that one. "Only those with the most to lose can truly make a sacrifice for the greater good. We don't have to lose each other, we can go there, achieve what we need to and then come home and leave it all to others from then on. If we don't we'll end up losing what we already have anyway. Sometime down the line one or other of us will die in a raid. Our child needs to live in peace."

Balen smiled. "Children."

Raven smiled. "Let's see how I go with one first. By the way I didn't know that Kurt was one of your oldest friends."

Balen smiled. "Him and the doctor. I went to school with both of them. We grew up in the same neighbourhood and used to play together when we were boys. When we formed Transition X they treated it as a sort of club, we all did. The chosen few could join. Then all this happened. I never expected all of this. But it couldn't have worked out better if I had planned it. Kurt is now Acting Commander here. He's the one person who I know has the same ideals as me and who will carry on with what we have started.

He also knows it is only until we come back and he is happy with that. The power won't go to his head.

I was talking to Ryjel last night when I realised I hadn't told you. It seems that Carl and his father were knocking off LexCorp merchandise among other people's lorries. They hit their deliveries regularly and they were pretty damned stupid about it. They took the ease with which they were stealing stuff as being their own skill. It turned out that LexCorp was setting up runs with marked merchandise. Then then infiltrated the Mart. Your meetings with Carl and his father made our place a prime target.

It goes deeper than that. The reason we got to take you so easily without anyone talking was that the Mart had set up a slavery ring. The women that were going missing were being shipped out by them.

Raven looked up tearfully. "We lost so many good people. I'm just glad our people got out of there."

.

6

Raven smiled. "It has been a long journey and I have a feeling that there's a longer journey to come. What happens if they won't accept what happened here?"

Balen looked at her seriously. "Then they will execute me and probably you as well. You have to be ready for that. I would rather go there by myself first and see how things are. Then I can send for you afterwards."

Raven thought about it. "Not a chance. I know you. Out of some foolish notion that you are protecting me you would leave me here and my life would be a living hell. I don't want to spend a day without you. I couldn't, not now."

Balen looked at her seriously. "And you think I would want to live a day knowing that I could have prevented you being harmed."

Raven laughed. "I'll walk beside you, not in front of behind."

Balen laughed and the worried lines melted from his face. "Now if you wouldn't mind I think I need to sleep. Leave me to my well-deserved agony. Whatever decision I've made I'm not going anywhere at the moment." Balen rolled back onto the bed and held his head, moaning. Raven pulled the covers over him, kissed him on the forehead and poured some water into his glass. She then left the room and went downstairs.

Frank was waiting for her in the yard. He looked worried. He fell in beside her as she went towards the barn. His voice was steady and calm. "Has he made his decision?"

Raven smiled. "I think he has but he's not doing anything until later. He's in no fit state to see anyone at the moment."

Frank smiled back. "So, how do you feel about it?"

Raven looked serious. "I will do what I have to do. If my friends and animals are safe here, I'll go with him and hopefully keep him safe and help him. I can't ask for more than that at the moment."

Frank walked along beside her in silence. She seemed lost in her own thoughts, so he left her to it.

Later that evening Lord Balen came downstairs. He had showered and looked far better than he had when she had left him that morning. He went to the kitchen and made himself a cup of dandelion coffee and one for Raven and took it out to her. She was sitting on a low wall watching the activities in the yard. She looked up and as he walked over and sat down beside her. "How are you feeling?"

He smiled. "Much better thank you and I've had time to think and make my decision final. I'm going to talk to Ryjel next but I wanted to talk to you first. Raven, it is a lot to ask you and I know you've told me already but this is the last chance to back out. Will you come with me? I would rather you didn't but I can see the logic and I know I can't stop you."

Raven smiled. "I will come with you but I will be careful. I've got a lot to lose now. None of us know how long we have got. To waste a day I could have spent with you would be more awful than I could possibly imagine. If we want to be together I will move heaven and earth to make sure that we are. Whatever it costs me."

Balen looked serious. "Even if it costs your life?"

Raven smiled and drank a mouthful of coffee. "Even if it means drinking more of this awful dandelion coffee."

Balen laughed. "Now that is serious." He put his arm around her. "Well I guess I'd better go and tell Ryjel and we can then tell the others. If we've set this place up right we should be able to leave without it falling apart. I know we'd like to think that we're indispensable but I doubt it. We have good people here. Well, here goes. We'll be going tomorrow morning. Pack the bare essentials. You'll be wearing uniform at the HQ and that is provided." He stood up and walked across the yard to the house.

Balen went to the guest room where Ryjel and the others were meeting. It as neatly furnished with bunk beds and each bed had its own locker. Ryjel was in mid flow when Balen knocked and walked in. Ryjel looked over to him and smiled. "My Lord Balen, I trust that you are feeling well."

Balen gave an embarrassed cough. "I am feeling much better thank you. I have come to give you my decision."

Ryjel stood up and his men stood up with him. "You may speak in front of the men. Whichever is your decision we will of course support and stand by you."

Balen smiled. "We will be coming with you. I would be honoured to accept the title of Archangel."

Ryjel smiled broadly. "That is indeed good news. We have been discussing how best we can present the news of Archangel's death. It is going to involve very careful planning. You said "we", I trust that you mean that Raven will be accompanying you?"

Balen smiled. "She will be."

Ryjel cast a sideways glance at his second in command who also smiled. "I am glad to hear it."

Balen noticed the glance and shifted his feet. "I trust that you will also ensure her safety."

Ryjel smiled thinly. "We wil do everything in our power to deliver her to TX HQ safely. It is indeed a wonderful situation that she will be joining you there. We are ready to depart at any time so if you let us know when would be convenient for you, we will make the appropriate arrangements."

Balen nodded. "I thank you. We will go in the morning so there it time to make sure everything is prepared here for our departure."

Ryjel bowed slightly. "It would be acceptable. I will make the necessary arrangements."

That night Balen and Raven dined in the barn with everyone else. When the meal had ended and the plates had been cleared away he stood up and tapped a glass to get everyone's attention. He cleared his throat. "As you know after the death of Archangel I am the next in line of Command. I have been offered the position of Archangel and I have accepted. I will be travelling to our Headquarters to make the necessary arrangements.

This may not be a surprise to some of you, but it will be to others. I have confidence that you will be able to run this place most ably in our absence. Raven will be accompanying me, as will Frank.

I have left written instructions as to what needs to be done and I have also spoken to those who will be taking over both my responsibilities and Raven's while I am away. I must assure you that I intend this to be a temporary measure until a permanent solution to certain problems can be found."

The barn was silent, the only sound was the gentle occasional noise of an animal out in the other barn. Everyone looked horrified.

Balen coughed. "As soon as I am able I will return. So you power hungry mongrels can stop eyeing up my office."

A nervous ripple of laughter made its way around the room but few managed a genuine smile. Balen put his hand on Raven's shoulder. "We are both greatly saddened to have to go. Some of you have known me for years, others are just coming to know us now. I hope that in the future we will get a chance to know you all a lot better. So all it remains for me to say is that I wish you luck and I hope that you will look after the place while we're away."

Balen sat down to thunderous applause. He looked at Raven who was looking sad. He smiled at her. "Shall we go and spend some time together before we have to go? I have one thing I have to do, and I'll be up."

Balen stood up. "Now if you'd like to enjoy the rest of the evening there are one or two things I need to deal with." He stood up as did Raven and they walked out.

Raven went straight upstairs. Balen caught Frank's attention as he left the barn and Frank followed them.

Frank and Balen walked up the field behind the barn. Frank was the first to break the silence. "Other than the obvious, what is the matter? Something is on your mind."

Balen looked up at the clear sky and the sparkling stars against the deep blue background. "Back in the day I would have been sitting down there with a piece of paper writing about stars. Now that I can see them so clearly, I have no time to write about them."

Frank smiled. "That is often the way."

Balen stopped walking. "If you come with us you are going to die."

Franks's smile faded. "Well, that was direct. What makes you think that?"

Balen turned to face him. "Because that is what is going to happen to us. They aren't taking me back to become Archangel. I'm no fool. They are taking me back so that I can stand trial for his death and if they can catch Raven as well then they will. I'm going to let them."

Frank looked horrified. "Why would you want to do that?"

Balen took a deep breath. "Because it is the only way this place is going to survive. If I don't then the new Archangel won't stop until he has me executed. I know these people enough to know that they will defend the place and us.

If they catch Raven she will be executed then as well. She will have to watch more friends die in the process. There has been too much bloodshed. I know that she would suffer all the more if I didn't take her with me. We are going to die Frank. I've seen the look on the Guards' faces, they aren't that good at covering it up. Perhaps I do deserve to die. I started this organisation after all. It was my stupid game that brought it all about."

Frank shook his head. "I beg to differ. It was me who started all of this, and it is NEMESIS who deserves to die. I suppose if we both die it could be said to be justified but Raven?"

Balen kicked a stone. "They need someone to blame. They don't know you are NEMESIS, and you are only a fraction of him anyway. They have lost so many people and they can't get retribution for them. They can transfer that hurt onto me and unfortunately onto Raven. What I do ask is that if they are not planning to execute her immediately and are planning torture and a slow death and I can't get to her first I want you to kill her. Make it swift and make it painless.

You may stand a chance of getting away as you are only under my orders and they will probably want someone to come back here and report. I hope that will be the case but I can't guarantee anything. So it is not certain really, just probable that you will die."

Frank smiled. "I'm coming with you, whatever the risk, whatever you say."

Balen smiled back. "It is selfish of me but I'm glad of that. Tomorrow we will have to put on the best act of our lives. I want those people to honestly believe that we are going out there to try and make a difference. Leave them that at least for a little while. I have already mentioned my fears to Raven.

I want to have one more night with her if it is going to be my last on earth. I know what is coming and it is going to be hardest for her. I can't spare her it, but I can do what I can to make it as easy as possible.

Will you promise me you will kill her if it comes to that?"

Frank looked at the floor. "That is a hard promise to make me give you. Is there any way you can think of that you can argue your way out of it?"

Balen took a deep breath. "My only chance is to present that file and Archangel's mental illness. We weren't in a position to do anything else as he had given the order to kill me. That file is essential. It is in my office in my desk. Can I give it to you tonight to keep it safe? Our lives depend on it. Other than that Archangel's men saw him cut down in cold blood in front of them."

Frank smiled. "Let's get it now."

They got up and walked together. Balen continued as they walked. "You are one of my men. They will assume that you were acting under my orders and that I gave some sort of a signal to kill him. Though would I think he would do that, he is, I mean was, my brother after all."

Frank looked thoughtful. "What does the law state. Do you remember the exact wording?"

Balen thought for a moment. "If any person who is a member of Transition X takes the life of another member unlawfully then their life shall be forfeit. I have condemned Raven by making her my wife. I never thought of it at the time. If I had not then she would not have been a member. I cannot believe that I was that stupid."

Frank started at the door before opening it. "Would the child be spared? Would they spare her to have the child?"

Balen shook his head and then they fell silent as Ryjel was leaving the building. He smiled at them both and went out into the yard. Then he continued. "She is my wife, my crimes are her crimes. Archangel died after I had conceived the child, the child would be deemed as guilty as we are."

Frank glared at Balen. "That is unreasonable."

Balen shook his head as they went upstairs. "I know. I didn't think about it at the time but some of the laws my brother added in were extremely harsh. It didn't matter you see; it was just a game. None of this was supposed to happen."

Frank let out an ironic laugh. "What do you actually mean by it being just a game?"

Balen smiled. "We were writing a roleplaying game. What we created was the background, but my father found it, liked it and implemented it."

Frank shook his head. "If I knew what circumstances had been unleashed, I might have been inclined to have rethought the shutdown. I did it with knowledge of what was going to happen. You are both innocent."

Balen stared at Frank. "What do you mean?"

Frank shook his head. "Neither you nor Raven gave the order for any of those people to be killed. In fact there is no blood on your hands at all. I killed all of your men who came to the farm. Those that the farm boys shot at were only wounded. I finished them off. I was not ordered to do so. I didn't really give Raven the chance to stop me. I also killed Archangel because he was going to kill you. Neither of you either gave an order or carried out any of the killings. You were both innocent."

Balen shrugged. "Not in the eyes of the law, I doubt we can prove it anyway. You are a person under my command now and you were under Raven's command when you eliminated my men. You might think of it as defence but the Agents at HQ aren't going to see it that way. I know I'm going to die. I must go back now. You have a choice and I would strongly advise you not to come with us. I need to go back to my room and I want to spend what little time I have left with my wife." They had got to the office. He took the file out of the drawer and gave it to Frank. "Keep it safe."

Frank put a hand on his arm. "You know this could all still work out."

Balen smiled. "It could, but at the moment I doubt it." He turned and went to his room.

Frank put the file into his boiler suit and zipped it up. He then went out and sat and looked at the stars.

The morning was overcast and grey. There was a slight drizzle in the air as Lord Balen, Frank and Raven climbed into the van. Just about everyone had turned out to see them go and it had taken two hours to say goodbye to everyone. Instructions had been given, notes had been left and when they finally drove off with the members of Transition X both Balen and Raven were satisfied that they had covered anything that they could think of with those taking over their duties.

They drove through the morning and into the afternoon. Initially this was through the relatively unspoilt countryside but as they neared the cities the road became more broken up b craters and potholes. Villages that they passed were either highly defended or abandoned. Where they were defended, they often had to take a detour to get around them.

There were few animals in the fields but the farms that they passed were all boarded and defended in a similar way to their farm had been and the Compound. Finally they came to their destination.

They drove over a hill and they could see it in the distance. It was a square stately home which stood resplendent in the middle of a walled estate and surrounded by thick mixed woodland. There was a stone gate house in the outer wall and both the gatehouse and walls were intact. A platform had been constructed around the top of the wall so that the guards could patrol and they could see these people from a distance making their way around the walls at regular intervals.

Within the grounds there were areas set aside for camping. Neat military tents had been erected in rows in the middle of the Estate. There were animals there. Areas had been hastily converted into animal compounds and a small farm on the estate was brimming with animals and bustling with activity.

As they approached the main gatehouse a couple of guards came out to open the large wooden gates and the van drove through. They drove up the sweeping gravelled drive. Ash trees lined the route and the grass was deep green. It was immaculately tended and small bushes and ornamental shrubs were laid out in beds around it. It was green as far as the woodland that circled the house.

The house itself had many windows. The main door was at the tpo of a flight of white stone stairs. A line of guards was waiting, standing to attention, assault rifles in hand. Balen tensed as they approached the house.

Raven too looked nervous. Balen took Raven's hand and squeezed it gently. She looked over at him nervously and bit her lip.

The van drew to a stop and the driver switched the engine off. Balen got out and helped Raven down. He took a deep breath and turned to face the guards. Frank got down from the seat behind the driver's one and he also turned to face the guards.

Ryjel had stepped down from the van on the other side and he slowly walked around it to stand in front of it. He took a long sweeping look down the line of guards and smiled. "Take them prisoner."

As a unit the men moved and pointed their rifles at the trio. Balen stepped in front of Raven and Frank moved in closer. Balen hissed. "Frank, do we stand a chance?"

Frank smiled ironically. "Not a hope. We have a choice, surrender or die."

Balen put his hands up followed by Raven and finally Frank. A guard stepped forwards and searched them for weapons and he found the file under Frank's boiler suit. He also found the arsenal of weapons that Frank had secreted about his person and then he stepped back.

When he was sure they were no longer armed Ryjel walked around the van just out of reach of the trio. "You don't think I was seriously going to bring you back to take over after you murdered your own brother did you? You will both stand trial for what you have done. You Frank will stand witness to what has happened so that you can report back afterwards. Take them away. Take Raven to The Factory. I want Frank and Balen in separate cells. I want them incarcerated until the trial and execution is over."

Raven managed a smile. "So it's going to be a fair trial then?"

Balen winced even before Ryjel walked over and reached up to cup her neck in his hand. The Guards were behind him. He looked her in the eyes and saw her hatred. He shook his head slightly as he stuck a mini tranquilizer, which was a bulb of liquid with a hypodermic needle, into her neck and squeezed the liquid into her. "Murdering Bitch!" He faked hitting her hard around the head. He was ready and caught her as she fell. "Take her to The Factory." He reached into his boiler suit and pulled out a Medical File. "Take that to the Medical Officer. My notes and orders are attached."

Two guards stepped forwards and they carried her away as Balen stepped forwards. Ryjel shouted. "Stand still or we will fire."

The guards stepped forwards and pushed them around the back of the house to a stable block which had been adapted to make prison cells. Ryjel followed them. "Put them as far apart as you can so that they cannot communicate. Cover the windows and leave them in the dark. I will issue my orders as to what you are to do to them later. They will be called to trial tomorrow when the Agents arrive. Tonight they are ours to do with as we wish."

The guards chained Balen to a chair. Ryjel walked over. "I am sure that you will receive everything that you deserve. Think on that."

They then chained Frank and left them.

They carried Raven to The Factory. The building had been one of the spas. They carried her down into the "Ward". There were lines of women strapped to shaped beds which just fitted their bodies in various stages of pregnancy. There were some who had obviously been there so long the muscles of their legs showed signs of atropine. They all had stoma bags and tubes which fed their urine into bags which hung from the beds.

They took Raven to an end bed, removed her boiler suit, and lay her on the bed and strapped her down. As with the other women they put a cage over her face with a tube which went down her throat for breathing and so that she couldn't speak and a feeding tube.

A doctor walked down the ward, slowly and deliberately and he was handed the file. He looked at the note. He then read the notes and nodded. He then did a full examination. The bed was such that it was easy to pull her legs up into stirrups as the bed moved and he didn't have to take the restraints off. He consulted the notes while he made his examination. "Prepare her for surgery." He then walked off.

In the morning two guards came for Balen and Frank. They opened the door and the bright morning sunshine cut into the pitch blackness. Balen shut his eyes and listened as they crossed the room and unchained him. He opened his eyes again slowly so that they became accustomed to the light. He let them lead him. They took him out of the cell and he looked around. Frank was brought out to join him.

They passed through what was a side entrance which led to a long corridor and then through a small room with a table in the middle of it. There were double doors at the end of this room which were open. The room beyond as stately. Tapestries hung on the walls and huge vaulted windows were made of stained glass at the top. In the centre of the room was a huge wooden dining table and seated around it were what looked like officials dressed in black suits with a white shirt and black tie.

Frank was taken to a high-backed chair and handcuffed to it.

The twenty-five chairs around the table were filled with people that Balen didn't recognise. Ryjel took his place at the head of the table.

When he had made himself comfortable, he looked down the table at Balen. Ryjel spoke in a slow and deliberate voice. "We are here to witness the trial of the Commander of X345. His wife has been taken to The Factory and introduced into Program X. She too is on trial and will be judged in her absence. Both are deemed to be members of Transition X and bound by our laws.

You have all read the report of how our men were sent to the farm where Raven was in charge and none of them returned.

You have all read the reports from myself and the Guards as to how Lord Balen, had High Commander Archangel, his own brother, assassinated while he was carrying out his duties and had given a lawful command for Lord Balen to be executed.

What say you? You only need to say guilty or not guilty. By Law I have to remind you that the penalty for Murder is death by whatever means is deemed suitable by Head of the High Council for the day. I have such honour of being the High Council today. So what say you? He was looking Balen in the eye as he spoke and smiled when he had finished speaking.

Frank coughed. "I believe that by your laws the defendants have the right for all the facts in the matter to be set on the table. I request that the file I brought with me be presented."

Ryjel turned to the Guards. "Present the file."

The Guard snapped his heels together. "What file sir? We did not see any file."

Ryjel glared at the Guard. "You have removed evidence from a trial. This is a crime punishable by death. Take this man outside and shoot him."

The Guards stepped forwards and took the stunned guard outside. A single shot rang out and they returned.

Ryjel faced the Agents who were looking a little shocked. "As you know we have a splinter group working against us. I took the liberty of replacing the papers in the file which the rogue guard burnt with the contents of the file for the Kitchen Rotas. The file with the information which has been requested is now presented to the Agents for consideration." He pulled a file out from his boiler suit and handed it to the first Agent so that it could be passed around. Frank if you would like to continue."

Frank nodded. "The facts can only be presented by an individual who has such information and was present at the events in question. I am such a person. I claim Right of Speech under Section 27, Subsection 2.11.45 of the Article of Law, Seventeenth Edition. That is page 469 if you would like to look it up."

The assembled jury looked at each other in amazement. A guard brought over one of the many assembled volumes of books with white covers and opened the book at the page in question. "Where the Defendant shall be deemed as being the perpetrator by want of having been the Instigator of the action such Defendant should have the right to call the Perpetrator of the said action to explain to the Party of the Second Part the exact situation as defined by what he or she has seen and can prove to be true."

Ryjel smiled. "Wel that is hardly going to be of any use now is it? Even if you testify that you shot those people and the two Defendants are innocent you can't prove it." He looked at the Agents of the Jury and they were laughing. "I'm sorry Frank, nice try and I'm truly impressed as to how you managed to find that little gem but it won't do them any good. As I said, there is now proof."

Frank smiled. "Actually, you are wrong."

Ryjel stopped laughing. "What do you mean? Go on, produce some recording of the whole incident. I've checked that you have nothing on you, no cameras and no playback devices. The jury must vote today, and you may not go and retrieve anything."

Ryjel was beginning to get a little nervous as the Agents had left the file on the table and not opened it. He shuffled his feet and looked at the assembled Agents who had begun to mutter to each other.

Frank laughed. "I can play you back both incidents."

Ryjel looked at him with a very puzzled look and then laughed. "I would like to know how."

Frank smiled. "By your Law you are not permitted to intimidate a witness. Now that I count as a witness, I ask that my hands are freed and that I be made able to make my statement."

Ryjel looked puzzled. "You seem to know our laws remarkably well for a non-member."

Frank smiled coldly. "Yes, I do, don't I? So free my hands. You can keep a couple of your armed guards with their weapons pointed at me. I really don't mind."

Ryjel nodded to the guard and he unlocked Frank's handcuffs. Frank stood up and rubbed his wrists. He walked into a clear space where everyone could see him. "Now let me make my statement. I, Frank was present on both occasions in question and I will testify that I was the perpetrator of all deaths that occurred at both incidents. On both occasions I was acting without orders and under my own initiative. On the first occasion I purposely avoided allowing Raven any information about what I as about to do. On the second occasion I was in possession of prior information that the party of the first part, Michael James Anthony Morgan, hereinafter called Archangel was not of a right mind. Considering previous reports from eminent psychiatrists and the likelihood that he was schizophrenic with a multiple personality I deemed that Commander Balen was in danger of losing his life.

As stated in your law in Book 2356 of the Collection of New Statutes, page 342, starting at line 6798 "If any member of Transition X attempts or succeeds in taking a life of another member unlawfully his life shall be forfeit." At the point in question all present would have been able to justify that Archangel was not in his right mind and Commander Ryjel had been presented with hard written evidence of Archangel's mental instability by way of a report made by the psychiatrist handling his case. According to Law of Command, Book 56, Page 346 "Any individual of rank who is deemed to be mentally unstable or under the influence of another shall be deemed as not sanctioned to issue any command". The command to have Lord Balen shot was therefore not legal as Archangel did not at that time have the authority to give the order. Therefore to order him shot was against your laws and his life was forfeit."

Ryjel looked astounded. He then thought of something. "But you are not a member of Transition X. It clearly says in our laws that a person who is not a member of Transition X may not be protected by our Laws. Nice try and you have no proof."

Frank turned to face the jury and so that Balen could see him as well. He took his right hand and removed the prosthetic cover to his eye. Underneath they could see the metal eye which was part of his make-up. "I am Nemesis. By your laws I am not defined as a "person" so as I am not a person I am therefore protected by your laws, or rather, he is. I am his property. You asked for proof. I will give you proof."

He turned to the blank wall. "If you would be so kind as to pull the curtains and I strongly suggest that you do what I say I will begin."

The Guards didn't wait for a command from Commander Ryjel. They pulled the curtain and returned to their positions.

Frank then projected the recorded image, firstly of his conversations at the Farm and his assault on Lord Balen's men and then a full recording of the events in the yard at the farm from his vantage point at the window. It included amplified sound where Lord Balen clearly stated, "Don't kill him."

When he was finished, he replaced his eye cover. "I believe that I have complied with your laws, and you will accept that Lord Balen and Lady Raven are completely innocent of all crimes."

The Jury of Agents spoke one by one saying. "Not Guilty".

Frank smiled. "As Lord Balen is deemed to be not guilty and therefore has no blemish on his record, I trust that there is no objection to him taking up his position as Archangel."

Ryjel smiled and sat down. The Head Juror stood up. "Lord Balen, we would like to offer you the position of Archangel. Will you accept?"

Balen was stunned but spoke clearly. "I accept."

Action was fast and furious. The word got around and there was mayhem. Many of the Transition X people had been unhappy about certain things for a long time. Those who were more than happy with the sadism rose up against them. The result was swift. Many of those who had been Acolytes of Michael were swiftly executed as Ryjel had seen that they were informed and armed. They also broke into "The Factory" and liberated as many of the women as they could safely remove from their beds. Husbands and fathers went to find their family who had been taken there. Many of the Archangel Guard also went there to find their wives and loved ones.

They took the Head Surgeon who had been pivotal in the inhumane way women had been treated out into the yard and they shot him.

The Head of Process got his notebook out. "Now I will make the necessary arrangements for your instatement as Archangel."

Gunfire was heard in the yard, and they went to the windows. There was a general riot going on and people were being dragged out and shot. The Header of Process looked down. "It seems that those who supported Archangel Michael's sadistic regime are being removed so that there will be no need for a long and drawn out process to deal with them.

Now I will make the necessary arrangements for your instatement as Archangel to be logged on our records. I must extend our condolences on the death of your brother. You will of course be afforded all the benefits that accompany the position and all rights and rank that go with it. Congratulations Lord Balen."

Balen smiled. "I thank you. If you can look after what has to be done, I would like to find out what has happened to my wife after she was taken to The Factory."

There was a look of horror and shock on the faces of the Agents. The Head bowed his head. "The Factory is a terrible place instigated by your father and expanded upon by your brother. Women are treated like machines there, machines to turn out babies." There were tears in his eyes. "My dear sister was taken there, she did not return."

There was a knock at the door. It was opened and a tall man in TX Uniform entered. He stood to attention. The "Head" looked at him. "Please speak."

The man looked grave. "There has been action in the ranks. Anyone who had been proven to be part of the splinter group has been executed. The Members have also raided The Factory. They have killed many of the medical staff who were responsible for heinous experiments on the women there. The women have been liberated though those who were too weak to walk or unable to be moved have been left in the care of Orderlies and those who have expressed their views to be contrary to the Head Surgeon's plan."

Balen looked in horror at the Agents. "I understand that you have protocol."

The Head Agent cut him off. "Go find your wife!"

Ryjel spoke up. "May I be permitted to go with Lord Balen?"

Balen turned on him. "Why should you be allowed to go? You sent her there."

Ryjel looked down. "I would rather explain in private."

Balen, who by now was unchained stood up. "Ryjel, explain now or face the consequences and this had better be good."

Ryjel blushed. "It is an awkward subject you may not want spoken of in public. I feel that Raven's private parts should not be the subject of public disclosure."

Balen almost screamed at him. "What are you saying?"

Ryjel looked down. "I was in a conversation with The Doc at Archangel's wake and he said that there was something that was worrying him about Raven's pregnancy and that could cause problems in natural birth. That it might mean no more children. I told him about the Head Surgeon. He is a bastard and has treated women like cattle but he is the best in his field. I knew he was going to be the first up against the wall but he could help Raven. Ethically you would not have allowed her anywhere near him but I was told she needed the surgery.

I was given Raven's Medical Notes by The Doc so I gave them to him with a note that she was to be a long term "breeder". Oh this is so distasteful! Why are you making me say this in public? He made me understand all sorts of unpleasant details about lady things, a place where I never intend to go! I commanded the Head Surgeon to repair the damage so that she can not only have this baby naturally but she will be able to carry many more children for you. Oh why are you making me say all this? Go to your wife. She is hopefully recovering from an operation which will help her. He might have been a bastard, but he was at the forefront of his profession and the most likely to be able to help. I'm a dead man walking anyway. I didn't realise I'd taken the Kitchen Rota to swap with Archangel's File."

Balen smiled. "No I would rather you hadn't spoken about my wife's lady parts in public, but I thank you for what you have done. Shall we go and see if she is alright?"

Balen, Frank and Ryjel left the room. Ryjel led the way. He got to the grey concrete stairs going down and he looked truly terrified. "This is a place of horror. I have heard rumours, and it is truly a place of pain. Women are kept here for years to have baby after baby. They are put on a stoma bag and their pee goes into a bag. They have a pipe down their throats and their heads are caged so their only view is the ceiling. They wait to give birth and then they are impregnated again. I have been told many who have been here for years have legs like sticks, no muscles. I don't want to go in there but I do want to get Raven out of there. That is why I sedated her. The Doc gave me something discreet. I didn't want her to see it."

Frank went first. Balen walked with Ryjel who was physically shaking. Frank opened the door. Many of the beds were now empty where those who could walk had been taken away. Those who were as bad as he explained were still laying on the beds. They had sheets thrown over them to cover them up and their head cages had been removed.

There was a curtain pulled around at the end of the ward. They had checked every occupied bed, she wasn't there. They came to the end and Frank pulled back the curtain. There was someone laying on the bed. She had a tube down her throat and a cage over her face. Someone had thrown a sheet over her to preserve her modesty. Balen ran to her, fearing the worst. He pulled the sheet off and Ryjel looked away horrified. She seemed untouched.

Balen put a hand on her. "I had feared that he would have, you know, put one of those bags on her."

Ryjel could hardly talk, he was so traumatised. "I put a note that she was not to be linked to that system as she was to be taken to Archangel for his pleasure. It was the only way I could think to stop him!" Ryjel ran to the notes at the end of the bed. "Please, oh please have done the procedure before they killed him." He read the notes. "He has done the procedure. Notes say that it was successful. No follow up notes, no recommendations, deliver to Archangel for his pleasure in four days." He looked up at Balen, hopefully.

Balen smiled and put the sheet back over her as he realised what he had done. Frank smiled. "I'm a machine, and he's not interested so I wouldn't worry."

Ryjel smiled. "I would rather my sister-in-law was treated with more dignity."

Both Frank and Balen stared at him.

Ryjel smiled. "I told Raven, I was handfasted to your brother."

Balen smiled. "Thank you Brother-in-Law."

Frank walked over to Raven. "She is breathing well. There aren't any drips or blood bags so no blood loss. She is probably still recovering from the operation. Not sure about moving her but I'm sure we don't want to leave her in this place."

They found a gurney and put her gently on there and covered her before going to wheel her out. Then they remembered there was no lift and only the stairs. Balen lifted her gently from the gurney and carried her up the stairs.

He took her into the main building.

The Agents were still in the Meeting Room deliberating what to do. Balen handed Raven to Frank. He walked into the meeting room. "We need to discuss the Offensive. Can we convene a meeting for this afternoon?"

The Agent looked at Balen and at Frank carrying Raven. "I am sure that you will want to freshen up and rest after your traumatic night.

We cannot apologise enough for what has happened to all of you.

If you would rather spend your time with your wife, we are happy for Ryjel to handle the day-to-day matters. As your brother's life bonded partner we are bound by the Law to follow his orders."

Balen smiled. "I would like to see my new quarters and I would like to offer our hospitality to our friend, Frank, or should I say Nemesis."

Balen was led to his new quarters which had been his brother's room. They walked inside and Ryjel closed the door. All around the room were mementos that he remembered from family holidays and bits and pieces of his past. There were photos everywhere.

The maid was still in the room. She was changing the bed. She showed Balen the bed stripped and when he smiled, she picked up a pile of sheets and a blanket. She saw Frank holding Raven and hurriedly made the bed. She pulled the sheets back so that Frank could gently lay her down. The maid then lovingly pulled the sheets over Raven. "Poor Bambino, bad day, bad things, pretty bambino." She stroked her hair.

There was a knock on the door. They all jumped. The maid stood by the bed. Raven moaned and moved so she grabbed Raven's hand and held it. Frank went to the door as Balen and Ryjel took up a defensive stance.

There was a doctor standing there. He looked tired and there was blood on his white coat. "I have come to inform you of what I know about Raven. I am sorry I was not there when you came for her but there has been a lot to do. I have been in surgery since the Redemption reversing matters."

Balen was about to step forwards, but Ryjel put a hand on his arm. "This is Doctor Gravens, he was about fourth in command and by what I understand he was the one who helped the women as much as he could. That is why he is still living. He may have information."

The doctor nodded. "I did an examination. She has a lot of older injuries which are healing. The procedure went well. That was The Surgeon's forte but he was pleased and in about four days she should be available for "active duty"." The baby is healthy. We don't have a scanner as that was computer run so we can't tell you if it is a boy or a girl. She is still under the sedation. I ensured it was heavy as I had a forewarning of what was going to happen. There was no point her seeing what is happening down there.

I have moved the women who are able to walk to more comfortable accommodation. Many of them are the daughters and wives of people here. Some were the sisters of Archangel's Guard. Those who have been in the

Hospital a long time will take time to rehabilitate.

This is a delicate matter but as Archangel I need your permission. Many of the women do not want to carry the babies to full term. Do I have your permission to undergo terminations?"

Balen was shocked. He didn't know what to say. "Let them settle down for a day and make sure that they are fed and comfortable. I will speak with Raven when she is awake. I would like to know her thoughts."

The doctor smiled. "Thank you. May I go sir. I do not want to leave the women unattended, and I have a lot of minor surgery to attend to."

Balen smiled. "Thank you. I will speak to you tomorrow."

Balen collapsed into a chair. The maid had replenished the tea and coffee making facilities. She was going to ask to leave but she stopped and put the kettle on. "Tea, Coffee?" Her accent was strong.

Balen looked up. "Thank you. Coffee please."

She made him a coffee and teas as asked for for Frank and Ryjel. "Big heroes, big heroes. Many thanks." She put her hand on each of their arms. "Many thank yous. My bambino, in The Factory, many thank yous. May I go?"

Balen smiled. "You may go. Thank you."

When she had gone Balen looked up. Frank was sitting on a chair beside Raven's bed holding her hand. Ryjel was standing looking awkward. Balen offered him a seat. He sat down, looking thankful.

Balen looked up. "Frank, Nemesis, how?"

Frank looked up. "I opened a cloning facility and grew some accelerated growth clones. I took people who had already passed away and grew clones to a suitable age. I downloaded their lives and then took them on as my own as the persona for the safe farms. I needed no cognitive development of the brain. I used those clones as the human part of the cyborg which is in essence me.

I now understand why you live such short lives. What I am feeling is not physical, but it is unbearably painful. I think I understand what you call "love". My love for this human makes me hurt to see her like this. I now understand that people are different when they are put in certain situations. I now understand.

Am I still welcome?"

Balen smiled. "Of course you are. What you did back there was remarkable. I owe you our lives. What you did with shutting the power down, well I'm not in a position to judge. What we do now and what we create will be a testament to whether it was right or wrong. Now is when we need you most.

Up until now we have survived. Now we must build a new world. As leader of Transition X that will make it easier. As Managing Director of LexCorp, I will have the ability to implement the creation."

Frank looked confused.

Balen sighed. "I know, not what I expected. My father had a majority shareholding of LexCorp. The other shareholder was my mother. When my father died the shareholding would have passed to my brother. On his death the shareholding would pass to me as his next of kin. My father wrote his Will and he made us write ours. I know now that was because he was intending to father children and he didn't want them to have any claim over his money."

He got up and went to an ornate desk. "I can't believe they still have the desk." He felt underneath and opened a panel and pulled out a leather briefcase. He opened it and pulled out three Wills. "There you go. With these papers we have the power to build the New World. I just hope and pray that we are the "good men and women" and we create a better one.

I am going to call a Meeting this afternoon so that I can be fully instated as Archangel. Frank, I'd like you as my "Lawyer", you seem quite good at it. You can start by reading the Wills and making sure that everything is watertight. I then want you to ensure that I can take over LexCorp. It shouldn't be hard.

We are also going to have to work on that manifesto my brother has so comprehensively corrupted to come up with something more reasonable. Will you work with me on that one? Nobody without experience should ever try to write rules or a plan for a new world, especially two drunk teenagers in Brighton!"

Ryjel, you have helped so much. I would like to instate you as my Second in Command as you are more than used to the role. If you would manage things for me out there. I seem to have some paperwork to do."

Ryjel smiled. "I will indeed look after everything out there. Your brother so often was unable to do anything. I was mostly running the place anyway. I will put in regular reports."

Balen smiled. "Good, you can come and read them to me when we all have our relaxing time with the odd glass of brandy. You are family after all."

Ryjel smiled. "Thank you."

Frank looked up. "I am happy to do whatever you ask. I had hoped that I could have kept surveillance over Raven."

Balen smiled. "I'm having my office in here for now and you are more than welcome to watch over Raven. I don't want her out of your sight other than the time that she is with me, privately. Can you contact LexCorp and put the take-over in motion. I can then focus on the meeting here."

Later that afternoon Balen called a meeting of the Council while Frank watched over Raven in the private chambers. Balen stood at the head of the table and the Council Members as they were now known, rather than "Agents" which had been Archangel's term, sat attentively waiting.

"Council, in accordance with our Law I ask if I may assume the title and rights of Archangel. I claim this as I am next in line and entitled to the position. I confirm that there is no legal impediment which prohibits me from taking this position. Do I have your approval?"

The Council looked stunned. The member who had earlier acted as the Head Juror turned to Lord Balen. "It is not customary for us to be able to accept or deny anyone taking this position. It is already your right."

Balen smiled kindly. "I know but I want to give you the option. If you do not wish to choose me, you may choose another."

Each in turn raised their hand, stated their name and stated. "I accept you as Archangel."

The Council Member stood up. "I, Athame, Head of the High Council of the Transition, in accordance with our Law and with the acceptance of all present declare that you are now Archangel."

Archangel smiled. "As you know, I am Gabriel Alexander Morgan. I was one of the original authors of the Laws and one of the Founders of the Organisation. In accordance with my right as set out in the Law I may amend any Law at any time. I choose to amend the Law and to adapt the manifesto."

There was a gasp around the room. Athame stood up. "This is unprecedented, but it is acceptable by our Laws We accept that the Rules and Laws will be changed."

Archangel smiled. "Then I ask that anyone who would submit their comments and suggestions should do so by the end of tomorrow."

There was a mumble around the room and Athame spoke again. "Are you asking for our opinion on this?"

Archangel looked him in the eye. "I am. You have run the Organisation. You know what works and what doesn't. We have a chance for change."

Athame looked down and Archangel could clearly see the relieved smile on the man's face. "If I may speak and this is completely out of turn I realise but we would like to welcome you to Transition X Headquarters and to express our heartfelt thanks that you are in a position to change the Laws as they stand." He looked around and everyone at the table nodded. "For too long we have been bound by these Laws and I think I can speak for everyone at the table when I say that on occasion these have been Laws that we do not agree with."

Balen looked around the faces. There was a knock at the door. Ryjel came in. "I have a message from Frank, he cannot leave Raven. He handed him a note. It was long and thin and had obviously been tied to a pigeon's leg. He read it and smiled. "Now I must turn my attention to Lex Corporation. You will all know by now that my brother, the former Archangel, was suffering from an extremely fragile mental state. That may have affected his judgment on many things.

I understand that Michael was under the belief that the new Managing Director of Lex Corp intended to bring down Transition X. I understand that where they have been following his orders they have caused considerable damage to Transition X, under the name of Black Troop.

As you may or may not know my brother had multiple personalities. Michael was the Managing Director of LexCorp."

There were gasps and shocked noises around the table. Athame stood up. "This is stunning and devastating news. LexCorp has caused the deaths of many hundreds of our people. To think that was one of our own."

Balen held his hand up. "When Michael was in his other personality, he was no longer Michael. He is gone, and the Directorship has fallen to me. I have confirmation here. Now we can really make a difference.

If you have any ideas I am going to retire to my room and write a communication to LexCorp as we need to know the current situation. Then we can take a look at what we are dealing with. This is not a time to sit in an Ivory Tower and decree Laws. It is a time to see what is happening and try to sort this mess out.

7

Raven woke up in a four poster bed in a room she did not recognise. It smelt of incense and was lit with candles. She thought that she was dreaming. The bed was comfortable, and the room elegantly cluttered with ornaments and photographs.

Frank noticed that she had woken. He was sitting at the dressing table. What had been on the dressing table was now in a box underneath it and he had covered the table with papers so he could be near to Raven as Balen had so many daily duties.

Raven was still a little dizzy and was in pain. "Frank."

Frank turned on the stool he had been sitting on. "You are awake, that is good." He got up and took the top off a pot of tablets which was on the desk amongst the papers. He tipped out a couple of white tablets and poured a glass of water and handed them to Raven. "Here, the doctor said to take these. They will help with the pain. You'll be fine in a few days."

Raven took the tablets and a drink of the water, and they started to work almost immediately. "What happened?"

Frank smiled. "Ryjel had a talk with The Doc at the Compound and Doc gave him your medical notes and one of those stealth tranquilizers he put together. You know the ones with the little bulb of tranquilizer and a needle which you can hide in your hand. He doped you so you didn't have to see what was going on. He put a note on your records to the Surgeon to repair some damage you had."

Raven started to sit up in a panic. Frank put his hand on her shoulder. "I need to.."

Frank looked stern. "You need to rest. If you don't then whatever he did will get undone, probably. I can't ask him, Ryjel was quite right, the Surgeon is now dead.

There had been dissent in the ranks for a very long time due to

Archangel's erratic behaviour and the rise of the "Splinter Group" was all the nutcases in Transition X who wanted more rules and the whole world to follow suit.

We got the Jury to see sense and Balen and yourself were found not guilty. Balen is now Archangel and although he has been sitting with you every moment he can, he had to pick now to go and do his rounds!"

Raven looked around the room. "Where am I?"

Frank looked around the room. "You are in your new room, which used to be Michael's. I think you might like to do something with the decor."

Raven caught sight of the broken doll with the melted face wrapped in old lace and pearls. She shuddered. Frank saw what she was looking at and threw it into the wastepaper bin. She then looked at him. "What happened to the women?"

Frank smiled. "As soon as the judgment was given the Transition X men went to The Factory to liberate their womenfolk. Apparently Michael had taken all the women there, even their wives, daughters and anyone female in the Archangel Guard. As you can imagine the anger was running high about that one, particularly as Michael was impregnating them himself!

The Surgeon had been undertaking some research and experimentation of his own. It was understandable that he was the first target of their anger. They took him out into the yard and shot him. It saved Balen the choice as ethically he would have had to have had him shot. Ryjel knew that which was why he got the work done on you first.

Those who could walk and who were able have gone back with their life partners and families. Those who can't have been put in accommodation for now. Those who are not able to leave The Factory are under the care of the one doctor who had been trying to help them. Thankfully it was known and he was spared the "Inquisition". Some of them have been there years and it is going to take a long time to rehabilitate them."

Raven tried to sit up. Frank helped her. "I want to help them. It was hell in there. I need to talk to them, and we need to find out what they want to do."

Frank looked at her blankly.

Raven smiled and reached up and stroked his cheek. "Those women have been forced to be pregnant. Many may not what to carry those babies so the sooner they can sort that out the better."

Frank looked down. "I'm not good with that sort of thing. I still think as a machine sometimes. You are healing but if we take you carefully and put you in a wheelchair, we could probably find you a room where you could speak to them. It isn't really something Balen would be best dealing with.

I will go and find him as he will want to know you are awake."

Frank left Raven to look around the room. Some of the imagery was beautiful, some was grotesquely hideous. There were a lot of dolls which had been part melted. Raven shuddered. She didn't want to get out of bed but she didn't want to look at them either so she settled for looking down at the bed cover which was a beautiful tapestry style which depicted a Medieval scene of deer and trees.

Balen ran into the room and hugged her. She hugged him back and they kissed which passion. "I love you Raven."

Raven smiled. "I love you too Balen. That place was hell. But I understand why Ryjel did it. Are you ok with him?"

Balen sat down beside her on the bed and put his arm around her. "I'm fine with our new Brother-in-Law. I've kept him as Second in Command and he has been invaluable with sorting things out. He has thrown himself into work."

Raven smiled. "Not surprising. He probably needs that."

Balen looked blank.

Raven smiled. "He's just lost his life partner, he's devastated. He needs to focus, and it sounds as though he's got the purpose he needs. Keep an eye on him, he has mourned but it is going to hit him. I'm sure there is plenty to do."

Balen smiled. "There is, unpicking the horrors that Michael set up for one. His rules were draconian and comprehensive." He went to the wardrobe and opened it. There were papers piled three feet high in five piles. "Those are the laws we haven't got to yet! Frank has been great help. He can at least speed read and write at fast speed. I think he's regretting taking computers and printers off line for that." They laughed.

Raven leant her head on his shoulder. "Balen, that place was hell. The women need help as much now as liberating them. Can I do something about that?"

Balen thought about it. "You are spending at least a week getting over that surgery as I don't want anything reversed and as the Surgeon is dead, I can't ask him."

Raven smiled. "If I'm in a wheelchair and in a room and people come to me then what harm can that do?"

Balen thought about it. "There is still a fear that there are some of the splinter group left who were not caught out by their fellow members. You would not be safe."

Raven smiled. "Then bring someone from the farm to be with me as security. The obvious would be to bring The Doc and Storm here. Women would be happier if there isn't a male guard in the room if they want to talk and Storm is very understanding. The Doc isn't really needed at the Compound."

Balen smiled. "I'll sort out bringing them over."

Raven went to speak.

Balen smiled. "No, I'm not bringing Oberon. He'll jump up and that could harm you. I'll bring him over in a week, he's fine where he is."

Raven laughed. "How did you know?"

Balen kissed her. "Because I know you. How are you feeling?"

Raven smiled. "They are good painkillers. I was sore but I'm a lot better now."

Balen kissed her. "I'm sorry my love, I was in a meeting with the Council, I'm going to have to go back. Frank can sit with you."

Raven smiled. "I'll be ok on my own."

Balen laughed. "You are joking, I am not going to leave you on your own. We aren't totally sure about who is still here. I'll request that Storm and The Doc move over here. The pigeon post seems to be very quick."

Raven smiled. "Bit like owls."

Balen looked confused.

Raven laughed. "You haven't read Harry Potter then?"

Balen shook his head. He kissed her and left. Frank had been waiting outside, he came back in.

Raven looked up at him. "Frank, can you put those horrible things in a box for me please? I can't bear looking at them."

Frank went around the room with a box and put the melted dolls away. He brought things so that Raven could look at them and slipped some other unpleasant things into the box before Raven noticed them. They spent the day doing that so by the time Balen came back the room had a far better feel to it.

Balen was exhausted. The meeting with the Council had gone on all day and he had had no sleep the night before chained to the chair worrying about what was happening to Raven. It was nearly twelve when he finally got to the bedroom.

Raven and Frank were talking when he came in. Frank was still working on the Laws but he was talking to Raven about them. He had got about two inches down on the first pile in the wardrobe. The pages were on one side of the table, each marked up with notes to put to the Council.

Frank got up as Balen walked in. "I'll bid you both a good night."

Balen smiled. "Good night Frank, has she had her painkillers tonight?"

Frank handed him the bottle. "She is due two now but I thought you'd probably want to give them to her when you go to sleep. The doctor has also put a pot of sleeping tablets there. He said she might have nightmares about what happened so for the first couple of nights it might be a good idea. What do you think Raven?"

Raven looked at Balen who was exhausted. "I think that the last thing Balen needs is to be roused from his well-earned sleep by me screaming my head off. Yes, I'll take the sleeping tablets if we are going to be safe here. I'm assuming there is a guard on the door."

Balen nodded his head. "As always, we are guarded. Ryjel picked them, and he vouched for them. He's been a rock."

Frank smiled and left the room as Balen took two tablets from each pot and handed them to Raven. He then got undressed and they fell asleep in each other's arms.

In the morning Balen had another meeting with the Council. It was going to be like that until they had sorted out the Laws. Frank carried Raven downstairs and to a light and airy room with a big bay window. He smiled as he looked around and sat Raven in the armchair with a table beside her with a notebook and paper, water and a glass and a pile of files.

There was a knock at the door and Ryjel came in. He had a huge bunch of flowers which had been tied with some garden twine. He smiled as he came in. "Flowers for my beautiful Sister-in-Law, special delivery and picked myself this morning." He found a vase and put the flowers in it.

Raven smiled and held her arms up so he could come over for a hug. "Lovely to see you Ryjel. They are beautiful, thank you. Do you have time to sit?"

Frank had positioned the sofa opposite the chair and a coffee table in the middle. Ryjel sat down. "I don't have long, there is so much to do but I'll visit when I can. I heard about what you are setting up. Some of the women used to be guards and in "The Unit" before Michael incarcerated them. They have asked if they can be your "Personal Guard" and would like to help with bringing the women to speak to you. Would you like to speak to them first?"

Raven was looking at the flowers. "That sounds like a wonderful idea. When can they visit?"

Ryjel laughed. "You are Archangel's wife; they visit when you tell them to! You'll have to get used to that. When would you like them to visit."

Raven looked at the huge pile of files beside her. Ryjel noticed it. She laughed. "Looks like as soon as possible."

Frank sat down beside Ryjel. "I want to be here guarding you. Storm will be here this morning with the Doc no doubt. I'll leave it to you to sort all that out."

Balen was in the Council Meeting Room. They had convened at 7am and had already gone through the first of the Laws. There were so many they had decided to start at the beginning and work through.

Athame was reading out the Law, they were quickly discussing it, then rewriting, or keeping it. Jenkins, an elderly Council Member had a pile of white paper in front of him and he was writing the new Laws as they were decided.

They were in full flow when there was a knock at the door and an envelope was brought in for Balen. He opened it. It was a communication from LexCorp acknowledging his ownership of the shares. There was also an enquiry as to the whereabouts of his mother. He looked up. "This is the acknowledgement of my majority shareholding in LexCorp."

The next two months involved setting up the new "Laws" which would govern Transition X. The reams of Laws which Michael had put in place were draconian. The new laws had to be practical and "liveable" and that took time.

Storm and Doc arrived and they set about making The Factory more of a hospital and began working with the Transition X doctor to rehabilitate the women who had been there for a longer time. One by one Raven met with the women who were in various stages of pregnancy. They were seen initially on their own but then when all the women had had at least one meeting with Raven they were able to request a second. Some came with their life partners who needed to make a joint decision as to what they should do.

As Ryjel had training in Mental Illness from his life before he joined Transition X he helped with a meeting that all the women had asked for. Those who had partners brought them along and they had decided to make the decision as a group. They discussed it and unanimously decided that they wanted nothing to do with Michael and they all wanted a termination.

Two months later, Raven looked up from the many sheets of reports and took a deep breath. Her report was coming along and her diary for the day was full. There was about half an hour spare to get some lunch but after that, meetings all afternoon.

Of course, her report had to be handwritten which meant it took ages. She had just been through the discipline sheets, and they had been graded into the trays according to their severity. Each one had been reported on and she had added an extra category of recommended punishment which usually involved some form of tidying up.

She picked up the report for the last month and compared it, then to the month before. She smiled as she saw that the worst "offenders" had not transgressed this month. Their regular reports for insubordination were notable by their absence. She shrugged, perhaps she was right, she had told Balen to hold fire on their punishment as everyone had to get used to new rules and in many cases, there had just been mistakes. There were after all a lot of them.

As the rules got easier to follow fewer people were reported for transgressions. What had been a half hour run through a list of what amounted to pretty much minor mischief evolved into hardly anything.

She tapped the pages of her report to line them up and stapled them together on the left-hand corner. Throwing them into the top tray she stacked the minor miscreant trays underneath and moved the stack to a side table, job done.

Her next job was to go through the feed stock and allocate the feeding sessions for the next week. She stopped for a moment to contemplate the days when feeding was much more freeform, and the animals had what she felt they wanted that day. Now the feed was measured and allocated, and it was her task every morning to write that allocation which had to be worked out for each animal according to its weight the night before. The sheets would then be collected, and the feed weighted and delivered.

She hadn't seen the animals in nearly a month, or perhaps longer. They were not fitted into her schedule which Balen gave her every morning. There was little point, but she got the same sheet as all his close court got, each designated with their tasks. The only difference being that she was sometimes allocated time with him.

Raven picked up the sheet and compared it to yesterday. The animals weighed the same, they pretty much always did so she copied the figures over, stapled the sheets and broke with protocol, she got up with the intention of delivering them to the feed shed officer herself rather than waiting for the postal worker to arrive.

She hadn't seen the yard for a while, and she was astounded at how it had changed. It was clean, tidy and the vehicles which were parked there were in a regimented line, painted black with the Transition X logo prominently visible.

She walked past the vegetable garden which had been "rustic charm" in the style of a Monastic Garden the last time she had seen it. Now it was quite different. The vegetables grew in regimented lines, the watering system going in beside them to ensure each plant had it's quota and no more. Gardeners prowled hunting weeds though by the look of it no weed would dare to break the soil.

Food was being gathered, meticulously wiped to replace each speck of soil back into the growing bed. Each vegetable had its place in a grid made of string and as it was harvested it had it's number taken down and it was weighed and inspected. The empty slot was then turned over with a trowel and a cup of what looked like compost was added, mixed in and a seed was placed in the prepared soil. Notes were taken and the plant was left to grow, monitored daily.

The gardeners walked up the rows, measuring the size of the plants and noting this on the sheets they carried around on clip boards.

Raven felt a hand on her arm. It was one of the security division. "Sorry Raven, Balen's orders, nobody is to be away from their allocated station, and I can see from my sheet that you should be in the office."

She glanced at the offered sheet on yet another clipboard and noted her place. She smiled at the officer. I thought I would deliver the figures myself this morning.

The guard gasped. "Please don't make my job any harder. Get back to your office as soon as physically possible and I won't record this. Don't tell him or I will be demoted or worse."

She took a couple of steps, and she was in agony, her waters had broken. The guard noticed and called for help. She was taken straight to The Doc and within the hour a baby boy was born.

Balen ran from his meeting. He took the steps two at a time. The Factory had now been transformed. The grey breeze block walls had been painted white and there were pictures on the walls. The lines of beds had gone, replaced by curtained "booths".

He ran to Raven who was sitting up in bed with a little bundle wrapped in white towels. She looked up. "Meet your son."

There was much celebration that night and by the morning the Doc was busy handing out painkillers and other hangover remedies.

Raven was allowed a little time to recover but soon enough she was seated in her "Day Room" and back to doing the work. The rules and routines were still a bit draconian but with nearly three thousand people to organise she could see why. There had to be a rota for the Dining Hall at least.

The days were long, and she rarely saw Balen until bedtime and rarely then. He was tired then, so was she and the best they could manage was to fall asleep together. He felt different, but he was tired, that was to be expected. She would be understanding.

The baby was named Raphael, and he was constantly with Raven who managed to juggle her paperwork and raising him.

The Doc and Storm had been called back to the Compound as they were trying to set up a hospital there. Raven had been sad to see them go but she could see the practicality. They had a medical team at the HQ, so it made sense.

Not long afterwards Frank was also sent back to the Compound as they needed him to set up the Laws there.

It was a stormy night and Raven was still working. Balen was in a meeting with the Council as there had been some food stolen from the Warehouse and they were trying to work out what had happened so were interviewing people.

Raphael was two weeks old when Raven came back from the bathroom and went to feed him. He was unconscious. She screamed and ran him down to the Infirmary. Balen was called but within the hour the doctor came out to say that Raphael had died.

Raven demanded to see him, but the doctor said that it was not wise. Balen was too busy comforting Raven and clinging to her, so they went back to their room.

The days passed into six months.

Another day was over. Raven stepped inside the room after a quick trip to the bathroom and leant against the door. She was also right on time as there was a knock on the door and the paperwork was collected.

Sebastian was a regular collector. He was in his early teens, shy and rarely looked her in the eye. He never spoke and she made him jump when she said "Hello."

He nearly dropped the paperwork. He seemed nervous although he had seen her almost every day for a few months. He looked up shyly and mumbled "Hello." He then took the paperwork swiftly and nearly ran out of the door.

Raven went to the window. Her view was across the lawns to the maze. She looked out there every morning but this morning she looked out with new eyes. She looked at things in a more analytical way and what had seemed before to be innocent marching and training now seemed somehow sinister. Those people who were marching were immaculately dressed. Not in itself an issue other than the uniforms they now wore were no longer the black boiler suits synonymous with Transition X. They wore actual uniforms. Black with red trim, the Transition X symbol clearly emblazoned on their breast pocket. Each wore a bar just below the symbol. She reached for her pair of binoculars and took a closer look.

The soldiers marched neatly in patterns. That looked smart but what she found disturbing was that they had the same haircut. She took in a deep breath and held it in then let it out slowly. The degree of control was beginning to trouble her. So was Balen.

She hadn't seen him alone and they hadn't been physical for a long time. He was so busy now he needed time to work late and do what he needed to do. The loss of their child had been a rift between them, and his distance didn't help. He was always tired and never had the time to talk with her. What did trouble her was that he seemed different. It wasn't something she had thought about but lately she had seen that cold look in his eyes she had seen when they had first met. He was also excluding her from what was going on. She was "summoned" when he wanted to see her and then dutifully returned to her rooms when he had other things to do. But uneasy the head that wears the crown. Also, she missed Frank and Ryjel rarely had time to visit as Balen was working him hard keeping everyone in check.

She swung the binoculars around but couldn't get much of a view other than the grass, the lake, and the perimeter wall. She did notice that a walkway had been added on the inside of the perimeter. It seemed odd and realistic at the same time. Odd in that they were supposed to be building a new world and, in her mind, all the disruptive elements had pretty much been wiped out in the shut down due to their habit of shooting each other. The degree of training and discipline seemed excessive for a world which they had discussed would hopefully be a "New Eden". This looked and felt wrong, and she had no idea how to find out.

She put the binoculars down and picked up her mug. It was a long shot that it would be a good excuse, but she got a real wish for a mug of hot chocolate and as there were no sachets in her room the kitchen would be the best way to get what she wanted.

Like a naughty schoolgirl she opened her door and looked left and right.

She didn't need to, there was a guard outside her door.

The guard snapped to attention. "Madam, do you need something?" Her voice was steady, but her eyes said otherwise.

Raven sighed internally as she knew how this would go. "I am just going to get a mug of hot chocolate."

The guard flinched. "I will arrange that for you."

Raven managed her kindest smile. "I will go and get my own thank you. I can manage."

The guard looked stricken. "But Madam, we are here to attend to your needs."

It didn't feel like it. Now she felt like a pet or a prisoner and more importantly she wanted to know what Balen was up to that he didn't want her to know about.

She backed away and closed the door.

There was a knock at the door and a middle-aged women brought her a mug of chocolate on a tray. The mug was on a saucer. She handed Raven the tray which Raven thought was odd and walked away quickly. The guard shut the door.

Raven went to her desk and put the tray down. She didn't want the hot chocolate, so she left it there and went back to thinking. Then she changed her mind, feeling guilty that produce was limited, and the woman had brought it to her. She lifted the mug to drink and there was a folded note underneath.

She picked the note up and opened it. It read. "Frank is in trouble. Nothing is as it seems. The Crimson Heart are in control. I love you, Balen" Raven hid the message in one of the dolls which she had kept as it was a pretty fairy.

The colour drained from the guard's face as she opened the door. She looked at her shoes and looked really awkward.

Raven pulled herself up to her full height. "Where is Frank?"

The guard did a goldfish impersonation as her mouth opened and closed but no words came out.

Raven glared at her. "Tell me, where is Frank?" She felt sorry for the guard and sympathized with her position but she needed to know. "Take me to him."

The guard looked confused and was obviously going over his orders to work out what her response should be. She maintained her glare and the boiler suited guard was caught in the headlights. Then she smiled kindly and added. "Please".

That caught her off guard and she turned on her heels and walked down the corridor. Raven followed and now she was worried as Frank was supposed to be at the Farm.

They waked down the carpeted corridor which was lined with works of art which had been accumulated over the past months. This part of the house she was familiar with, but they turned right down a corridor and down some stairs into a part of the house she didn't recognise. The carpet became more industrial and there were no pictures on the wall. The doors changed from residential to bland office type doors and the lighting from chandeliers to the battery powered lights which could be changed for recharging. The light was dim and there was a metallic smell and feel to the place.

So far, they had only made one turn so that was easy to remember. The second turn was left and down a corridor to a set of stairs which went down. The stairs were stone, uncarpeted and there was a prevailing odour of damp.

There were no doors in the corridor for about a hundred yards and then the corridor opened into a large room with doors off of it. There was a desk and chair with in and out trays and a dim light which illuminated the papers which were being looked at by a bespectacled weedy looking man with mousy hair and a rat like face.

He looked up. "What is the meaning of this?"

The guard stood to attention. "Raven has requested to have an interview with Frank."

Ratman looked at the pair of them as if the guard had gone mad. "Where is the paperwork and the authority from Lord Balen?"

Raven felt for the guard who looked as if he wanted the earth to open up and swallow him up. She thought for a moment. "I am Raven, if you wish to upset Lord Balen you will stand in my way and upset me. I wish to speak with Frank. I am sure that Frank will spare me some time from his important duties."

The guard stared at her at a loss. Ratman looked a little confused, his authoritative ordered brain unable to cope with the break in protocol. There was also something else. Raven could feel it. They were trying to work out if she was being sarcastic. That truly terrified her as she knew something was "up". She smiled, trying to play on the sarcasm to camouflage her lack of knowledge of the situation.

She looked at Ratman in the face and in a haughty tone she insisted. "Take me to Frank."

Ratman stood up and as he took a step back, he nearly tipped his office revolving chair over. It teetered and returned to upright. He stepped to the side and opened a drawer and took out a key. He turned and went to one of the doors. Raven followed him, trepidation chilling her very heart. This was very, very wrong. Why was the android locked away, the very android who had put Balen in his position. More worrying, why had Frank let that happen.

Part of her hoped he would be in a secluded office of his own request where he could work on what he needed to work on. As the door swung back she realised that was far from the truth.

The android known as Frank was chained to a chair in the corner. Angry gashes revealed the silver of his endoskeleton and pipework ran from his systems, wires and tubes protruding from where his flesh had been removed.

His chin was on his chest but as Raven entered the room he looked up. His eyes seemed lifeless; the spark she had always liked was gone. Lights flashed on the wall and a keyboard flickered into action out of sleep mode. Recognition flashed across his face. He almost managed a smile. It was a painful wincing smile. "Well, they could have shut off my pain receptors couldn't they?" His voice was broken but still recognisable.

Raven had to think fast and swallow the shock she felt. "Balen has sent me to work on your systems. You two, leave us." She glared at the guard and Ratman. "You know my position here and my clearance is unquestionable. Balen has requested that I undertake certain tasks. I should not be disturbed and Balen himself does not want to be disturbed. I will be submitting a full report and I am sure he would not be pleased if this is drawn to anyone's attention and if I am disturbed. Leave us."

They both looked terrified, turned on their heels and left. Her gamble had paid off. It was obvious that Balen had not assumed she would do anything, so he had left her "status" as assumed. That was enough.

When the door had shut Raven looked around the room to check for cameras. She hadn't expected to see any as the sensitivity of what they had done to Frank was something he no doubt preferred that nobody knew about.

She crossed the room and knelt in front of Frank. "What can I do to help?"

Frank seemed to think for a while. The seconds felt like hours. "I have run system check. Without the controller here the system seems to be activated. This system is unviable. That in itself is an issue for me now but not an unsurmountable problem.

I assume that Balen is responsible for this and that his sociopathic and megalomaniac tendencies have got the better of him. I had hoped that his affection for you would have kept them buried but as they say power corrupts and absolute power corrupts absolutely. I am sorry Raven, Balen has reverted to type. It was a problem which arose in his brother and the sibling seems to have the same issues. I tried to control him or at least to see him through issues but he is thriving in the midst of his new power. He is creating the peace he wants to see by total control and the elimination of anyone who opposes him. We may have limited time. He is attempting to reconnect the internet using my system so that he has control of it. I cannot allow that to happen.

The infrastructure is sufficiently damaged that he would not find it easy. I need to ensure he cannot do this."

Raven looked around the room. "What can I do to help?"

Frank smiled; it was close to his old smile she knew so well. "I don't need to tell you that it will be dangerous with little chance of success, but I don't want to be completely gone. I would have done but I need to stay to oppose him. Obviously not from here. The obvious thing would be to upload my consciousness onto a memory stick and then destroy this body. But, that would mean you would be discovered. Also, the programmers are pretty primitive so I think there could be another way. Are you willing?"

Raven didn't need to think about it. "Of course."

"Very well, go to the console. There is a box of memory sticks under the counter. Take out two. Put them both into the ports on the laptop and press "return". That will download two copies of me onto the sticks, might as well have a back-up plan. I then want you to leave me here. I am going to crash the system. That will effectively destroy my CPU and "mind" and any programs running, I will crash it with the virus I have been creating. So keep those memory sticks away from anything here!"

Raven did as she was told and returned to Frank when the system had completed the download. She put the sticks into her pocket. "So what now?"

Frank smiled. I need you to go to Madame Tussauds in London. The building still stands but it is closed and barricaded. There is an exhibit there for the Terminator. I had made provision for something like this to happen or for this unit to be destroyed. There is a port behind the right ear. Put one of the sticks in there and the system will do the rest. It is an independent system with its own power system. I will be back." He laughed but she had no idea why. "Oh never mind."

Paper was churning out of an ancient printer. "Take that and give it to the guard outside. It states an order from Balen never to mention that you came here. Your timing is perfect as they want my system to come online tonight so you might as well get ready for an almighty bang. The two sheets also printed are orders to take you to the Warehouse, a place where they get supplies. It is printed but it is Balen's handwriting so they won't question it.

There is enough dissension here that in the chaos there won't be any effective opposition and it should be assumed it was a miscalculation on the part of the computer operators.

Your main problem will be dealing with Balen's control. Transition X have supreme control and he runs the country like a police state, supreme control of everything. The only chance is to stay in the country areas as he does not deem them a threat.

Go pack a bag sweetheart, you are on the road again."

Raven put her hand out to touch Frank's arm. He looked up at her and smiled. "Frank, how did it get to this?"

Frank looked into her eyes, and it felt as though he was looking into her soul. "Humanity wanted a saviour. They need guidance and Balen was happy to be worshipped. He provided the security they needed in the crisis, and he systematically eliminated anyone who could challenge this supremacy by being a potential leader. He shot the wolves and kept the sheople.

Why would they question him as out of the chaos he found a way to be a god by providing for them. They handed over their individuality and sacrificed their freewill on the altar of security.

I can pre-empt your next question. Why is this a problem? Is free will overrated when people are starving? I can answer that. On the face of it perhaps but the assassination squads have a lot of power and they have already eliminated anyone who is not of use. That includes anyone over fifty and anyone who questions authority. There are rules for everything, and he seeks a perfection in the countries of the world. Anyone who doesn't fit is removed. He has recreated the gas chambers and created a new source of animal feed in the process. Of course, a smaller population is easier to feed. There is a control on breeding amongst humans and Transition X has a breeding program. They dictate who mates, which has no relation to who is married, and currently all children are to be removed into the schools he is having built at four years old. He has already had all children under two years old culled.

Raven looked horrified. "I don't know what to say."

Frank looked stunned. "Now this is awkward. I was already out of touch by the time your son was taken from you. I was informed that it had been a decision to remove the child from the compound as he would be a distraction when you had other work to do and being a mother wouldn't be the best use of your skills."

Raven glared at him. "What? You mean my child lives? Where is he?"

Frank shook his head. "I was not there and I can see now that was all part of Balen's cold and calculated plan. My programming did lack some of the humanity which would have alerted me to the unrealistic situation but to me it seemed practical, and I was just getting on with what practically needed doing. In six months Balen has achieved complete control. I for my part was instrumental in part for it as it made sense. I had been led to believe that his association with you had given him that edge of humanity. I am not a psychologist, so I didn't notice the transition. Then one day the rules were amended as the structure was in place and his unquestionable dictatorship was launched to applause and elation.

Launched on the backs of the poor he removed everything from everyone and put it all into his control. He then allocated things according to people's use to him. He keeps it that way. People work they get fed and a roof over their heads. The more use they are the better their accommodation but let him down and you are eliminated. He had people bringing their own children to the incinerators.

This is not something you can fight now and all I am suggesting is that you get away and go find the Resistance. You would be invaluable in their ranks.

Now go. Return to your room and collect your things, only what you can carry without it being obvious and go."

Raven kissed Frank on his forehead and left the room, her head spinning.

Raven sat on her bed looking out of the window. The Autumnal golds and yellows had driven away the green of summer and there was a definite chill in the air. The troops marched and the sentries patrolled. This place had felt safe and all she could think about was that she had to leave.

Her thoughts confused her and images of Balen swirled around her consciousness. Over and over, she analysed their last time together. She was looking for something that would reassure her that she was doing the right thing. It was a big ask to take everything in and walk away from what had been her home. An even bigger ask for her to believe her child had not died and was out there somewhere.

Natural caution made her think it over repeatedly. Yes, she could believe that Balen could be dictatorial, he had been before she met him. But she knew him or she thought she did. He was overworked that was true but that would not have hidden the softness in his eyes and that she knew he loved her. He had given her no reason to doubt him other than having not seen him for a while. She looked at her diary and was horrified to see that it was nearly six months.

In those months the rules had become harsher and there had been a few things she found distasteful about reports she had read. Some she should have read, some she had got hold of as she was still Raven, despite being Archangel's Wife or whatever title he had bestowed on her. None of the titles seemed to carry much weight or open too many doors. It had taken having a keen eye and the ability to grab papers when she could. Then she would return them saying they had got mixed up with hers. Simple but effective as nobody wanted to upset any apple carts or admit they had messed up. By what she had heard Balen was very intolerant of any sort of mistake.

Could he have become the dictator he was being accused of being? He had it in him which made it believable but what was said was excessive and she would have said he would not be capable of that.

The soldiers marched, on and on. The sun was making its way across the skyline, lower in the sky than earlier in the year, the seasons were marching on. Life was marching on, but she had life. So many were gone, and she had barely had time to mourn them. There was nobody left from her farm now at HQ. They were all gone. She was trapped in an alien-controlled world, and it hit her like a bolt that she was almost pleased that there was an excuse to break free and get out there again.

What confused her was what was going on and she was very unhappy at having to take everything on say so with no back up evidence. It was such a big ask to expect her to walk away and enter what was obviously a hostile world where she would have a value as something that Balen cared about. Also, if he was such a dictator, he, and by association she, would have natural enemies.

Who should she trust? A megalomaniac AI who had instigated the deaths of millions without losing sleep or a previously vicious dictator who had convinced her that he wasn't like that. Everyone she knew from the farm was gone, including most of the animals and she was now part of a Dictatorial Organisation where there were rules for everything and she herself was part of the machine which was controlling people's lives, allegedly. That was the point, she had no proof.

She hadn't seen Balen much but he had told her it was going to be like that. They had trouble on the Eastern Countries, and he had left to handle it personally as it was such a threat to everyone's freedom. That was what they had told her. There had been correspondence from him, that she knew, she had seen the reports and orders coming in, in passing when she dropped off her reports. Now her reports were collected so her source of information was cut off. She knew he was busy; she didn't expect a love note, they weren't like that, not now. Losing the baby had come between them and they had started arguing and being distant. He had stormed out saying he had too much to deal with to handle it. She had hoped for something and now she had it and the covert way it was delivered worried her more.

That note was from Balen and if he was at the HQ then someone was lying.

She had not seen Frank for much longer. Again not that she expected to. He was not a friend, he was a machine, or rather is a machine. One with quite an agenda which may not have gone to plan. What came to mind straight away was that he hadn't shut down the computer systems, he had merely shut everyone else out of it.

That would mean that the internet still existed and with it all the other AIs. It had been a huge thing to shut it all down and if it was all shut down how come he could give her a memory stick to activate another version of himself. Surely if he can activate an "independent" unit so could anyone else. Even if he had planted a virus there were going to be systems outside the "net".

Would other AIs have tolerated being assassinated? Being shut down was effectively death and if Nemesis could infiltrate systems how many military and civilian systems had done the same. It was not beyond belief that everything was controlled. So in truth, who was Nemesis? Was he the "be all and end all" of computers or was he just one of many and there was more out beyond that wall than expected.

If so then was there a plan here to send her out to create other Nemesis programs and units to try to combat these other systems? Or was she overthinking it all.

The bottom line was whether Balen was a merciless dictator or a misunderstood man. Or was Nemesis in charge and framing him or using him to create the world that Nemesis wants?

That was confusing enough to send her to the kettle for a coffee.

She was shaking and it made no sense. The world seemed to close in on her and she couldn't think. She reached for the Anti Depressants that the doctor had given her. She took one and hoped she would feel better. She didn't.

She walked across the soft carpet and checked there was enough water in the kettle. She flipped the switch and it leapt to life. She looked at it. Her mind going through the evidence. The power was generated so that explained their power system. Nothing there that Nemesis would or should have destroyed which couldn't be rekindled. The kettle was basic, no computer parts, so why not?

If they had "things" then so would other people. So what control did Transition X have? What made them "top dog" other than that they had good weaponry. That opened a whole train of thought about other organisations. Most of them would have wiped each other out but there had to be some survivors. Outside the walls it could be a war zone. Inside the "compound" was relatively peaceful, no it was peaceful. A peace that was protected by the sentries on the wall and the standing army which was training daily.

Why would Balen have to do such a thing to Frank? Surely a controlled world was what Nemesis wanted. So now another aspect to worry about.

The kettle was boiled so she put a spoonful of coffee into the cup, a sachet of milk and then poured the water. The simplicity of the action after the complications of surviving post shutdown was not lost on her.

As a prisoner in her room, she had no access elsewhere to find out what was going on. There was no way she could trust the guard or ask her. Balen was away anyway. Whether she stayed or left was up to her and her doubts were making that decision very, very hard. If she was wrong the repercussions would be severe. She would be potentially handing herself over to Balen's enemies as leverage. If she stayed, then she would have crossed Nemesis if what he was saying was true or false. Now as she sipped her coffee she wanted to scream.

What she wanted most was to talk to Balen. He wasn't there and that left a huge hole in her life. Memories flooded back of the days they had spent in the early days of taking over Transition X. The changes he had made had been for the best. The changes now were reverting things and taking them far beyond what they had originally been.

As she thought it through the pieces began to fall into place. With every transgression instigated by the "soldiers" and those who lived in the complex Balen had brought in another rule to make sure things went smoothly. Rule after rule piled up and there had been a change in him as well. As when she had first met him, he was keeping everything ordered again. Pens were lined up; his desk went from an ordered chaos of papers to neat trays and the paperwork increased from one report to a report on everything. It had always been the situation that he was grasping at anything he could to keep the peace with a pit of vipers waiting for him to mess up. Not everyone was happy with the transition from the old Archangel to the new. Balen's brother had had quite a following and they were hard to win over.

The new rules helped and giving them positions on the Committee he had set up. For good or bad it had silenced them and made his position more secure as they had nothing to gain by removing him. That was all she could cling to now that he was "away" and she was left with the dilemma that he was "different".

Why would he do that to Frank? They were not friends, but it was a bit excessive and excess was not something she would associate with Balen.

There was a knock at the door which she almost welcomed to drag herself from her thoughts. She went to the door and opened it. It was her habit that she would do that rather than ask someone to come in and of habit she had her foot behind the door so nobody could push the door in. In that way the room felt like her sanctuary, not her prison.

She opened the door just enough to see who was out there.

Balen stood in the corridor. His face was bruised, and he had his arm in a makeshift sling. He put his other hand up to push the door open. Raven took her foot away and let him in.

He stepped inside, shut the door, and leaned up against it. He was out of breath and took breaths between words. "Things aren't going well. That bastard Frank, or should I say Nemesis has an android version of me and a few of himself. By what I can work out he has a factory somewhere. I'm screwed Raven. They were going to kill me, but Ryjel managed to arrange an escape. I thought you had betrayed me. I was told that you were with Frank and that I was there because you had asked him to as I was as insane as Michael."

Raven put her arms around him but while stroking his hair she checked there were no ports in the nape of his neck or behind his ears.

Balen managed a smile. "Subtly done and you were right to check. I am definitely me though the way this body feels I think.."

Raven put her finger on his lips. "Don't even say it. Well Frank certainly has an agenda. He has a version of himself in the lock up rooms disassembled or at least with pipes coming out of him."

Balen looked down at her and stroked her hair. "By what I have been told by those still loyal to me that is the version of him which is running the systems. It seems that he did not shut things down as much as he made out. He left some options for himself, not least a fully functioning factory to make his own army of robots or androids, whatever you call them."

He said there was going to be an explosive time tonight and that I should escape before then and get to Madame Tussauds where he has an android which could be booted up with his consciousness or a clone of himself or something. He mentioned I should get help from The Resistance."

Balen half smiled. "Yes, and they would trust you, meet with you and then he would know where they are and eliminate them. I would put money on whatever he gave you being a tracking device. Glad you didn't carry that one out. Problem is now what do we do?"

Raven looked at him sincerely. "What is the situation?"

Balen shook his head. "Frank has "me" in charge, well his version of me. I was locked up in the basement in case he needed me later at any time. He has been writing his own rules and running this place for the past six months. I fell for it, all of it when our son died. I would have agreed to anything, and I just wanted him to handle things as I couldn't cope. I do not know how long he has been planning this, but his plan is bigger than I first thought. It has gone over and over in my mind that there was no coincidence that he was "brought" into my life, with the old Archangel being my brother.

He used your "success" to ensure I had to take notice of you. Whether he had a plan for "us" or not is irrelevant, what he needed was for Transition X to take him into their fold. Then one by one he has eliminated everyone around you so that you would be easier to manipulate. Putting a rift between us would mean you were not likely to come looking for me. If you did you would find a far less "amenable" Balen in charge which you are likely to accept as I hardly appeared "nice" when you met me. I've been in that cell for six months.

Raven looked thoughtful. "My love. I was with you in that time. Or I thought I was. I was understanding when you were tired and didn't want me. Being rejected so many times hurt me. So I backed off and accepted it. So what do we do next? We cannot stay here, and I have no idea how we can get out. Will he know you have escaped?"

Balen thought about it. "Probably not. He is a creature of assumptions. He sets something up, checks it is working but then assumes it will stay that way. I should be dead by now and my body disposed of. I would be if it wasn't for Ryjel. This is human intervention, and he would not allow for that in his plans. He is expecting you to "escape" and will probably make it easy for you. He may even let someone else go if they are with you. He likely won't check. He may well just keep everyone out of the way so you can go and rely on devices and bugs. Didn't you realise that it couldn't have been me. I'd never want a night I couldn't show you how much I want you if the option was there."

Raven smirked. "Perhaps it is the only way to know you, are you? Well he wants me to get out and I would want to take someone with me. But I don't associate with anyone so that falls flat. What about one of the guards? Would it be realistic if I took one of the guards with me?"

Balen thought about it. "Debatable as I have no idea which are androids and which are human. Anyway, your guards are female!"

Raven looked at the door. "Is there a guard out there now?"

Balen smiled. "No, I would assume that the guard has been removed to make your escape easier. Do you have anything I can change into?"

Raven shook her head. "Only boiler suits here."

Balen looked around the room. "Anything you need to take?"

Raven looked around. "No, wish I could take the dog though."

Balen looked at his shoes. "I wasn't going to tell you. Frank could see no use for the dogs, and they wouldn't behave for the androids so he had all but Oberon shot. He kept Oberon in case he had to keep you sweet. At least we didn't bring any others from the Compound."

Raven glared at Balen. "How do you know? Didn't you have a say?"

Balen met her glare. "It was one of the first things he did when he locked me up. He told me to keep me unbalanced along with many other very, very upsetting things which I will not tell you about. I was losing it over our baby dying. It took me a long time to get my head together. It was Ryjel who helped. He's definitely not on side with Nemesis but he has made Nemesis think he is. He has been my rock. It was him who made it possible for me to escape and kept me informed."

Raven thought for a moment. "Then Oberon is coming with us."

Balen grimaced. "You can't be serious. So, we have to break the dog out too? Then he would be useful to let us know if we are dealing with an android. Travelling incognito with a long-haired white German Shepherd does increase the odds of us being caught though."

Raven gave him one of those don't even think of crossing me looks. "For one he is a Belgian Shepherd, and he would not survive if we left him as Frank would have no use for him." Raven picked up her shoulder bag which she had long ago packed with essentials as a "go bag" and slung it over her shoulder. She went to the door and Balen followed her.

The corridor was, as they had expected, empty. Raven didn't hesitate, she strode down the corridor and almost ran down the spiral stairs, down another corridor closely followed by Balen, into a back kitchen where she opened the window and climbed out.

The loamy soil outside the window clearly displayed her footprints so she walked backwards covering them over, Balen behind her.

As they were behind a low bush, they were able to duck down so as not to be seen from the grass where troops were marching. They were all eyes front anyway so they could easily get around the corner and into the hydrangea bushes. The rooms which had been used as kennels were just across a pathway. Raven put a hand on Balen's arm. "Best I get him." Balen nodded and ducked down into the undergrowth.

Raven swiftly moved across the path. She opened the door to the shed and stepped into the rustic interior. The woodwork had seen better days and there was a strong smell of disinfectant which nearly choked her.

She whispered "Oberon" and it was answered by a whimper. The room was empty other than a bag of dog food and a water carrier as there was no obvious water source. No sign of a lead either. There was a door in the far wall where the whimper came from. She went straight to it, opened the door and Oberon took a flying leap at her, paws around her neck and his tongue gave her a good face wash. Raven hugged him, sinking her face into his soft fur.

The room was clinically clean. An empty dog bowl and one full of water were neatly placed. There was no bed or lead. Raven shrugged. "Come on boy, heel."

They left together, Oberon walking perfectly to heel and rejoined Balen in the bushes. Oberon gave Balen a lick on his hand and they ran as a group to where cars were parked. Balen was following Raven and whispered. "You can't be serious. You are going to take a car?"

Raven half turned. "No, I am going to take my car. The one you gave me and the one with the survival kit in the boot."

Her Jeep was where she had left it and so was the key, resting on the tyre on the passenger side. She opened the back door and Oberon jumped in. Balen jumped into the back and ducked down into the footwell, and she jumped into the driver's seat. The total lack of technology on the ancient vehicle meant it still worked. "Right, say nothing. It is going to have a tracker on it and we will dump it when we are as far away as we can get."

Raven drove the jeep out of the yard and up the track to the main gates. The gates opened for her, and she drove out. Once outside she stopped for Balen to get in the front and then she put her foot down and they tore down the country lanes. It wasn't lost on her that the tank was full. She smiled. "Helpful that they filled the tank first." Balen nodded.

Oberon was laying on the back seat watching the scenery go past.

Raven drove until the petrol ran out. They then got out and opened the door for Oberon who jumped out and cocked his leg up the back wheel. They both laughed, a relaxed laugh, the first for a long time.

Raven beckoned Balen away from the car and when they were far enough away she whispered. "Ok so the car is going to have a tracker on it and likely things on it could have as well. I have no idea how to tell."

Balen thought about it. "Well, if all the computers were down, I wouldn't worry but it is all too evident that that is not the case. As far as Frank is concerned you have done what he asked. I would also suggest that we give Oberon a good look over for recent scars as well."

After an hour they were sure that Oberon was bug free and his collar lay in the dust, cut open and the tracker clearly visible. Similar trackers were found in various parts of the packing and what was left was packed into the larger backpack which Raven handed to Balen.

Balen looked around. "London is that way I can just about work out. You were driving towards it that should throw Frank off the scent. He will assume you are doing what you were told. So where are we going?"

"The last place he would expect us to go. As far away from England as possible. I was reading about a private project in Spain, in the wilds. There are still sailings, or we could get a private boat and get across. Then all we must do is cross Spain."

Balen looked confused. "So, no plans to overthrow Frank then?"

Raven raised an eyebrow. "The world is in a state of anarchy if what I have heard is true but that is all way out of date. His plan worked in part but not in its entirety. The rules are draconian but there is no effective force against him. If we approach The Resistance, then that is what he planned. If they have a serious uprising before the population is fed up with the current regime they will be eliminated. I agree we need to make contact but only in a minor way and if the opportunity arises."

Balen smiled and hugged her. "When did you turn into the General?"

Raven hugged him back. "That is exactly what Frank is getting wrong. The strength in humanity comes out when tested not when allocated a task. You taught me a lot. I listen, I learn, and I have watched a lot of films. I could also be very wrong. So, it is up to you. What do you think?"

8

. Raven looked at the mess. "We can't risk having missed one. It is a shame, but I think we may have to leave the car here and go on on foot."

Balen moved a box with his foot. "I think you could be right. I think that we have gone through the bits we can take with us, but the rest could let us down. So, I guess we are in for a long walk."

Oberon strolled over and sat down next to Raven who gently stroked his head. He looked up at her lovingly. "Yes, a long walk but to where?"

Balen pulled the map he had taken from the pile out of his pocket. "We passed villages, and I don't know about you, but I didn't see anyone."

Raven walked over and looked at the map. "You wouldn't as before the shutdown they were holiday homes and Air BnB places. As few people lived in the villages and they had no infrastructure they were unlikely to be inhabited. That is good for us as we don't really have a plan yet. We will have to have an idea as to what to do."

Balen smiled "I was a bit lost as to what to do at the compound let alone out here. What was certain was that we had a dilemma. Knowledge cannot be un-learnt, the knowledge of what people had, albeit disastrous in places is for many people what they want.

Even back before Nemesis turned everything off there was talk and people were trying to make a difference. The problem was that what was needed had to be a fresh start. They tried various plans and took on the buzz words with a passion. Of course, as reality was revealed in a world where everyone could record there were serious doubts thrown on what people were doing. The first of course was recycling. It was discovered that carefully sorted recycling was being thrown on landfill or sent abroad to be disposed of. Electric cars were powered by electricity which came from coal powered power stations and the amount of lithium needed and the disposal of the old batteries afterwards was another issue. There were so many issues, but I am sure you know that."

Raven shook her head. "Actually no, I lived on the farm and only had that and what was around me as information. I knew there was a problem but like a lot of people I believed it was someone else's. The price of feed fluctuated; the cost of food went up. I saw the news, but I have long believed that the people are shown so little of what the world is really like until it bites them on the bum."

Balen put his arms around her. "Well you are not far wrong. Companies had to make money and lots of it so they grabbed the best way they could do it rather than what would have been the best for the world. You know yourself that a single field if managed with aquaponics and hydroponics can produce so much more. If they had focused on local food generation rather than paperwork and the need for good presentation the mess may not have happened. Farmers initially enjoyed their EU bonuses which was no encouragement to grow excessive amounts of food to feed the masses.

I read somewhere that the subsidies were originally introduced alongside quotas which ensured that everyone had a fair-trade option. In a world of increasing population and fuel bills perhaps it would have been better to have encouraged farmers to grow more and take on the intensive farming that would feed those near them, to diversify to be able to have multiple crops which dovetailed and helped each other. Vegetables and meat on the same farm so that the compost from one fed the other. Literally grazing animals on the crop fields for a season and then planting a crop so no need for expensive manure and intensive worming schedules as life cycles of the bugs were broken up. You see, you taught me a lot Raven. I now understand that perhaps having a dual use type of cattle which could produce meat and milk would mean that the byproduct would be meat and the product milk. With a less chemical based raising system perhaps there would be less allergies and then again, the oats grown would bring the straw needed to feed the cattle so everything would be symbiotic.

Of course, that would have meant that the general population would have to cut their cloth and only eat what was in season. Chefs did talk about it for a while but then the credit crunch came, and people only wanted cheap food.

You would have thought that when Britain left the main part of Europe they would have looked to a more sustainable and "feed themselves" attitude. What did they do? They jumped on the carbon zero bandwagon and rather than planting food producing hedgerows they took up the farmland by planting trees. Rather than the "old way" of letting every four or five trees in a hedgerow grow they cut down the farming area to make the country reliant on other countries for imports which were hauled halfway around the world and which were still cheaper than produce produced in the UK. That these goods were allowed in was remarkable.

Of course, the reliance on certain countries was fuelled by the needs generated by the media. Things like toys encouraged plastics which might as well be single use when the children got fed up with them. Toys were big business and plastic rubbish took over from handmade local toys. Can't blame them though.

The world was designed that way and it fed commerce. Money revolved around it as did recycled cardboard being shipped many miles using a ton of fuel to become packaging to come back with plastic toys. Even the shipping containers were one use, well some of them were.

That was the world that Nemesis tried to destroy to put people back to having to grow their own food and obviously to cut down numbers.

But things have gone wrong as far as he is concerned. The brave new world seems to be people struggling to hold onto the old world and trying to recreate it. They want the old world back; they are not looking forwards.

The strongest have formed gangs and they are destroying anything the others are trying to create. The law of the jungle now prevails and rather than being able to plan a new world out of the ashes we are firefighting and trying to calm and quell the problems. Hence all the rules.

Nemesis is reacting as any machine would, practically. More rules, more executions and he needs absolute control. You aren't going to like this but, in many ways, I think he may be right. We cannot build while the gang lords are destroying. He knew it was a risk, but his gamble did not pay off. Here is quiet as you say but, in the cities, it is anarchy and all-out war. Same all over the world and the old enmities are magnified.

The Rebellion are not one of these groups. They are trying to set up order and food growing. But that has nothing to do with Frank and his rules and that has made him their enemy."

Raven looked up at him "I agree as from up my hill I was able to see things clearly and live the simple life but as you say people want the old world. Oh boy, 2020 hindsight, perhaps better to innovate rather than eradicate. I had an idea way back about recycled plastic lego bricks in larger sizes being used as farm buildings. It would have been great. If made solid it would be so easy to take a shed apart, disinfect it and then rebuild to suit whatever animals it is for. But we can't unbreak the world. It also looks as though you have lost whatever influence you had as well. If Frank has made "another you" then even if you do join The Rebellion it is going to have no real power. What can we do?"

Balen was looking exhausted. "You always want to "do" but at the moment all we can do is survive. The clues were all out there for humanity. Even in a house or flat people could grow their own but let's face it, vegetables are boring without being made into something and not everyone can cook. People want their quick food burger in a bright coloured box and the best that happened there was when the companies started to ethically source. Then it is a case of "so what".

The hippie sitting in a field eating mung beans and polluting the ozone layer with their bodily functions had no power at all. Only people with the money had the say but when they started blasting rockets into space, they lost any "green" credentials. It was an insane time before the crash, but it is an insane time now and worse because what "could" have been done has been done. The return to Eden is not as easy as taking away the toys as no doubt they have the factories up and running again, they are not that reliant on computers.

To say that Nemesis had an overinflated estimation of his own power is an understatement. That is probably why his response is active and vicious. I spoke out against him, and his reaction was instant. He must have had an android me waiting and I was very soon removed. It was only because I still had friends and those who believed in the old plan that I survived at all.

In truth I still believe that the "sanctuary sites" without the fall would have worked. Take those who want to grow things and put them in a place where they can grow for the masses, not for the favoured few. The organic Farm Shops are lovely but by their nature they are expensive and most likely ego trips or conscience cleaners for those who want to tip their hat at being green. Green was an overused buzzword anyway.

With hindsight what we needed was to turn more of the country over to agriculture and food growth and to improve the cities while keeping people there. Dead villages where once there had been thriving communities because people wanted a second home was a rot which eat into the fabric as farms became tourist attractions, not food producing. They were almost apologetic about the food their produced."

Raven looked around. "It is easy to get sentimental about animals. Take the goats, I couldn't kill any for meat but when you think about it they were not practical for meat anyway. For that you needed a cow where a lot of people can eat from one animal and the rest of it can be used. If that is what applies to a male calf, and they had bred dual use animals then the wastage on the dairy farms would have been cut back. Killing male calves was a wasted resource and the practicality of raising them for meat makes the whole system symbiotic as the manure they produce can feed the vegetables. Alongside aquaponics and hydroponics using their manure as the plant feed but controlled as an island Britain could have led the world into a new Dawn. But no they had to fixate on the problems not the solutions.

How environmentally disastrous was it to bring in vehicles which everyone had to "have" in a few years. So, all those old cars had to be scrapped. Better to bring in an adaptation kit and adapt all the old cars so nothing gets scrapped. Then I am no mechanic and ideas come cheap. The car companies were multi-million-pound corporations, they want to bring out new cars as the sales of the old ones do not bring them any reward. It is in their interest to make people scrap them and buy their new ones. Never mind that there wasn't enough power for them all and China had to rip up villages to build coal fired power stations."

Balen laughed ironically. "And they are probably working still. That is the problem, we did not achieve anything as the back-up of the people wanting to change was not there. Force them and they will fight against it. The volunteer and the conscript."

Raven smiled. "Sorry to be selfish about this but where does this leave us?"

Balen kissed her. "Up a creek without the canoe."

Raven thought about it. "Could we return to the farm? We could try to begin again with it and perhaps encourage others to build similar colonies."

Balen shook his head. "Not with the gangs about. They would raid right from the start. But there is a core in Transition X who still believe in the old ways. If we could find a safe place and then "call them" that might be a start. We need to create the new Eden, the Cradle of Life."

Raven looked down; she had been hopeful. "Where? Not here. The climate in Britain means that there needs to be intervention and all those things are gone. That is the trouble, humanity just wanted to "do", so they did. They took plants and animals out of their natural environment and country and then spent their life trying to compensate. Take the goats, the Anglo Nubians were African origin so a whole world of problems keeping them warm in winter and the energy going into heat lamps for the kids etc. In their own environment they would kid naturally with no need for all that. Even worms and fluke are exacerbated by a damp climate and enclosing animals on and in an unnatural environment. The Enclosure Acts started all that. But if we want crops we can't have goats mooching and munching.

In the latter days of the farm I was getting more interested in foraging and Forest Gardening. Literally liberating the plants and letting them grow and then going to find them not making them grow in lines. Of course, that works on a small population but not to feed the masses."

Balen looked thoughtful. "Well, I did think about that and before Frank had his run in with me, I moved the loyal Transition X followers to Transition X Spain. They are in Malaga. So, it would be practical to go there. That included your people from the farm."

Raven laughed. "Long walk."

Balen smiled. "We will need a new vehicle. Something with a good engine, no technology which can run on anything."

Raven thought about it. "That sounds like a tank. What do the military vehicles run on?"

Balen laughed. "Military vehicles are adapted to run on anything. Of course, getting hold of them is not easy as the gangs grabbed all they could." There was a glint in Balen's eye which Raven noticed.

"I have seen that look before. It is the "I know something you don't look.

Come on, you are leading this conversation aren't you."

"There is a vague possibility that the vehicle I hid when I sent the operatives abroad may well be still there."

9

The wind blew gently through the leaves sending them fluttering down on the couple who walked side by side down the abandoned road with the white Belgian Shepherd running around them. The leaves were piling up and the couple tried to walk without disturbing them, ever conscious of not revealing they had passed that way.

The fields were empty, animals had long since gone. There were no signs of habitation and as dusk fell, they both got their torches out in readiness but utilised the last of the light to get as far as they could before they had to become such obvious targets.

There were houses but they seemed abandoned. Some had been wrecked and obviously looted, some seemed intact though there were no signs of any vehicles. They passed a few houses, and the drives were covered in leaves.

Balen was looking at the house they were just about to pass. It was up a long drive and looked abandoned. There were no signs of broken windows. "Shall we try that one as somewhere for the night? There is a chance if it hasn't been looted that there may be food there."

Raven looked nervous. "I don't know but it looks like nobody has been in or out for a while. What do we do? Just walk up to the front door and knock and see if anyone answers."

Balen laughed. "Pretty much not a daft idea really. It would show we were not attacking if there is someone at home."

They walked slowly up the drive, watching intently for any movement but they didn't see any. The house was large and set on two storeys with a balcony around the bottom and painted white. Large patio doors faced the drive and there was a large glass door which was obviously the front door. There was a doorbell but they both relaxed when they saw the key safe on the wall. Balen reached for the door bell. "Pretty likely it is not inhabited and a holiday home but unlikely there is any food here."

Raven looked disappointed. "Well unless it is a holiday home they don't let out and they have a stash of all their favourite food."

Balen pressed the doorbell and waited. Then he knocked. "We can but hope. Even if it is unoccupied, we will have to be careful about getting in. No need to alert anyone that there is someone here."

They waited and there was no movement from the house, so they went around the back. Oberon was sniffing around and cocked his leg in a few spots before joining them by the back door.

The back door obviously led into the kitchen. It was a solid wood type with a glass panel, so Balen picked up a rock and broke the glass. He reached in and let them both in. "There is no way of knowing if the owners are still alive and I doubt they will be back for a while."

They went inside and started opening cupboards. Everything was neat and tidy, clean and new. It didn't look like any of the pots and pans had been used at all. There was a pin board which had plenty of take away menus, so they were giving up hope of finding any food worth eating when Raven opened the pantry. She took a step back. It was very well stocked. Tins were piled high, tins with long sell by dates. There was rice and pasta and a bookcase full of survival books.

They looked at each other totally unable to believe their good luck. There was also a set of car keys hanging on a hook at the end of the bookcase. Balen looked at the keys in disbelief. "Well, I might as well go and find out." He took the keys and went back out of the back door and went to the garage.

He hesitated when he came to the garage door and went to a window which was high up in the wall. It was one of those concrete garages made of panels, so he found a patio chair and had a look in. The doors were ordinary wooden doors which seemed to have an ordinary lock. There didn't seem to be any devices attached to the door, but he was very suspicious. This was just too good and too easy. Someone was a survivalist, and it was so very unlikely that they would not set traps.

He jumped physically as Raven put a hand on his shoulder. He whipped around but relaxed as he saw her. She held out a piece of paper.

Balen took it and began to read. "To whoever this may concern. I had intended for us to use what is here and to survive but my wife died on the first day of the blackout. I do not want to continue and survive without her, so I am going to take the coward's way out. I apologise if it upsets you to find me, but I hope by way of apology that you accept all that I would offer you with my best wishes for your survival. Nothing is trapped, help yourself."

Balen was still nervous and pushed Raven behind him as he went to the door and put the key in the lock, turned the key and opened the door. There was a car in the garage, a Land Rover and when Balen got inside and turned the key he discovered it had a full tank of petrol and there were petrol cans in the garage which were also full.

Balen popped the back door and loaded the petrol in. "It is a gift but as we cannot stay we had better load the car with as much as we can fit in and get ready to move on. The car will make the journey a lot easier.

They did as he said and loaded the back of the car with as much as would fit. They then covered it over, locked the garage and returned to the house. The power was of course out but the survivalist had left a gas cooker. After blacking out the windows in a small room, which looked like a study they cooked themselves a meal and opened a bottle of wine. Balen raised an eyebrow but gratefully accepted the offered crystal glass full of deep red liquid.

Raven smiled as they sat together on the small sofa in the room and lit another candle as the last one burnt down. Raven stroked Oberon who was lying beside her and got up. "I have to go and see if the owner is upstairs. We owe it to him."

Balen glared at her. "You are kidding of course."

Raven smiled. "It is worrying me. Our benefactor should not pass unacknowledged."

Balen shook his head and smiled. "Ok, I will come with you."

They walked slowly up the stairs carrying a torch, just enough to see the stairs.

Upstairs all the curtains were closed so Balen's initial worry about the torch revealing they were there was unfounded. The landing was devoid of furniture. Country scene prints hung on the wall and the five white doors were firmly shut in their white painted frames. The magnolia hardly any contrast in the faded light.

The first room was a bedroom and by the looks of it a guest room with a pair of twin beds. It was immaculately clean, and catalogue coordinated. The carpet looked as though nobody had ever walked on it. The en-suite was similarly clean and in order. A floral soap dispenser stood sentinel on the sink.

Raven closed the door behind them, and they went to the next room. This was set out as a child's room. Everything was immaculately placed as before, toys strategically left ready for action. Raven and Balen looked at each other, the poignancy of the un-played with toys not lost on them.

Balen looked down at her. There were tears in his eyes. "There isn't a day I don't think about Raphael."

Raven froze for a moment and then stared at Balen. "Balen, Frank said that our child had not died and had been taken so I was not distracted from my work."

Balen looked thunderstruck. "That can't be true. Why do you think he said that?"

Raven looked slightly sinister. "Why do you think?"

Balen shook his head. "I would never order our child taken from us. I was totally serious when I said that I fell apart, that wasn't a story. Surely you wouldn't believe I would do that. I love Raphael, I wanted to be the father to him that I never had." Then he looked thoughtful. "Did you see his body? I'm thinking back and I'm beginning to worry."

Raven thought about it, back to that dark night. "Actually no, it was a wild night. You said I shouldn't see him. No, I remembered that wrongly, it was the doctor. Oh God Balen, I thought you were lying to me. You were so distant, I thought you'd taken our baby! Did you see him, did you see our boy?"

Balen looked at the floor. "No, I was more interested in seeing that you were ok than looking at the boy. But we buried him."

Raven looked worried. "We thought we did. It could have been an empty casket or another baby. Frank handled everything. I was in no state mentally to think about it. I lost it after that. We argued and you stormed out. You were cold after that."

Balen put his arms around her. "Argued about what? We never argued. Raven, this is really nasty, that wasn't me. You have been sharing our bed with one of Frank's androids!" He winced a little as he jolted his shoulder this time "Ok, not for now but something else we need to investigate. I trusted Frank far too much. But then he thinks that I am dead so we may just stand a chance here. I would put money on it that if the child were alive he is with my brother's child. He probably has them there to use them later. I know where he was sent, and Nemesis would know that too. I sent him with someone trusted to someone I totally trusted. If Raphael is there too then I'd say we should go and get them both. Nemesis is counting on you really hating me for taking your child and you'd have no idea where he is so there is no chance that you would find him anyway."

Raven broke away from Balen and picked up a teddy bear from the crib. She held it and there were tears in her eyes. Balen put his arms around her again as she collapsed onto the floor and crouched in a ball. He whispered. "That anyone could take our child from us, from you. We will find him." He held his hand out. Raven took it and he pulled her to stand up. "Come on soldier, we've got a long way to go. If he's alive we will find him."

They backed out of the room and reverently closed the door.

The next room was the main bedroom, and their benevolent host was laying as if asleep on the bed. A pack of pills lay beside him, and he looked at peace other than showing signs of decay. He was an old, old man, at least in his eighties. There was a piece of paper in his hand.

Balen took the paper from the non-existent grip and read it out loud. "If these are my last words, I had better make it a good one. I had a good life and despite my wife's ideas I do not feel I would survive very well in the world which is coming. If you have found me and you are reading this then all I ask is that you bury me before you leave. You can take anything else that you like. Good luck." Balen folded the note and put it in the old man's pocket. He then turned to Raven. "We can do that in the morning."

They quickly opened the other two doors, a bathroom and another bedroom and then went downstairs.

Balen poured them both a drink. "To welcome complications."

Raven looked puzzled but they clinked glasses. "Not sure what you mean."

Balen smiled. "As I said I know where Michael's child is. That is going to cause complications. Travelling with a child. Fortunately, if he is alive, he isn't far from here. I think we both need to know."

Oberon wagged his tail. He hadn't followed them upstairs; he had kept guard at the bottom of the stairs.

Balen put his glass down and he took Raven's glass from her and put it down. He kissed her neck. "It has been a long time my love and I really, really want you. It has been unbearable. Do you want to make love?"

Raven smiled. "Of course I do. I really want you. All those nights lying beside what I thought was you, being unwanted. I really want you. I thought you'd never ask but I'm so used to you not wanting me that I didn't know how to ask. I didn't want to be turned down again."

Balen lifted the coffee table off of the large soft fur rug. He took her hands in his and pulled her to stand up. He kissed her then he licked down her neck. He then ran his tongue down her chest until he came to the zip of her boiler suit. He caught the zip in his mouth and pulled it down, following it down until he was kneeling in front of her.

She reached to touch his boiler suit and he caught her hand. "No, that comes later. This is for your pleasure. I want to touch, I want this to last." He reached up and pulled her suit off of her, letting it fall to the ground as he kissed her breasts, running his tongue around her nipples and biting gently as he ran his hands over her, feeling all parts of her, feeling the softness of her skin and the warm and wet as he reached between her legs. He wanted her, he had to hold back. He then ran his tongue down her stomach. He laid her down on the fur rug and took his boiler suit off. She reached and grabbed his manhood and began to stroke it. He grabbed her hand. "My love, after so long if you want me to last, don't touch!" He kissed her passionately and they made love in the candlelight.

The morning dawned bright. They found food to cook for breakfast and eat well. They made food for the journey and spent the morning enjoying being in a home. They knew they had to go but a bit of normality was nice. Then Balen and Raven went to the garage, found a spade, and kept to the deal. They buried the old man. They transplanted some of the flowers onto his grave and then loaded the car with what they thought would be useful and drove off. There was no point in staying. Playing Mr and Mrs Normal had started to hurt both of them.

They drove for a couple of hours until they came to a cottage at the end of a lane. It was a classic postcard cottage with a neat garden laid to cottage flowers. Balen seemed to know where he was going. He looked around. "Quite a few memories of this place."

Raven looked nervous. Balen took a hand off of the steering wheel long enough to put a reassuring hand on her knee as the car rolled to a holt. "Be careful."

The car rolled to a halt and Balen put the brakes on. He opened the door. "Raven, stay here. Get ready to get out of here quick."

Balen walked around the car and opened the front gate. He walked slowly up the path to the front door. There were toys on the path. He reached out to knock but the door opened before he could reach it. The door swung open and a lady of about sixty almost leapt at him. He was caught off guard and the two nearly fell over. They kept their balance and hugged.

Raven nearly jumped out of the car to help until she realised that the woman was hugging him. The hug went on and on but finally they stepped apart. Balen followed her inside.

The farmhouse kitchen was untidy with baby bottles, toys and other things strewn around the room. Balen looked around the room. "Is my baby here?"

The woman turned and slapped Balen across the face. "Your child, you remembered him, did you? I am glad to see you son but abandoning the poor boy so young is unforgivable."

Balen opened his mouth and considered his words. "Mum, I didn't. Do you know about Frank?"

Balen's mother glared at him. "Do you think they tell me anything? A couple of your soldiers came here years ago, and I was given your brother's child to look after. Then they turn up six months ago and bring another one. They told me that you were dumping your child with me as well as you all have too much to do and I must not contact you under any circumstances. Your brother well I could understand that the child could be a threat. So when you took him from that place and sent him here that was fair enough. You, you never change. Handing your responsibilities over to someone else. You have five minutes, explain yourself. Go on, convince me of something different."

Balen had to think on his feet, and he knew that years of prejudice which had previously been justified would stand against him. "Mother, I have changed in this crazy world. I met Raven and she showed me that there was more to life, more meaning. I am or rather was Archangel after Frank killed my brother."

Balen's mother put a hand on his arm. "Hold on a minute Balen, you can't just tell me that my son is dead like that and carry on!"

Balen thought about it. "I am sorry. That was thoughtless. Sadly yes,

Michael is dead. He was constantly having episodes. He slipped into his personalities, and he ordered me killed. When his guards didn't do it, he tried to do it himself and Frank shot him."

His mother was holding back the tears. "Who is Frank?"

Balen was struggling for how to explain things and what to say. "Frank, and this is where I might lose you, is an android who is Nemesis, the Artificial Intelligence who shut down the computers. He has been manipulating us for his own ends, didn't want the child around and told us he was dead. Mother, we were told our baby died days after he was born. I would never have abandoned Raphael, never, like I'd never abandon Raven. This is totally weird I know but Nemesis has kept me prisoner, I escaped and Raven and I have come here to find our child as Nemesis told us he was still alive. He told Raven I had sent him away. We had a lot of trackers on us, we cleared them off."

The scowl could have soured cheese. "You seriously want me to believe that drivel?"

Balen stared her in the eye. "Yes, because it is true."

Balen's mother laughed. "You know I believe you. You are lucky that Ryjel, who was your second in command came and told me the truth a while back in case Frank tried something to harm the child. He left me weaponry which of course I didn't need but he was a polite young man, so I humoured him. So, what now?"

Balen smiled. "We have come for our child. The problem is that it was Nemesis who told Raven her child was still alive so he might be intending an attack here."

Balen's mother smiled as well. "Highly likely, so you have now destroyed our life here. There are things you must do. Firstly, you had better introduce me to the mother of my grandson and secondly, we had better discuss what is best for both the boys. Your father will be back in a bit. It is time you met him. I assume you know that you and Michael had different fathers." Balen nodded and looked completely stunned.

Balen hugged her. "Thank you mum for understanding."

Balen's mother smiled. "I always have, and I always will."

Balen left the house and felt a certain chill as he approached the car. Raven was watching him approach. "Raven, long story but that lady is my mother, Eleanor, and she has been looking after the boys. She would like to meet you".

Raven smiled. "Of course, she does." She leapt out of the car and they both went into the house.

Eleanor had tea in the pot and biscuits on a plate which she offered as soon as they came in. "Tea, biscuits and obviously no need for an introduction. It would seem my wayward son has returned with some half-baked idea to take his son and nephew."

Raven took the offered cup and saucer. "Thank you. I would of course want to take my son with me. I would also like to see him. Has Balen told you what happened?"

The old woman smiled. "Of course, my dear, Gabriel here has told me a wild story. It is a crazy world and no doubt you both have a lot to do if I have the situation right. What I am saying is that neither of you would have time to look after a six-month-old and the two year old. He is a little monster in a loveable way."

Oberon chose that moment to introduce himself. He trotted in and sat down beside Raven and looked up at Balen's mother who looked down and smiled, took a biscuit off the plate, and gave it to him. "And I gather a dog as well. Complete happy families in one package. So, what is this handsome chap called?"

Raven smiled. "Oberon."

The mother smiled. "Good name, good strong name."

Balen looked confused. "What are you saying mum?"

She smiled. "Well looking after the children is not easy and they know me. I am guessing if you are here that things are not going well with Transition X or you would have come in an official capacity. If you take the children, you will need someone to look after them. I will have to speak to Asha and see what he wants to do.

They have had their breakfasts and no doubt meeting you will be exciting enough."

They followed Elaine in silent trepidation. She took them upstairs and opened the door on what was obviously the nursery. The four year old was building a tower.

Elaine walked over and picked up the baby from its cot and walked over to Raven. "Now dear always support his head. Here, take him, he's yours."

Raven did what she was told and cradled the little boy. "Hello little one, I am your mother." She looked up at Balen.

There were tears in his eyes and he stroked the baby's face. "Hello little one, and I am your father."

The baby looked up at them with his baby blue eyes and held up a hand and touched Balen's nose.

Raven looked up for a moment. "What did they call him?"

Balen's mother was lost in the moment. Then she composed herself. "They kept his name as Raphael. Your nephew has been called Elijah."

Balen smiled. "At this rate we are going to need a people carrier."

Raven smiled at Elaine. She had to be in her late sixties and her slim build was almost skeletal. She was immaculately dressed in a twin set with a string of pearls around her aged neck. Her eyes however were bright, and she didn't seem to miss a thing. She smiled back. "Well Raven I am thinking he is not going to have it all his own way now. The children must come first but I am guessing that whatever damn fool plan he has come up with has to come a very close second and may well get us all killed."

Raven shook her head and looked at Balen who smiled. It was a relaxed smile as he watched his mother. "Well not so much of a damn fool plan this time as our options are very limited.

Frank as the embodiment of Nemesis has control. I am guessing if I keep my head down and we just leave this country he will probably not pursue us as he thinks I am dead. He told Raven about Raphael on purpose and perhaps it was his plan all along to get us out of the picture or to make sure that Raven really hated me. Either way there is only one plan I can see as viable and that is to go to Spain and try to develop ways of farming which anyone can take up.

Frank will have enough here with the gangs, and it is not just the UK, it is worldwide. All we can hope to do is to avoid the cities and find somewhere."

Raven looked hopefully at Balen's mother. She smiled at Raven. "By the way you can call me Elaine. I can see your logic and in truth if Frank had wanted to trap you then waiting here may well have got him what he wants. How can we ever hope to second guess how a machine is going to think. You can of course remove any sentimentality but should you both have been spurred on by anything happening to those two your justifiable anger would have been intense, and we all know what that means." Balen looked sheepish. "Well, you may look like that. You were a complete pain in the butt for most of your life and a complete worry to me and your father. But I heard how you brought Transition X together and the way you developed the farm. I have my spies and you will probably find out that I know more than you think. I kept the Archangel children safe because I kept a man on the inside. Frank is a working AI, he cannot trouble himself with trivia and we made sure these two were just that." She smirked.

Balen looked even more interested. "What do you mean? Why would Frank think they were trivia if he mentioned Raphael to Raven?"

Elaine laughed. "Who mentioned Raphael to Raven?"

Raven looked confused. "A version of Frank who is in the basement."

Elaine smiled. "You mean Frank Junior? Well his history is somewhat checkered. He had faulty programming when created. One of the first off the production line. So, Frank not wanting to destroy himself put him in the basement to use him to run the systems around the place. It wasn't a huge job for my man to reprogram the thinking part of the system to keep an eye on things. He was reprogrammed a few weeks back so anything he says now is not us."

Raven's mouth was by now open, and she looked stunned. "How, I mean…"

Balen smiled too. "My mother was not always an old lady and we

Nemesis tend to forget the wealth and breadth of the knowledge an elderly person can contain. My mother once worked for MI6 in Counterintelligence and was a Field Operative for several years."

Elaine grinned. "Until my knees couldn't take the strain anymore and after the replacement, they put me out to pasture. Nice pension mind you." She smiled at Raven. "I'd better tell you the truth here. Yes I was with Michael's father for a number of years. He was a vicious, spiteful man who made my life unpleasant. I did give him a son but I found out what he was doing with the Spas. That was the last night I spent with him.

I started seeing Asha about then. He was my Healer, my rock and my love. The result of that love was you Balen. I had hoped that I would be set free but he officially claimed you as his son and it all continued. I loved both boys so I didn't really want to leave Michael either. I bought this place years ago. This and the small farm in Spain I had hoped to retire to with your father. Yes Balen, your thoughts of going there are probably guided by your time there as a child. I was sometimes allowed to take you there. So, as it is a small place in a slightly remote area which was bought with good old-fashioned paperwork before the onset of computers it would be a place that Nemesis probably knows nothing about. Unless it has been taken over which is unlikely there should be no remarkable incidents that could be picked up when we go there.

Raphael needs to sleep. I know it is hard to be parted from him now but don't worry, he will be fine. Let's put him back in his basket so he can sleep."

Raven gently laid him in his basket and pulled the covers over him.

Elaine smiled. "Now, let me get lunch on and we will discuss the plan for travelling. I have a vehicle of course; one we might find a bit more useful than yours, but I suggest that at least to start with we take both. Come and have a look."

Balen followed his mother like a well-behaved dog. Raven followed him, amused by his behaviour. They went down the hallway and out of the back door. There was a neat garden at the back, manicured lawn, and a path across it which was broken up by a stone-built gazebo.

They crossed the lawn and went through a gate at the back of the garden which led to some sheds and a barn. Elaine went to the barn with a grin on her face. "I had been hoping to use this little lady for a long time."

The well-maintained wooden barn door swung open to reveal a shiny silver airstream Winnebago. Elaine looked at it with some pride.

Balen shook his head. "Well, that will be inconspicuous."

Elaine laughed. "Any vehicle moving about will be noticed and this little beauty is at least convenient. Come inside."

Elaine opened the door and went inside and they followed. She opened a wardrobe door and touched a panel which slid down to reveal an arsenal of weaponry.

Balen gasped. "Mother, are these legal?" As he took in the automatic weapons as well as bows, arrows, crossbows, and other assorted items.

Elaine ran her fingers over her Beretta 92R. "My job had certain privilege."

Raven smiled, amused at how uncomfortable Balen looked. "I should say so. This is truly amazing."

Elaine was busy looking at her toys. "It will come in alright. I would suggest we take your vehicle as well and perhaps go and swap your vehicle for the one Balen no doubt has hidden somewhere. Yes, I do know about that."

Balen looked stunned. "Who the heck is your man on the inside? I thought only Jake knew about that."

Elaine was laughing out loud by that point. "Well until Michael transferred him earlier this year, I had a very good informant. You mean Jake who used to work for MI6 at one point. His father was my working partner on a few missions. You two used to play together as children. His cousin Rijel has been very helpful as well."

Balen looked surprised. "I remember playing with him, that was why I trusted him. I didn't know that Rijel was his cousin."

Elaine glanced at him. "And so you should. It was him who reprogrammed Frank Junior. He has been my liaison and worked with me to get you both to this position. Did you like the corpse in the bedroom? That was the contingency plan in case you decided not to come and find me. I hope you collected the goodies from there."

Balen was clearly sulking. "I feel like I have been played like a computer game. How did you know we would stop at that house?"

Elaine looked very pleased with herself. "Well, I had to guess some of it. I assumed that you would take Raven's car so I knew how far you would get on the petrol in there. If you were going after Balen's car then you would take the road far from the one which led there but with the easy option to double back or cross across. There were two possible roads, so I set up a house on both routes. That house was the first that did not have broken front windows. I set that up too.

The only complication was that Raven did not tell you about Raphael still being alive straight away. But the result was the same. Yes, I played you like a fiddle my boy."

Balen put on a fake look of anger then smiled. "Totally well done there. You planned and executed that with some finesse, and I had no idea."

Elaine was checking through the cupboards. "Well, what we have to hope is that it was well enough planned that Nemesis doesn't have a clue. The whole plan falls down if we can't get to Spain and if he catches us."

Raven was looking around the camper van with a smile on her face. "Now this will make life a lot more comfortable."

Oberon jumped on the sofa. Elaine glared at him, and he jumped off, came over to her and sat down so she could stroke his head. "Good boy, so you are going to come with us, are you?" Then she looked at Raven. "There used to be a lot of paperwork to take a dog abroad. We will be going in through a port at night. We don't have the month to allow for a Rabies Vaccination."

Balen smiled. "All the dogs are vaccinated against Rabies. It was a directive from before my time which I kept to. Archangel was terrified of dogs and had seen a film about a dog with it when he was a kid."

Elaine thought about it. "Oh yes, I remember that. He didn't sleep for a week! Handy now as if there is a problem at least he has had the vaccination and who knows what is happening with animals after the shutdown. He'll be ok, don't worry.

There was a clatter at the door and Balen jumped to his feet. Elaine laughed. "That will be Asha. Excuse me, I had better warn him."

She walked out into the kitchen. "Asha, glad you are back. I have a surprise for you. Or a shock." She laughed. "Sit down. I did say that there was a possibility that Balen would make it here. He has turned up, with his wife."

A deep, silky voice answered. "That is wonderful news, they made it safely. Did they find the house? Oh good. Well planned my love, I knew they would be alright. Well, do I get to meet my son after all these years?"

Elaine came in first and behind her there was a tall man, about six foot two who had long grey hair which would have been waist length, it was tied back neatly. He wore loose fitting clothing, a smock, and jeans. He also had a very long beard. His eyes sparkled mischievously. He stepped forwards and held his hand out to Balen. "I'm not sure how I should greet my son after a lifetime. Would a handshake be appropriate?"

Balen stood up and walked over to him. They were nearly the same height though Balen was slightly shorter but the family resemblance was clear. "This is a very welcome surprise."

Asha smiled. "Well I am very glad to hear it. And I have a daughter in law as well, this is indeed a joyous day. I am pleased to meet you Raven. I can see what my son sees in you. You have a beautiful boy by the way.

I assume that Balen had a good excuse?"

Elaine smiled. "They were told that the baby was dead."

Asha held his arms out. "Come here my boy. You have had an awful time of it." He hugged Balen and Balen hugged him back. He stepped back and walked over to Raven. "It must have been a living hell thinking you had lost your child. You were angry? Why were you angry?"

Raven looked confused. Then she thought about it. "I was angry because I was told that it was Balen who had taken him so that he wasn't a distraction."

Asha held his arms out. "My child, that was the cruellest thing that anyone could have done. But there is more. On the journey we will talk, no doubt. You can talk to me about anything." Asha stepped forwards and he hugged her. It felt like he was taking the pain of the world away. There was such a gentleness about him. "There child, you have a father and a mother in law now and nobody is going to harm you again if we have anything to do with it."

Elaine smiled. "Well, we will get a good lunch under our belt and then we can set off. Might as well get a little way on the way tonight. The longer we stay here the more dangerous it could be."

They sat around the table in silence enjoying a good meal. She cooked them a full roast dinner under the premise that that would be a meal they would not get for a while. After the meal they packed things and moved things for her to the camper. Asha did the washing up and put things away and made sure there were no signs of how many had been there. The children were installed in the camper van, both vehicles had a copy of the planned route. The car went first, the camper behind and they set off at a fast pace to cover as many miles as possible the first day.

Balen was driving the car, Raven in the passenger seat. Asha was driving the camper but the last moment Elaine had got out of the camper and strapped the baby basket on the back seat so that he could get used to their voices. He was quiet as a lamb and absolutely no trouble. There was the occasional sound from him and when they were talking a giggle.

The roads were clear while they were in the "wilds" of Somerset. They cut down to the coast, it was a risk but there were better roads, and they could not risk getting the camper stuck on a country road. Elaine had not only marked the route on the map she had written it out.

The road was clear of debris which had been something they were worried about. There were cars on the road, old ones. As they drove along shops were open although by the look of them through the window stock was low. There were also horses and carts bringing produce to the shops which had tables outside as well where people were selling items which looked handmade.

It was quiet. They had expected gunshots but there were none. People even waved when they went past as a car was rare. People were walking dogs, walking children and as they passed a school the playground was full of children playing.

The only signs that anything had been wrong were the odd repaired gunshot hole. There were abandoned cars, but they had notes under the windscreen. They stopped to take a look. It was someone's name and address and an apology for leaving the car there.

They were driving along and suddenly the two cars which passed them flashed them and turned off the road either into garages which were offered by locals who waved them in or down between houses. A man jumped out into the road and held out a flag.

Balen came to a stop, his hands on his gun he wound the window down. The man was in his mid-fifties and dressed in an anorak and chinos. The flag was white with an orange cross on it. When the window was run down, he stayed a respectable distance and spoke in a very officious voice. "Greetings traveller. You must be new around here. The flashing lights mean that there is a Transition X convoy coming. If you have any reason to avoid them then turn down the next road and let them past."

Balen gave Raven a nervous glance. "What do you think? It could be a trap."

The man had stepped away and gone to the camper behind. He had obviously said the same thing as he was searching in his pockets and pulled out a card or something which he was showing Elaine. He saluted and she indicated to turn left and pulled off. Balen put the car in gear and pulled away as well. The man waved and put his card away and ran back into his house.

They pulled down the side road and pulled out of sight around the corner. Balen jumped out of the car and went to hide in the undergrowth. He came back a short while later. "Damn straight there was a convoy. Heavy machinery and cover vehicles. They went straight through the village and as far as I can see they have kept going."

Raven smiled. "It looks like Frank's control isn't as complete as he thought. Nothing seems that different."

Balen got back in the car and they turned around and rejoined the road. They passed a supermarket. It was no longer stacked shelves but tables with people coming and going selling what they had. A van had arrived and there were people unloading it by hand. The goods were carried inside. The supermarket was smaller but there certainly was food available.

They drove on through the evening. As dusk turned to night the houses they passed were lit up, mostly by lanterns. They also had candles burning in their gardens in glass jar lanterns and the whole road had a party feel to it. People walked around carrying the jar lanterns and the pub had windows open and was serving people through the windows by candlelight.

Driving past some people waved, the people in the pub raised their mixture of glasses and mugs. What they did notice was that people took their mugs for a refill and there were very few glasses about.

The road stretched out in front of them, the cat's eyes directing them on their way as there were no streetlights to light their way. As they left the village the countryside was dark, and their headlights were starkly noticeable.

Elaine indicated left and Balen turned off into a side road and stopped when he found somewhere the camper could stop as well. Elaine leapt out of the camper and came to their window. "We had better stop for the night. We'll stand out for miles around if we keep on going. Grab what you need and junior and come to the camper. We can black out the windows and we should be inconspicuous."

Balen smirked. "Well inconspicuous other than the shiny silver camper van."

Elaine shook her head. "Not for long. Open that gate, we can pull off into the field and park there. Park your vehicle parallel to the door and about eight feet away." She got into the camper and Balen returned to the car after opening the metal farm gate, moving the car in, and closing it behind them.

Elaine had moved the camper to the other side of the hedge so it wasn't clearly visible from the road and Balen parked his car beside it. Elaine and Asha then climbed out of the car as did Raven and Balen.

Elaine was looking about. "This should do nicely. Now, Raven I suggest you change the baby out here ready for bed. Wouldn't want the smell in the van. Balen, come and give me us hand while Raven settles the baby into his basket."

Balen followed her around the camper to a compartment near the back. She lifted it and there was a roll of camouflage netting which was neatly rolled. He looked to her for directions. "Grab that end of it and we can lay it out the length of the camper."

Asha also knew what to do and once unfolded and laid out she got out a box full of tent pegs and a hammer. She pulled out the end of the cammo netting and started to peg it down. Balen fetched the pegs, she did the hammering and soon enough that end was secured down.

Asha then pulled it a little open and went to one end, indicating that Balen went to the other end. There was a rope which went through the middle, she took one end and indicated that Balen should take the other. They then rolled the cammo netting over the camper and the vehicle parked next to it.

Next she took out telescopic poles and from under the netting she built a framework and pulled it upwards until both camper and vehicle were under a cammo tent which she then pegged down, leaving a couple of exits.

Job done she went into the camper, Balen in tow.

Raven was sitting beside Raphael's Moses Basket and he was clearly asleep. Elijah was sitting on the floor and had just completed building his tower. Elaine smiled. "He's a tenacious little bugger you know. He spent all the journey trying to build that tower and every time it fell over, he started again." She reached down and picked up his cuddly tiger and gave it to him. She then picked him up and carried him to the cot bed and put him in. He held his arms up and she gave him another cuddle before he laid down and went to sleep.

Elaine then went to the kitchen area. "Right now for something for us to eat." She went to the cupboard and got out some vegetables and began cutting them up.

"I suppose you don't really know much about what happened in the real world from your ivory tower. Well people just rebuilt. To start with there was chaos and people tried to loot but when Transition X joined in with dealing with them most of the trouble causers were wiped out early on.

I am sorry to say that early on Transition X were seen as a bit of a problem as people don't like the level of control they tried to exert and that was when we started communicating with the CB radio. With the trouble causers mostly gone we managed to get a supply line set up for food from the farms to the towns. I have no idea what is happening in the cities, that is more Transition X and they left us to manage ourselves.

The first year will be hard as of course the farmers are still geared up to grow commercial crops but next year they should be ok as everyone came up with all the seed they could get their hands on and we are hoping they will manage to grow actual food.

Us old ones remembered when things were like that anyway and what they used to call "Farm Gate Sales" so we started all that up again. The farms sell their goods directly to the people although of course money has no value anymore. Too many people had relied on the banks and of course overnight all that was gone. Millionaires were broke overnight and what you had physically mattered. Not so important to those who lived hand to mouth, so it was a great leveller. Suddenly those with skills were much more important than someone in IT. A brave new world overnight which I gather was what was intended. Well, we got it.

Actually, it wasn't too bad. People were either antisocial or most of them were the trouble causers so didn't last long. The rest of us just banded together and got on with it. Those with generators shared the power and others brought their petrol. For the first year we shared around what food we had, after that well there was enough as we started producing it. There wasn't even a need to dig into the food in tins which many had stockpiled. There had been a fear of trouble after covid, and many had kept their stash up to date. They mostly still have it as far as I know. Ok what people eat has changed and many more are working on the farms in exchange for food, either as security or working there as of course there are no big tractors left, they had too much computer technology on them.

You can't get rid of the knowledge people have and their memory of what they had. It is a different world but just one without computers and a lot of the imported plastic rubbish we had grown to rely on.

As we had the CB radio we have managed to keep in touch with others across Europe. It seems similar everywhere. I think they have got some of the factories started up again. Only the ones they could adapt which didn't rely on too much computer assistance. Which of course was most of them."

She had finished chopping the vegetables and got out some premade pastry and rolled that out, put it in a dish and got some chopped up meat out and fried it off. The aroma was filling the camper making Balen and Raven feel very hungry. Asha came in. He had been securing everything outside.

Elaine smiled. "No point getting too keen as this will take nearly an hour to cook with the gas." She put the pie in the oven and got four glasses out and bottles of beer. She cracked the metal tops off on the bottle opener on the wall and set them down on the table.

Balen poured his glass and took a sip. "There were good intentions, and we did have a plan. Particularly in the cities there had to be an iron fist to stop the riots. With Nemesis now there is an issue. He wanted a completely new start and the rebuilding of the things he tried to destroy has turned him into a complete megalomaniac dictator."

Elaine took drink of her beer. She looked at the bottle. "Bierre Moretti, not my favourite but that sort of thing is hard to find. Well, megalomaniac dictator, seems they aren't that rare. I loved my son but even at a young age your brother wasn't exactly normal. A dictator suited him well with his phobias and control issues. You too if you care to admit it. I am proud of you that you backed away and even prouder that he thought you a threat to his new controlled world. You may well be, just not yet. Exponential numbers, that is what comes to mind. Nemesis believes in multiplying his control so when he is challenged it messes with his understanding of things. His military computer status will compute the path of most damage to the enemy and sadly I think he believes humankind is his enemy, or at least the enemy of his plan."

Balen took another sip. "What plan? All he seems to be doing is attacking any group which gets organised and wiping out any military based or gang-based group. That and eliminating anyone who mentions things he doesn't agree with."

Elaine stared at the bottle. "Not so inhuman. We all fear what we don't understand. However much he reads, analyses the tries to pigeon hole humanity it will always amaze and in his case bemuse him. As a creature of absolutes that must be his enemy. We can't win, not now. All we can do is try to find an alternative and get you and the Archangel children far away. There will come a time, just not now. Don't worry, the people are aware that you are not you and that you are an android created by Nemesis. That is totally undermining what he is doing, and it will completely undermine him if he can't produce the real you if it comes to him being challenged.

That was how I got so much support when it came to helping you get clear of them. Do you seriously think that those roads are that clear normally?"

She went to the cupboard and brought out a road map. "We have to make our way to Weymouth in Dorset. It used to be a ferry port to Jersey and with a bit of adaptation it is now a route to Europe. We can't use the tunnel and other routes have been cut off by Nemesis."

Balen looked confused. "Are you serious? How on earth did Transition X miss that one?"

Elaine was busy with the map. "Well not so difficult really. Transition X is busy with the cities and other concerns like controlling the people who are here. They don't have time to worry about who is leaving. The ferries are very old and had been decommissioned. We got them from collectors who had the forethought to buy them and keep them hidden. Of course, a crossing costs an arm and a leg but thankfully we are able to pay and they are very discreet. It is our only hope and it will be quiet a drive."

Balen smiled. "Well, it isn't as if I have anything else to do now that I'm redundant."

Elaine fetched them fresh bottles, opened them and set them down. "Yes, well we all have that problem."

The moon was full and cast shadows across the grass field. A fox trotted across the open area, looking left and right as he went on his way. Somewhere an owl hooted and a cow in the next field mooed. Raven put Oberon out for his walk and stepped down behind him. He trotted off, ignoring the fox and she followed him.

We trotted along the hedgerow. The leaves were falling as it was a beech hedge and the dog roses had long since turned to hips. As Raven walked, she began to gather a few in a small bag she had in her pocket. Oberon didn't mind, he was happily sniffing and wandering.

He found a stone and threw it at her feet. She threw it for him a few times before he got bored and went off to look for something else to interest him and she went back to her berry picking.

Bats were flittering around as they came close to a stand of old beech trees. They swooped and fluttered, catching the myriad of night bugs and midges which threatened to bite. As they passed under the tree Raven stopped for a moment, allowing Oberon to run about as he wished. She looked up the field which sloped upwards, the moon clearly visible at the top.

She got out her compass and in the moonlight, she checked where she was standing and the direction. Again, as she had many other times, she wondered why the moon was in the wrong place.

All was still, even the animals were silent, that unnerved her. That wasn't natural. There was always some sort of a noise.

As if on cue Oberon came and sat beside her. She put her hand on his collar and they both crouched down as there was a gentle whirring sound. She pulled Oberon beside her and under the bush, conscious that he was a bright glowing white in the moonlight.

What came over was a large drone. The guns on the side of it were clearly visible in silhouette and as it entered the field it's lights came on, focusing on the fox which was the other side of the field minding his own business. It was a large dog fox, and he was sniffing around some rabbit holes.

There was a crack and a whizzing sound followed by a loud flash and a bang as the drone blew the fox to oblivion. It was too far away to hear the thud, thud of the sods of earth and fox hitting the floor.

Oberon whimpered but he stayed still. Thankfully there was no trace of light from the camper as the drone turned it's lights off and headed off towards the South East.

Raven didn't dare move. Then she saw a shadowy figure leave the camper and head towards where the fox had been obliterated. The sounds of the night were beginning again so she broke cover and let Oberon run to the figure, she was certain it was Balen.

Balen saw Oberon coming and braced for impact as the large German Shepherd jumped up to greet him, nearly pushing him over backwards. Raven crossed the field and he put his arms around her. "Just glad to know you are ok. When we heard the drone strike, we feared the worst."

Raven snuggled into his neck. "We were over by the stand of trees so out of sight. The fox wasn't so lucky. Why are they shooting foxes?"

Balen thought about it. "I have no idea. I didn't know they went in for pest control. Odd, but we probably won't find out, or then again perhaps mother can find out." The last comment came with an air of exasperation.

Raven smiled. "She is a very useful mother to have but a big shadow to grow up under."

Balen nodded. "Tell me about it, and father's shadow was larger. I shouldn't say that now. Asha is my real father."

Raven kept her silence. This was more than he had ever told her, and it was up to him to tell any more if he wanted to. She had assumed various things, all of which were wrong.

They went back to the camper where Elaine was waiting. Raven grinned at Balen. "Go on, you are itching to ask."

Balen glared at her. "Ok, I will. Do you know why Transition X are blowing up foxes?"

Elaine thought for a moment. "No."

Balen looked relieved.

Elaine put the kettle on and made them a hot chocolate. She then went to Raphael's cot as he was making a few noises. She took him outside and changed him, put him back to bed and then checked on Elijah who was sleeping, cuddling his tiger for comfort. She gently pulled the blanket over him and Mr Tiggs and stroked his hair.

She then pulled out a double bed for Balen and Raven and pulled out her double bed at the end and made them up with duvets and pillows. "I think we had better turn in. Enough excitement for one day and a long day tomorrow."

When everyone was settled, she turned the lights out.

10

Somewhere in the distance, hidden from view, a cockerel crowed his little heart out.

The autumn sun beat down on the green grass and there wasn't a cloud in the sky. Birds were singing and somewhere to the right a pair of donkeys breyed.

Elijah had woken up first. He stood up, hands on the side of his cot and looked about the strange surroundings. Raphael was making gentle quiet noises before he launched into a full out crying session.

Elaine woke up first, opened and eye and pretended to be asleep. Asha rolled over, allowing Raven and Balen to fall out of bed and take Raphael outside to change his nappy. She smirked as she waved to Elijah who laid back down. She turned over and went back to sleep.

Later that morning after they had enjoyed a cooked breakfast Raven and Balen were back in their car leading the way and the camper van followed as the miles rolled under their tyres.

The road was moderately busy. Cars were going about their business but there was no sign of any Transition X vehicles. The cars were all old, tech free and many showed signs of having been barn finds. Anything which could be used was being used.

There were a few horses on the roads. Teenagers who had been riding for fun were now obviously being sent out to pick up a pint of milk and a loaf or something similar. Makeshift paniers and saddle bags made of old shopping bags were rife and the riders rode with intent.

A farm lorry passed them, full of sheep with the shepherd clinging to the back desperately trying to hold onto his shotgun.

They passed village after village, each slightly different in their approach to life. Somewhere fortified and they had to answer questions, others were more open but the local snipers, who were not terribly good at hiding, were clearly visible watching them.

They had no wish to stop and no need to look for provisions, so they just kept driving on the road ahead.

Every larger village or town was avoided but by the stream of traffic on the roads around them that was normal.

It was later that day that they drove into Weymouth. They came in through Osmington, the thatch cottages now burnt out and the place was deserted. The white horse on their right was very much a grey horse and hard to make out. The caravan site a burnt-out wreck and the car garage abandoned. It was the same with the other areas of occupation and they drove very fast through Preston which seemed to be still a war zone.

The locals were trying to storm Home Bargains which was barricaded. Rival gangs were then taking shots at those who were trying to raid their shop. They in turn were firing back so thankfully they left the two vehicles to drive past unchallenged. They didn't stop, they put their foot down and turned at the roundabout to approach the town along the coast road.

Weymouth itself seemed peaceful. People were walking along the beach, dogs were playing and chasing balls and the traffic although somewhat heavy was moving fast. They came to what had been the Pavilion.

Asha flashed for them to stop. Elaine jumped out of the camper and came to Raven's window. "The Pavilion is a Refugee Centre for people who are on their way to cross via the ferry. We are booked already so we don't have to go in or wait our turn. We just need to drive around the side of it and they will put us on the next available space. We will go in front. Here are your papers." She passed Raven a sheet of paper.

"Don't open the window for anyone and when they wave you on board just go. They will show you where to go. If we can stay together then great, if not then come and find me. I'll take Raphael with me and Oberon too. It will make it easier for you. I don't need to tell you to lock the car and bring weaponry with you if you leave the car when we are on board. The boats are usually very peaceful. Everyone knows that it is a closed environment and there is no getting away. Come to the camper as it is a 48-hour crossing. We have provisions and won't need to leave the camper until we need to move off. Good luck."

Raven reached out of the window and grabbed Elaine's hand and squeezed it. Elaine reached in and stroked Raven's hair. Balen reached over and took Elaine's hand as well. His voice was broken a little. "Good luck. Well, this is it, we are leaving Britain."

Elaine smiled. "Hopefully."

Balen unlocked the car and Elaine reached in and took the Moses basket which contained Raphael. Raven got out, put Oberon's lead on and took him to the camper. When both were safely inside, she returned to the car. The camper went first with the car tailgating it. They came to the checkpoint and Elaine showed their papers. Then she opened the door, got out and gave the guard a hug. They chatted for a short while, shook hands and Elaine got back in and they were all waved through.

Balen looked at Raven. "Is there anyone that woman doesn't know?"

Raven laughed. "Be thankful, this is really, really handy."

It was as they were waved through straight onto the ferry, the last vehicles aboard and a couple of cross drivers had to wait for the next ferry. They had only just got their brakes on when the ferry door began to close. The engines shirred and the ropes were cast to the shore. The ferry pulled away and out to sea, full steam ahead. That was all it could do, sail and hope. There were no defences on board other than what people in the cars brought with them. There was no escort vessel. It relied on being a pointless target. Raven and Balen locked the car and gratefully climbed into the camper.

Elaine was sitting at the table. Raphael was beside her reaching for a mobile she had hung up for him. Asha sat opposite her. Elijah was on the floor at the far end trying to build his tower under the watchful eye of Mr Tiggs. There was a pot of tea and biscuits on the table. They sat down and so the long 24 hours began.

The ferry was making good headway when the crew spotted a gunship helicopter on the horizon. The crew member immediately grabbed the Tannoy. "We have a Code Red."

That sent most of the passengers to their bags to look that up on the information sheet they had been given. It sent Elaine to the weapons cabinet. Balen and Raven were watching her intently, waiting to see what she was going to say. She didn't say anything initially as she took out a ground to air missile launcher. Then she turned to them. "This is a decision we will have to make. If I take that ship down, then we will be a threat. If we hold our cool, then it could just fly over or destroy the ferry. Asha?"

Asha smiled. "It is your decision. Either could be right. You will know."

Elaine smiled back. "Hard call as once that missile is fired either by them or me there is no going back. The Code Red directive is return to the cars and stay there. The ferry does have fake crates on the top of it and if we are very lucky the gunship is just on manoeuvres and will ignore this as a goods carrier. That is why the stay in the car order. Anyone on deck could betray what is going on."

Balen stared at her. "How do they manage to get away with the sailings anyway. Surely Frank knows about them?"

Elaine smiled. "Did you?"

Balen looked at Raven for some sort of support. "Well, no, not at all."

Elaine rised an eyebrow. "Well then."

The gunship came closer. In the cargo hold they couldn't see anything but Elaine took the rocket launcher and positioned herself where she could get a slight view through the only porthole. Her slight body seemed really out of place, especially in her twinset, holding a huge military rocket launcer! She was tense, they could see that. Her stance was more military than mummy.

Advertisement

Privacy Settings

The sound of the rotor blades got closer. Raven picked up Raphael and cuddled him, Balen picked up Elijah as if he was handling a hand grenade but managed to sit the boy on his lap. The boy then cried as Mr Tiggs had fallen on the floor and Balen had to retrieve it to restore the calm. The moment seemed like hours. The metallic engine fuel aroma and the darkness of the hold closed in. They had turned the lights out in the camper, as had everyone else and they all sat in their vehicles in the darkness.

The sound of the rotor blades were getting closer and Elaine had begun to open the porthole. She left it ajar, at the ready. The rotor blades were becoming almost deafening but they both relaxed when they saw Elaine become more visibly relaxed as the blade sound became really loud and then deafening and then lessened as it headed off into the distance.

Elaine returned to the camper, unloaded and stashed away the rocket launcher. "Well, not today my old girl. Not today and hopefully not any day.

Well, we are hardly out of port yet and they are sniffing around. I would expect the captain to take a route which joins with the same route as the Plymouth Ferry. The times are worked out as the Plymouth Ferry is all but finished now. It is heavily policed by Transition X, and they use it as a troop route mainly. Apparently, it hasn't run for three weeks so we should have a clear run at this."

Balen looked worried. He grasped Raven's hand as he saw the terrified look on her face.

Asha noticed the worried looks. "You know something we don't about that ferry? It is bothering you."

Balen looked up. "I tried to get those who were loyal and the people from Raven's Farm over to Spain. That would have been a couple of weeks ago. Does that mean they didn't make it? Mum, do you know if they made it?"

Elaine smiled. "That ferry isn't running but there are others. They were Transition X, they probably took another route. Try not to worry. I know it is hard. You can't contact them, you know that. What I need us to do is to batten down the hatches as we will be going through the Bay of Biscay. That will be about twelve hours' time. So plenty of time to get that done. It is Autumn and the routes would have been closed in the old days. This is going to be boring as the captain won't allow anyone on deck. This makes sure that nobody can be seen either from the mainland or from drones. Some of those spy drones are just so small. If you want to take a look through that porthole, we are following the coast at the moment so as not to get out into the main channel until we have to. We should be somewhere near Torbay by now. Once we round the headland, we will join the Plymouth to Santander route."

Some of the other passengers were risking getting out of their cars. Many were stretching and then taking a little walk. They didn't move far from their cars, and they were avoiding each other. There was a definite attempt at making sure that nobody met anyone else eye to eye. They walked around and then went back to their cars.

The light was dim, so it wasn't pitch black. As it was still daylight some of the cars did risk putting their internal lights on for a while but not for long as they were warned by the crew to turn them off so that they didn't flatten their batteries. Those who had come prepared put on torches, the others had to sit in the dark.

The floor was hardly moving to start with. The sea was millpond calm but as a breeze increased the deck started to move slightly. Then came the rush for the sick bags. A crew member had opened the portal, and the bags were un-ceremonially thrown out but it did help to lessen the smell. The swell increased and those who had attempted to walk around decided to return to their cars and vans.

The hours rolled past, and the sun began to go down. What natural light there had been diminished and the hold became pitch black with pinpoints of light where people had torches.

Elaine had settled the children down and they sat around the table in silence for a few hours. Lost in their own thoughts as it was a time to catch up on the day. Somewhere a dog barked and Oberon jumped to his feet, almost taking the table with him. He ran to the door and answered with a resounding "Woof" before Asha put a hand on his head. "Steady boy. Someone is upset so no need for you to join in." Oberon wagged his tail and laid down across the doorway, licked his front paws and then put his nose on his paws and went to sleep.

The hours passed and Asha cooked some food. It was a whole selection of nibbles with a spicy Mediterranean twist which kept them occupied for quite a while. Again, there was little to say, the enormity of what they were doing had hit home.

Raven was looking at the road map. "It doesn't show the boat routes of course. Couldn't we have gone to France? It is closer."

Elaine watched Raven track the coast with her finger. "Yes, it is but the only routes across there are Transition X monitored. The Weymouth route is the only one which has managed to keep undetected, mostly because ferries also run to Jersey and Guernsey and for some reason they are left alone. This route is ignored as by this time of year the ferries aren't travelling with passengers even if they are Transition X ones. The Bay of Biscay would be too routh. We have to risk it as it is the only way. I am guessing that the captain will take the shortest crossing and hug the coastline around Brest and then work his way down the coast.

As the Basque Region is now pretty much a no go zone with the Basque Uprising in Bayonne, Santander has pretty much been abandoned as a port, that is where we can sneak in. Bilbao is pretty much a war zone but the uprising in Burgos has somehow managed to leave Santander out of the troubles."

Balen sat up. "What do you mean the uprising in Burgos? That is a non-entity of a place."

Asha laughed. "Well, that was what everyone thought but that is not the case. There is a group there known as the Coer Noir who have been meeting in back rooms for years. They are a quasi-religious sect which based its beliefs on an ancient cult who believe in "The Redemption" where all their sins will be exonerated. That gives them free reign to do what they want to pretty much.

They aspire to the idea that the ancient Annunaki will return, and a faction of that alien race will reward them for what they are doing. They had a stronghold around Chartres in France but that was eliminated when they started to have a stroke of bad luck and a local subgroup of the Catholic Church wiped them out. The whole of that coast is a war zone between Transition X and the Coer Noir and as they are covert Transition X have no idea who they are fighting."

Balen shook his head. "How do you know?"

Asha smiled. "Now wouldn't you like to know."

Balen scowled. "Yes, that was why I asked. Go on, tell me."

Asha took a deep breath. "Well, a lot of all this relies on ancient beliefs and organisations which go back, way back. Some say as far back as Thoth and Isis where they formed an ancient society to ensure that architecture still carried the pattern of the Temple of Solomon. It was long ago abandoned or so everyone thought. The thought of building the Temple of Solomon to the original design which had been lost, on the rock in Jerusalem, was not only outlandish it was downright impossible.

What they didn't know at the time was that a second plan was still going ahead. It relies on the EMF of people and building a network of energy. That did go ahead and culminated in the one person who had been to all the places going there and as she was a medium releasing the last tower of energy. If you believe all that, that awakened or was the flag for the Sacred Heart of Our Lady to rise again. They absolutely annihilated the Coer Noir in the region and have managed to hold their own against Transition X as well."

Elaine picked Raphael up and cuddled him as he had started putting the mobile in his mouth. She then thought about it and handed him to Raven. "Here, you need to bond with him. You have missed so much."

Raven took him and cuddled him. He amused himself by pulling at her hair.

Elaine smiled. "The troubles in the area have tied up Transition X resources so it is possible to sneak in, unload as quickly as possible, and get out to sea again. It is the only reason that the Santander route is still open. But a long way to go before then. We must get across the Bay and that is going to involve a very bumpy ride in this old ferry. But the weather report is fair at the moment and it looks like we are making good headway."

A loud metallic noise outside silenced Elaine. She immediately jumped to her feet, as did Balen and went to the window.

There was a bright light outside in the hold and one of the cars was on fire. The crew leapt into action to put it out, despite bullets which were flying around. The smoke was choking, and it was hard to see what was going on. There was a running gunfight going on by what they could hear. Elaine pulled Balen back and shut the door. "It is not our fight. We have the children here. We need to keep quiet and keep the door locked."

Out in the hold the gunfire was coming from two of the cars, the burning car was between them. Its driver lay dead on the deck and the two men who were firing at each other were bad shots. Everyone around them had hunkered down in their cars and they were hoping for the best.

The side door of the hold opened and armoured guards ran in. They had a mis matched combination of ex-military army surplus armour but enough to look effective against what they were up against. They evaluated the situation in a moment and split into two groups, they took aim and after both groups emptied several rounds into both cars all was silent. They walked up to the vehicles, guns at the ready and put a bullet into the heads of both assailants.

The crew had by then put the fire out and doused the car well to make sure there were no more problems. One of the armoured guards opened his visor. "Does anyone know what happened?"

A mousy looking man dressed in grey jacket and trousers with milk bottle thick glasses stepped out of his car which was nearby. "Well by what I saw it was like this. The man in the burnt-out car opened his door and scratched the door of that chappie." He pointed to one of the cars. "He got out of his car and they faced each other off. The man from the burning car being the one who did the scratching. They glared at each other and the man from that car shot him a few times and one of the bullets killed the wife of the man in that car over there and the young boy who was in the burning car. The boy in the car was smoking. You know it says he shouldn't have been. That man then started firing on the other man because of his wife and then you came in and stopped it."

The guard smiled. "Thank you."

By then the crew had carried the bodies away and all was calm. Mr Milk Bottles had got back in his car and the guards returned to their posts.

Balen and the others had been watching through the window. He stepped out to check on the other car which was securely locked and locked the door after him. He came straight back and locked himself in.

Elaine put the kettle on. "I suggest we stay in here for the rest of the journey. This camper is self-contained and we can't afford any mess ups. I know it is going to be boring but better bored than dead. If you want something to do then start reading the Rough Guide to Spain and we'll see if we can plan a route which keeps us out of trouble.

Raven sat down with her cup of tea. "Why did that kick off?"

Asha took his cup and sat down opposite her. "Well, when you are in a world where there are few possessions, the less you have the more you intensify how you feel about the few you have. They become territory, even if you have no home or "territory". The car got scratched. That was a personal attack and an affront to the man's manhood. Even though it was an accident it had to be defended. Rather than backing down and severely apologising the situation was antagonised by the other man standing up to the one who had his car scratched. In a situation where we are all vulnerable, he saw a situation where he could at least "fight back". Innocents got caught in the crossfire and breaking the rules caused another problem. Same here now as in the world. The disruptive elements have wiped themselves out. Hopefully we are left with the sensible and the meek."

Elaine was thinking. "This is going to be a slower crossing. After 48 hours it could get a little heated out there. In the old days people would have walked on deck or had access to cabins if they booked them and probably a bar and areas to walk around. The captain can't risk that, and did you see when we got on that the rooms are full of boxes. It must look authentic so there are no spaces for people to walk around.

People are going to feel claustrophobic and vulnerable. They are also going to be near people they probably only spend a few hours as day with. This could get "interesting". So, don't go outside. Keep the door locked and we do not open the door under any circumstances. Let them get through the journey as best they can and we stay in here, whatever happens."

Balen and Raven both nodded. Balen was looking out of the window as the lines of cars. "I would not like to be stuck in a car for 48 hours, but I suppose if it is the only way to survive and get out of the country then I suppose I would manage."

Asha pulled the curtains and blinds closed. "Don't even look outside. There will be some who will envy what we have. They could be dangerous. Best they forget about us."

The ferry sailed on in an empty sea. The storm clouds rolled across the sky, blotting out the moon and as the last rays disappeared the rain started. It was a gentle mist to start with but soon is escalated to a downpour. Then came the winds. Just as they rounded the headland at Brest the wind hit them, and the waves, sending the waves to colossal levels as they entered the Bay of Biscay.

Tempestuous waters bounced the ferry around. Cars began to slide and people scuttled about taking the ratchets from the side of the walls and fastening down their cars. Balen and Asha left the camper for a short while to do the same with the other car and the wheels of the camper. He forbade Elaine and Raven to follow him, moved fast and as he leapt back through the door Raven closed it and locked it.

In the camper Elaine and Raven had taken anything breakable which could have fallen out of the cupboards and put them in a box under the table. Just in time as the ship started to roll and so did the cars. Brakes on were enough but the ship rhythmically rolled, making walking difficult. Elaine had planned. She had flasks full of coffee and the mugs were replaced with metal camping ones. She poured everyone half a cup and they sat and looked out of the window at the totally uninteresting view.

Elijah was in his cot giggling. He had not long mastered walking on the boat and this new addition to his challenge amused him. He was trying to walk from one side of his cot to the other which was interrupted by the more than occasional land on his backside and climb back up again. But, he kept going and got to the other side, held onto the cot poles and let the ship make standing much more interesting for him.

Raphael was asleep, gently rocked by the huge waves which buffeted the outside of the ship. He was oblivious to the tremulous sound of the waves and wind and the ominous creaks of the ship.

Elaine got the map out and a pen and paper and although it was difficult began to plan a route through Spain. She flipped through her "Rough Guide to Spain" where she had made a few notes in the margin.

Raven was sitting next to her and was reading the notes. "What are they for?" She asked by way of starting a conversation more than needing to know the answer.

Elaine smiled. "Well, I made my own notes when I stayed in various places. It helps me to remember. I started with a travelling journal but that got complicated when I started writing other things in there, so I just wrote things down in the book and transferred them when I got home. Well, I intended to do that, but I never got around to it. Life is a bit busy. Well it looks like none of us get seasick. That is good, we'd certainly know that by now."

Asha nodded. "We ought to use this time to read some of the books I got hold of just before the move from home. I managed to get a book on growing in Spain, Aquaponics, and a Witch's Garden. The latter is because that interests me. I also have a book about Cadfael's Herb Garden somewhere in the packing. It is an interest, but I am hoping that we will be far enough from the town that we will be left alone enough to get on with whatever we want to. I was reading about Planting by the Moon and although that is a "new" idea now it is a very old thing. We are now back to very old things and ways. It doesn't hurt to get as far ahead as possible when it comes to ideas.

I was watching about how to make a chop and flip BIC tank growing system. Fish and plants growing in harmony. We will need a watering system but as the house didn't have water anyway nothing really changes. There is water there. We will have to purify it as we haven't been there for a while. There is no mains water but there may not be now anyway. It got like that for many as water for the farms was diverted to the ever-growing number of golf courses on the Costa Del Sol. Not an issue now as far as I know but then life has returned to normal in a lot of places. I haven't heard about anything going on there, that could be a very good thing. Or a very bad one."

I also watched something about fodderponics. They were sprouting seeds to feed to animals which gives 80% more nutritional return."

Raven smiled.

Elaine smiled back. "But I expect you know about those sorts of things. I forget that you had a smaller farm before you moved to the Transition X fortification. Did you try any of those things?"

Raven shook her head. "The day-to-day troubles were enough. Balen didn't exactly turn up as a farmer and the help I had was a bit limited. Not now though. I think between us we can come up with the already tried and tested plans and then take them to another level. I have long wondered about taking the water from the fish into a drip feed system which uses the soil as well. What thoughts have you had on water loss?"

Asha laughed. "Well, there you have got me. I didn't think down those lines. I have looked into getting the water to the plants. I never thought about stopping it going. I assume you mean evaporation and transpiration?"

Raven nodded. "If we are going to get precious water, we don't want it to just evaporate away. I was wondering about something I saw on a documentary years ago. A sheet of plastic as a "roof" over the plants and water them to the roots rather than surface. The plastic would draw the water up past the roots and then as the water evaporates it would hopefully coalesce on the plastic and run to the lowest point where we can collect it up. When it rains the other side of the plastic would do similarly and take the water into our tanks so that we can use it when we want to. If we add in a grey water system for the toilet and bathroom, we may well be able to cut water loss to a minimum."

Asha nodded agreement. "Well how are you going to stop the water just draining away?"

Raven thought for a moment. "Good point. Well, I assume we will be planting a new area so why don't we plant in "gulleys" lined with plastic or guttering. It would depend on the depth of the roots of what we are growing but at the end of the season it would be easy to lift the whole half tube, clear it out and reset and then place it back in the ground. It would stop all that back breaking bending down."

Elaine was taking that in. "Well, if we raise the tubes in the first place and angle them slightly or step them then we wouldn't have to bend down at all. We could then keep chickens underneath and if my thoughts are correct, they might well eat the bugs which would harm the plants. As we are not talking a commercial quantity, just enough for us I think that might work.

Just a thought here. It usually takes about a month for seed to germinate. How does it work with the shelf germination and sprouting so quickly? You can see where I am going with this. If we sprout seed in a mini version of the fodderponics would we jump our growing ahead a month?

We could keep the early, baby plants, seedlings in the guttering and then move some of them to a dug raised bed to go to maturity to either eat or produce seed."

Raven thought for a while. "We would have to find a way to isolate the root system of the seedlings if we are going to transplant them. I am sure we will have to try a few things to get that to work.

Another problem we would have with the water loss is how to get lost water back. 97-99% of water is lost to transpiration. Big problem if you are short of water. Although evaporation causes cooling which will help with growing the plants the main problem is to get the plants to transpire as they have to for photosynthesis and then grab it back.

When it comes to survival a hole helps. Put the plastic over it and you get what water there is. In a growing situation we would lose a lot to the breeze, which is probably why they put the water collection in a hole.

We could use a tarpaulin stretched between four poles with a stone and hole in the middle and gather the water to send out back to the plants. That would be a basic system but if we want to keep more water, we will have to enclose the system. In a hot country that could be terminal for the plants as the heat it would gather without a cooling breeze would be phenomenal.

So, we then have a choice of either using a fan to blow the humid air away and find a way to get the water out of it somewhere else or find some way to keep the "greenhouse" cool without ventilation."

Elaine thought about it while Balen looked lost. "Well, we could use Ammonium or Potassium Nitrate, but both have explosive applications so getting hold of them could be an issue. Possibly we could look at Baking Soda and Citric Acid. That can get down to -6 and the biproduct is water ahd carbon dioxide which the plants could use anyway. Of course, the extra water is no issue at all."

Raven smiled. "In the old world perhaps. What we really need is to raid a supermarket and get hold of commercial fridges and freezers as they have glass fronts and run the water through them as part of the cycle. It would feed the heat sensitive plants, but the water would leave chilled, particularly if we run it through the freezer. Some seeds need a frost to germinate, so we would still be able to grow them. I think after they are germinated, they are ok. We could also move parsnips in pots in there so that we can still have them in a warm climate.

Could we run a fridge and freezer on solar? That would be the problem. We would need something like that."

Asha thought about it. "Well during the day yes but of a nighttime we could shut off the system as transpiration is part of photosynthesis which doesn't happen at night as it needs sunlight."

Raven thought about it. "It would still be warm in there though. What would we do about that?"

Asha smiled. "Well, if we use cool packs cooled in the freezer that should bring the temperature down to start with which would give them a start. Or we could just keep it running. There would be a bonus as we can keep the lights on in the fridge to convince some plants of a longer growing season."

Raven looked at Balen who was looking totally bemused by now. "You mean we would be creating a closed hydroponics system or even aquaponics as we could chill the water going into the fish tank which would mean we could keep a fish tank in a polytunnel as well. I had wondered what to do about the water evaporating."

Balen smiled. "So, you could chill my swimming pool as well?"

Raven smiled. "We could and there would be plenty of ice for drinks."

Balen looked a little worried. "Then of course we have to get there first." As if on cue the sound of gunfire erupted outside. The whir and plunk as bullets ricocheting against the hull. Shouts and screams accompanied the din of automatic and single shot gunfire.

Elaine indicated that they should get down, they didn't need telling. She moved to the sofa and rolled up and had a look out of the window.

Outside was pandemonium. Anyone who had a weapon had it out, was trying to get it out, leaping for cover and people were using their car doors as cover to fire from. Guards came running down the back stairs before barricading them shut. Both sides of the hold were now securely locked, there was just the front stairwell which had the door open, and Elaine could just about make out a swarthy face dressed in black.

Elaine rolled off of the sofa she had been kneeling on to get a better view and crawled to the front of the vehicle. She took a peek. "Looks like it is bloody pirates. Ok, well they have come down the fore stairway and are firing from there. I'm guessing that there is a similar gunfight above. We wouldn't hear it from down here with all that din going on from the guns down here."

She went to other windows and pulled the curtains shut. "They have the rest of the stairwells barricaded shut. So just one area to worry about. Not a lot of use for cover, that is just a duck shoot when they stick their heads around to fire. I am guessing that our neighbours are not natural gunslingers by the number of holes in the hull beside the door. I think I had better give them a hand while we still have a ship. You three stay here. The guards are here, and they have some pretty tasty automatic weaponry. This could go on a bit and I'm more worried about the integrity of the hull now. Some of those shots are a bit wild!"

She reached the gun cupboard by crawling although no bullets were coming through the hull of the camper. They occasionally plinked off of the shell though. She took what looked like a rocket launcher out and an odd coloured cannister and loaded it. It had writing on it they couldn't make out, strange symbols. She also grabbed a loaded handgun.

She opened the door and aimed the rocket launcher at the walkway, fired and the cannister took off with a trail of smoke behind it and landed squarely in the doorway just as someone from above stepped forwards to shoot accompanied by a volley of chaotically aimed gunfire from the hold.

The someone fell in a hail of bullets as he neither dodged or stepped back. He seemed to stop in his tracks and as he fell many of the bullets thumped into him with little splashes of blood as he fell like a felled tree back into the stairwell.

Elaine raised an eyebrow. "And that was just the tail of the thing."

There was a loud "Boom" and yellow smoke billowed into the hold. It rose quickly, missing the people in the hold but it rose up the stairs and coalesced on the ceiling in the hold. Anyone it touched was instantly knocked out and tumbled down the stairs. They came tumbling down into the hold, out cold and clearly no threat but the people in the hold kept firing, mostly out of sheer terror. The gunfire upstairs petered out almost immediately after they stopped firing in the hold.

Elaine left the camper and made her way past the cars. People were tending to the wounded and trying to patch up their vehicles so they hardly missed the "Miss Marple" like lady in her twinset as she had left the rocket launcher in the camper.

The guards had by then got to the stairwell and had started putting a bullet into the heads of the sleeping pirates. Elaine smiled her approval and was watching when the guard with the most stripes came over to her. He was in his late twenties, tall, thin, attractive and a red head. She braced for what she knew was coming. "I don't think they are going to harm you now dear but I think you had better go back to your car. This is not going to be very pleasant." Then he noticed the Beretta in her hand. "Now grandma I don't think we need your help. Thank you though."

She shrugged and turned on her neat kitten heels and as she passed the doorway she put a neatly placed bullet between the eyes of one of the pirates who was almost out of view up the stairs. In her peripheral vision she saw the lead guard looked shocked, she smiled and went back to the camper as she whispered "Prat".

She opened the camper door and stepped inside and shut the door behind her. "Well, it will take them about an hour to clear away the bodies. I hope they remember to search them first. There will of course then be the problem of their ship. It will be nearby, and they no doubt landed in dinghies. This may or may not be over."

She then picked up the Rocket Launcher and returned it to the cupboard. "Good stuff that Mess13. Not sure what they really call it. We called it that as it often got us out of a real mess."

Balen had been eyeing it up. "So, what are those symbols? I don't recognise the language."

Elaine tapped the side of her nose. "Oh, go on then, I don't suppose it matters now. The symbols are I suppose "alien" though how you can call them that after all these years. We have a fair bit of alien technology we get to use. It is part of an exchange deal. I've fought alongside them, nice chaps, bit gung-ho but can't complain really. Not sure how many stayed after the shutdown. I haven't heard of or from any of them since. We did email for a while, just exchanging pleasantries. They weren't settling well though. Can't say as I blame them.

The cannister is a form of sleeping gas. Pretty much everything they gave us was to avoid civilian casualties. I think they all left on a transport out which was not affected by Nemesis. Don't blame them, this is not their world." She went to the window and looked out of the curtain. "Well, it is going to take a while for that one to sort out. "

Those with medical training were tending to the injured and there was a lot of wailing, ouching, and crying.

Elaine got a piece of paper out of her pocket and a small black pager like device. "I think we are settled and organised enough to see who will be joining us for the rest of the journey. Yes, I did a bit of a Nemesis myself. I have been recruiting for a while now and there are a few of the people on this boat. If they have survived, I think it is time we made contact.

I recognised some of them when we got on board. It was decided that to save any inconvenience with other travellers or any unwanted hangers on that we could keep this covert for as long as possible.

The pirate attack was unforeseen, but we can't do anything about that. I'm going to put in the code now and they will gradually contact us throughout the rest of the journey. When we leave the boat, we can then travel in convoy. That is why I was happy for you to bring the other vehicle. I notice you didn't bother with yours. I don't blame you, the one you have is much more comfortable."

Asha opened the door and let Oberon out, following him with a roll of doggie poo bags. Elaine went with him.

Raven leant back in her chair. "Your mother is somewhat astounding."

Balen smiled. "Tell me about it, try growing up in her household. No wonder I was such a rebel. She ran that house like a military installation, and I am guessing we can look forward to the farm being the same. Personally, I prefer your air of controlled chaos, it is much more comfortable. But I would put money on the people she has chosen being scientists, military and the like. I'm guessing she didn't nip down the local Women's Institute, but I could be wrong. That woman always amazes me."

Asha was following Oberon as he sniffed his way around the cars looking for the perfect place. She was near the wall of the boat when one of the guards came up to her. "Ok Miss Marple, what are you up to this time?" Asha kept an eye on them.

Elaine put her most innocent look on and stared wide eyed up at the guard who was at least two foot taller than her four-foot frame. "I am walking the dog."

Oberon on cue decided on the perfect spot and deposited the perfect distraction. Asha pulled out a bag, cleared it up and held the bag out. "Are there any bins on this boat?"

The guard smiled and pointed to a bin attached to the wall. "That one there do?"

Elaine smiled and put the bag in the bin. "It will do nicely thank you young man. Now I hope we won't be disturbed by any more of those ghastly pirates. Can I help you?"

The young man looked confused. "No, enjoy your walk." He turned on his heels and carried on with his patrol.

Elaine watched him go out of the corner of her eye, pretending to stroke Oberon. As she stood up the car window of the white Skoda Fabia next to her wound down and a dark-haired man handed her a piece of paper. She recognised it so took it from him, opened it and smiled. "Hello there Gerald, lovely to meet you and your family."

Gerald turned his head to look inside the car. "This is Anna, my wife and Tony and Mark my two sons. Anna is a good cook and Tony and Mark are both well skilled in the building trade. We are looking forward to the adventure."

Elaine smiled. "As are we. This is Asha, my husband. You are the first to make contact. Do you have all that you need?"

Gerald smiled back. "Well other than space. We are taking regular walks but that first twelve hours has been trying."

There was a squeaky "woof" from the car. Gerald jumped and looked sheepish. "I couldn't leave Pedro behind."

Tony lifted the short coated chihuahua and Oberon jumped up, the two met noses with an extreme amount of tail wagging.

Elaine smiled. "Dogs welcome. We are making a life, not a military establishment. I'm waiting for a whole raft of pets who are no doubt squirrelled around the cars."

Anna looked relieved. "I am so glad. I really didn't want to leave the little boy behind."

Asha shook his head. "That is understandable. We will care for any animal which joins us. But no doubt we could do with a ratter, any good?"

Anna smiled. Her golden curls swung as she shook her head. Her sweatshirt and jogging pants were immaculately pressed but she looked a little self-conscious.

Asha stroked Oberon who jumped down. "Well at some point come to the silver camper. I need to find whoever else is to join us, preferably before we dock in Santander."

They made their way through the cars by a different route. Two cars along the window rolled down and a similar piece of paper was held out. The battered camper van had seen a few miles and had taken a couple of dents from the recent exchange. The bright eyed twenty something who leant out to offer her the paper had waist length dreadlocks which screamed "surf dude". Elaine took the paper but pretty much knew who he was before she opened it. "Hello Archie, and of course Shade."

Shade lent forward to smile and raised a nervous hand. "Good to meet you." She was dressed in black with a good deal of lace involved. Around her neck hung a tri moon pewter necklace.

Asha smiled. "Bright blessings." Shade immediately relaxed.

Archie seemed a little tongue tied. He opened his mouth as if to speak and Shade elbowed him in the ribs. "Erm, well, you don't seem, well."

Elaine smiled reassuringly. "Well, we all get old. If you are lucky it will happen to you one day."

Archie flushed red as Elaine laughed and he mumbled. "I didn't mean to offend."

Elaine smiled. "You didn't. I can fight a lot of things; age is one battle I can't win but I can draw evenly by doing it disgracefully. You and your skills are very welcome. Go on, what pets have you brought with you?"

Shade jumped. "Well, we didn't know whether to mention. We have brought "Akita", she is a Siamese cross black moggie."

Elaine looked down at her immaculate shoes. "Well, I am hoping her name is after Akita assassin and that she is an excellent ratter."

Archie was grinning. "Exactly why we called her Akita."

Asha was already grinning when she looked up. "Good, well she is on the payroll then. We had better introduce her to Oberon and Pedro. I assume she is in a cage. Try and drop by the camper before we dock, don't bring Akita yet though, we will keep that introduction until we have a better situation."

Elaine smiled a goodbye and kept walking. Oberon helped by sniffing around. Most people were in their cars after the pirate raid, they had been milling around previously. Elaine picked the time because of this. It was easier to get around and she knew roughly what she was looking for.

She was doing a circuit of the cars so that she could get a general idea of what was there. The hull was fairly large but not large enough that she couldn't see the group of military jeeps in the middle. She caught Oberon's eye and sent him that way, he thankfully complied, a bit too much as he stopped to cock his leg on one of the wheels of the front jeep.

The driver stuck his head out and was about to shout when he saw Elaine. He leapt out of the jeep and lifted the tiny lady up. He was over six foot tall and built like a brick outhouse. He put her down, looking a little sheepish when he saw Asha until she hugged him back. "Good to see you Brad. Everyone here?"

Heads and waving hands were emerging from the jeeps. Brad pointed to each in turn. "Hamish "McSporran", Janice Vasgie, John Le Strange and Evan Snowdrop".

The latter was clearly an albino, wispy built and as she already knew the best sniper anywhere. She had no idea why she had selected him, but she thought at the time it could come in handy. Anyway, they had been a team for a long time so no need to split them up.

"Well, if you get a chance, drop by the camper. Ok, I have to ask, did you bring any pets with you?"

Brad looked down at the footwell next to him. "Well, we did sort of raid the military kennel before we left. We thought they would be useful. They are all well trained. We had been on guard duty before we left, and they were sort of part of our crew. We couldn't leave them. We do however have a good stash of dog food. We can also hunt so they won't go hungry."

Asha shook his head. "Oh well, we will manage. Names?"

Brad stopped to think. "Sheba, six-year-old German Shepherd, Brendon, six-year-old Rottweiler, Kaylee, two year old GSD, Frak, three year old GSD and Goliath, three year old Great Dane. He was the Commander's pet but when he got shot, he moved in with the rest. They are all inseparable."

Elaine smiled. "Of course, they are and oddly enough one for each of you. I'm feeling a little left out here. I seem to be he only one without. Oberon here came with Raven."

Brad laughed. "Well, I was going to mention him later, but we do have Beast. She sort of followed us. We thought she was a stray, so we took her in and she sort of became a bit of a mascot. She is a Cocker Spaniel. We found out just before we left that she had been part of the bomb squad before the "fall"."

On hearing her name Beast leapt over the chair and landed on the passenger seat. There was a bit of a growl from Sheba which was quickly silenced by a snap in her general direction. "She is a bit of a character." Brad whispered as he reached over to stroke her.

Oberon jumped up and investigated the jeep through the open window.

Beast landed on Brad's lap then sprang out of the window to land beside Oberon. Brad shook his head. "Well, there is loyalty for you. Then she does feel a little left out."

Oberon and Beast started play bouncing and running about chasing each other. Asha was mesmerised. Brad smiled. "I think she is going home with you. It is a bit crowded in here. I've got Goliath in the back."

Elaine watched the black working cocker as she ran about, totally unphased by Oberon's size. Then she shrugged her shoulders and said "Heel."

Beast immediately ran to her right side, sat down and looked up at her with dark brown bright eyes. Elaine leant down and stroked the silky black head. "Well Beast, are you as well behaved as that all the time?"

Not to be left out Oberon ran over and sat on her left. Brad and the others were laughing uncontrollably. Brad recovered his composure. "Well as spokesman for this lot I shall say that I think that by unanimous decision it is decreed that Beast shall be yours."

Asha was looking down at the dogs. "Well, it doesn't look like we have much choice here."

Elaine smiled and turned to go back to the camper. It was just as she turned that she noticed that the driver of a black van was watching her quite intently. She walked a bit closer to the van and the man was facing forwards as if he had never looked. It was then that Beast started running backwards and forwards next to the van. She seemed agitated. Elaine didn't hesitate. She pulled her weapon and shot the man in the head just as he was reaching inside his jacket.

The team were out of their jeeps in moments, and they had the door of the van open. The man had a suicide vest on, and his hand had been going for the button.

Elaine reached down to stroke Beast who was jumping in circles barking loudly. Brad reached in his pocket and threw her a ball and she happily laid down to play with it, snuzzling and rolling it with her paws.

The team stood back and Le Strange stepped up and went to the back door of the van. After a very careful check he opened the van to reveal boxes of explosives.

Elaine looked at Brad. "Well, I guess that Nemesis knows we are here. We can assume he knows our plan too."

Brad thought for a moment as the others crowded around. The other passengers were getting out of their vehicles for a look see and there was a general bubble of horrified conversation. It was well placed as there was enough explosives there to blow the ship out of the water.

Raven and Balen had by this time left the camper and had joined her. As had the others out of the other cars. Elaine smiled. "Well, the gang's all here."

Balen felt someone standing behind him. Then he heard a whisper in his ear. "I doubt you were the target, more likely me." Balen spun around to see a tall man with bleached blonde hair a, a Star Wars T Shirt, and blue jeans. The man was in his late fifties, slim and pale in the I have not seen the sun in a long-time way. "Don't you recognise me?"

Recognition dawned. "Well yes but I am guessing I wasn't supposed to. There is no such thing as coincidence so why are you here?"

Raven was confused as she didn't know who he was.

The man smiled. "I am here because I work for you. I had no idea you were on this ship as you were booked on the next one."

Elaine nodded. "That is true. The rest of the crew were due to travel earlier, all on different ferries, and we were then supposed to meet up in a car park in Santander. When I got signals from the beacons that they were all on this ferry we put the pedal to the metal and got on it too. But who are you and why would Nemesis want to blow up a whole ship to get rid of you?

The tall man smiled. "You got it in one. When Nemesis replaced you, I was expected to work for the "new" Balen. I knew there had been a replacement straight away. By conversation "below stairs" I was able to ascertain where you were. Recovery was not easy but thankfully nobody notices the serving staff and Ryjel and I were able to spirit you away in the laundry basket after you imbibed a rather doctored cup of tea. The rest was a case of getting you to a safe room, bringing you around and leaving you to sort out your own problems.

As to why they would blow me up, I know far too much. Unfortunately a rather chatty boot boy let the cat out of the bag and I was forced to make rather a speedy exit. As I had no idea where you might be going, I took the liberty of heading to visit my aunt in the Dolomites. As Santander is the only safe port for us travelling off radar fate has put us on the same boat."

Balen glared at him. "I am of course extremely grateful, but I have two questions. Firstly, how did you know I had been replaced and secondly why would Nemesis go to such lengths of blowing the whole ship up to blow you up?"

Hargreaves smiled. "The new Balen had good manners. I may have accidentally removed a copy of Nemesis' operating system which was his current back up, so it has all of his plans and thoughts. Nemesis may be an AI, but he is also a computer program."

Raven shook her head. "So who are you? I'm sorry but I haven't met you before."

Balen smiled. "This is Hargreaves. He was the "Butler" at HQ. He looked after the household and me when I was at the meetings. He took on the codename Alfred when he was doing covert stuff for me. It was him who warned me about Nemesis, but it was too late.

He realised that the Balen in charge wasn't me, found me and managed to bring me food and information in my cell."

Hargreaves nodded. "You will have to forgive me the homage to my favourite butler."

Elaine smiled. "Under the circumstances I would have said Parker was more appropriate. Your light fingeredness could well give us a huge advantage."

Hargreaves smiled. "Well in lieu of salary one sometimes does have to extract recompense in other ways. I do not consider it stealing and should Nemesis wish the copy reinstated I would of course oblige after a few adaptations of my own, call it interest." Hargreaves took a memory stick out of his pocket and gave it to Balen. "I would assume that the destruction of this stick would warrant the complete destruction of this vessel. I would assume that there was some way that Nemesis knew that I was on board."

The crowd which had assembled at the back of the van had long since dissipated. None of them had been able to get close enough to hear anything which had been said. That was mostly facilitated by the collection of dogs which had jumped out of the vehicles to make a perimeter around them.

The surf dude with the spliff had been the first to leave, closely followed by Beast who had growled at him until he dropped it and ran.

.

11

The boat sailed on across the choppy sea. It was now so rough that everyone had retired to their cars and some even had their seatbelts on.

Raven, Balen, Elaine, Asha and Hargreaves had settled down at the table in the camper van.

Hargreaves had taken a duster to the camper and had already sorted out the cupboards despite the way that the camper was swayed by the moving deck. He seemed to have sticky feet as he just got on with it.

Elaine was completely happy about this. She watched him. "I have never been one for housework and this gives me time to play with Beast." Beast seemed very happy to chase her ball up and down the caravan successfully waking up Raphael and Elijah who were totally transfixed with the new dog. Oberon found his spot under the table and stayed there while the running around was going on.

Balen and Raven were just watching what was going on. Raven looked out of the window for a while. "Absolutely nothing going on out there. I can't believe nobody is moving around. The boat isn't moving that much. Well then again, she saw one of the guards doing his patrol and he was all over the place, despite his sea legs. He was tossed from the wall to a car and ended up making his patrol by holding onto the cars.

Brad got out of the jeep and staggered his way to the camper with Sheba in tow. Sheba nearly fell over at one point, yelped, and then made her way carefully to Brad's side.

They made it to the camper and were about to knock on the door, but Raven opened the door just as Brad reached out. He gratefully grabbed the door jam and climbed inside. Sheba was about to jump in, thought better of it and stepped graciously up inside and laid down on the floor. Oberon came over, they sniffed noses and he sat down beside her.

Brad staggered across the rolling floor just as Hargreaves put the kettle on. Raven had made it back to the table and Brad pulled himself into the seat next to Elaine. Hargreaves made the tea, gave them each a cup and then as Raven glared at him angrily, he sighed, made himself a cup and sat down. Raven smiled. "Now that is better. You aren't Balen's butler anymore, you don't have to do all that."

Hargreaves smiled. "I thank you for that but if you don't mind, I would much prefer to fulfil my duties. I will however made some adjustments under the current circumstances." He then got up and shut the door before returning to Elijah first who laid down and he put a blanket over him and he picked Raphael up, rocked him to sleep and put him back in his cot. "Right, well here we are, all tickedy boo."

They sat around the table with their tea. Beast jumped up and sat on Elaine's lap. She was a bit big and had to sit part on the seat, but nobody seemed to mind. She laid her nose on her paws and went to sleep. Oberon and Sheba had both laid down and were asleep.

Raven looked around the camper. "Well, I am really glad you had this. It makes life a lot easier. How long to go now?"

Elaine thought about it. "I don't know exactly where we are, but we must be in the Bay of Biscay for it to be this rough. This is where it is either a long or a short journey depending on how the weather is and other factors. We could dock in the morning; it could be another day. I suppose we will find out in the morning. The crossing is choppy, but it could be a lot worse than this. I'd say we are doing well."

Balen had moved over to the window seat when Raven got out to let Brad in. He was then looking out of the window but there wasn't much to see. As it was getting late most people had decided to get an early night. They had turned their torches out and gradually the hold was getting darker and darker until eventually there were just the red security lights which covered the cars in a red eerie glow.

The other jeeps were in darkness as well. Brad leant over and looked for a moment. "Seems the crew have turned in. I said I would come over and see what the plan is. They weren't sure if we would all fit in here."

Elaine looked around. "Well, we can give it a try."

Brad made his way carefully back to the jeeps and knocked on the windows. One by one they woke up and joined him and climbed into the camper. Hargreaves had the kettle on, and he had found every mug in the place. He had to use the metal cups and the porcelain mugs.

Brad looked around the rather luxurious camper. "This is a lovely vehicle. Where did you get it from?"

Elaine smiled. "Well, it is actually a collaboration between Airstream and Winnebago. I wanted a Winnebago as this sleeps up to nine, but I wanted the shape of the Airstream so that I could incorporate the armour plating. So, I got them to work together and here we have the Airbago. It is as I said armour plated, including underneath in case we run over any mines. It has a few other adaptations I had put in. Yes, it cost me an arm and a leg but better to keep those limbs and under the circumstances now that money in the bank is worth nothing, I think I did the right thing.

At the moment I can't extend the sides so it will be a bit cosy, but I would suggest that we use the camper as "base camp"."

Balen smiled. "That's my mother, always practical. I agree, keep this as base camp, and have the jeeps as outriders. That will give us better protection if we are hit by Nemesis. At the moment we were relying on stealth. When he realises that this boat hasn't exploded, we are going to be back on his radar. I am guessing that the people who run it wouldn't kindly blow it up after we are all disembarked so we are going to have to assume that we are going to get company along the way.

We can't sleep everyone in here, but I suggest that we invite Gerald and his wife and Archie and his girlfriend to join us as well. It is time we pulled the team together or is that a risk in this confined space if we don't know if there are any other "operatives" on board?"

Raven thought about it. "They are probably asleep by now and their anonymity will be a slight protection. Brad, you, and the team have already revealed your colours. So, no you are losing nothing by being in here. I'm assuming your dogs will look after the cars."

Hargreaves had the kettle on again and was just doing the second round of drinks. Raven took a look out of the window, and all was quiet.

Balen had the map in front of him. "I would suggest that when we land at Santander, we take the A67 down to Palencia and go around Valladolid, head for Medina del Campo and then down to Salamanca. We need to avoid Madrid at all costs as that is a Nemesis stronghold. From Salamanca we can head directly south on the A66, through Plasencia.

Where we go after that will greatly depend on how the roads are. We need to go cross country but the A5 takes us too close to Madrid. We can either go down and pick up the 430 or we can try a smaller road to Guadalupe. We will have to see but if we aim for Salamanca to start with that will at least give us a destination should we get split up.

I'll assign two each of your vehicles to the two "civilian" transports, one is a camper, the other an ordinary car but neither would escape well if they come under attack.

We need them, they have the knowledge which will help us into the future. We have books but that is not the same."

Hamish looked up from his coffee. "We would never lose anyone willingly anyway. I clocked the two vehicles you spoke to Elaine. Neither have any protection as you say, and we will have sleeping problems. We have tents and they may well have. The camper is obviously sorted out but that leaves us and the people in the car.

I would suggest we try and acquire another camper if we can. Not going to be easy but we could try and buy or take one. There are bound to be abandoned vehicles."

Le Strange shook his head. "At the start perhaps. I doubt we'll find anything that useful." He was looking out of the window. "Then again, we don't know whether there is someone selling that sort of thing at the port. Again, we will have to see."

Elaine was looking about. "This sleeps nine, I am assuming that Archie and Shade only have one bed as that Volkswagen Camper was only really designed for festivals. The four in Gerald's car could be an issue. I suppose they came in what they had."

Evan smiled. "I bet that car is his pride and joy and we will have to crowbar them out of it. I think the first night under canvas and all the terrors that will bring to a civilian in this world should get the keys off of him."

They all laughed. It was graveyard humour, but it did lighten the mood.

The hours rolled on and eventually Hargreaves cleared the last of the coffee.

Elaine looked around the assembled people. "I would invite you to stay as we have enough beds, but we need the eyes out there so I'm sorry, it will be an uncomfortable night."

Janice smiled. "Totally logical and we will do one off one on so we should be covered. Have a good night."

They turned the lights off and waited for their night sight to stabilise before opening the camper door and returning to the cars. Once the dogs had been walked, they turned in for the night.

Same with the camper, Elaine and Asha took Oberon and Beast out and then climbed into their bed. Beast jumped up onto the bed and they didn't object as she cuddled up to her and fell asleep. She was made to sleep on the outside though as Asha put his arms around Elaine and they fell asleep together.

Raven and Balen had the other double bed. Oberon lay on the floor beside Raven who was stroking his fur.

All was quiet as they bounced their way across the Bay of Biscay. The swell was rhythmical though extreme and once they were used to it, it was as if they were being rocked to sleep.

On deck all was action. Hatches were of course battened down and so was the cargo, but the extremes of the swell had thrown a few ropes loose. The crew were onto dealing with that fast.

Out at sea all was dark, that was how they liked it. No ships as far as the horizon at least and shoreward in the distance the lights of the coast. They were of course sailing with no lights on and that close to the coast was dangerous but so was glowing like a light stick.

The boat sailed on through the night. Shifts changed and the port got closer and closer.

By dawn they had made good headway. So much so that they had to slow their passage to arrive after dark. There was a ship coming in, they had seen it from first light and that ship had priority and also, they didn't want to tangle with it. It was no cargo vessel and the worry that it was a Transition X vessel was enough to make them all cautious.

As they watched an orange plume erupted from the ship. This was followed by a loud bang and another plume of fire. The ship broke in two and was gone under the waves in minutes. Whatever had exploded it had done an excellent job of removing the ship.

The captain ordered the boat to speed up. He wanted to get his boat off the sea as soon as possible. He didn't want to land during the day, but he deemed it as the lesser of two evils.

The boat cut through the water and entered the straight which led to the port. The white buildings on either side were uninhabited, black burn marks testimony that there had been trouble in the past. The captain was aware of this. The whole port area had been subject to extreme looting and trouble when the power went down. Very little had been done to rebuild.

The dock was virtually empty. That was normal as well. People were now naturally cautious and as his boat was on the schedule to arrive at some point there was no paperwork to check. There was also no help, but he was used to that as well.

He sent a message down to the hold and down in the hold the drivers got ready to disembark.

This was a process they had no control over. They got to their vehicles and got ready to turn on the engines when the boat was safely docked and the door open. Asha was driving the camper and Balen and Raven had returned to the car leaving the children and Oberon in the Airbago. The rest were in their positions ready to go with an agreement to meet up as soon as they could when they had disembarked.

It was a nerve-wracking time as everyone was waiting but soon enough the doors opened, the ramp came down and they were able to disembark in the order designated by the guards.

They hit the concrete at a steady pace and drove off with the rest of the vehicles until the first of them came to a layby. They stopped as did all the others. They didn't get out of the vehicles when they had all stopped. They then travelled on in convoy.

Santander was almost abandoned. Most of the buildings showed signs of extreme gunfire and heavy weaponry and the shops were boarded up. There were people watching but only from cover and they disappeared when they realised they had been spotted.

Brad had the lead vehicle and he kept them going at quite a pace. He had weaponry on the seat beside him and as always, he was expecting trouble.

They cleared Santander and were out on the open road soon enough.

The roads were almost empty. There was a donkey cart driven by an aged farmer. He was keeping his eyes front and trying not to be noticed as the convoy drove past him. The cart was full of vegetables and he was heading towards the town.

He didn't look like he was a threat. He was trying not to get noticed. His donkey just plodded on.

They drove off into the distance.

The miles passed by. There were buildings in the distance, but they didn't see anyone moving about.

Brad put his foot down and the convoy made good progress. They didn't stop for a few hours but then as Gerald was flashing them, he slowed and they stopped the convoy. Brad jumped out and ran to the car. Gerald had rolled the window down as Brad approached. "Can we have a loo break please?"

Brad smiled. I'll find a good place to stop. We have made good progress so probably a good time to have a break."

Brad ran back to the camper and Elaine rolled the window down. "A break has been suggested. I'll pick a good spot, shall I?"

Elaine nodded. "Good idea.".

Brad went back to the jeep and pulled off. It took a few miles before he found a place to stop. They pulled over and there was a lot of running behind the bushes for those in the cars. Dogs stretched their legs and reluctantly got back in the vehicles, and they drove on.

Darkness was rolling in when they pulled off the main road and onto a side road. They found a place they could all stop, it was sheltered from the road.

The "Combat Crew" disappeared off to do a recon to make sure it was safe. They came back and reported in. Brad smiled. "All clear, no sign of anyone for miles. Could be time to bed down, get some sleep and then move on. It is a first night, probably best that people get to know each other."

Elaine nodded. Asha was playing with Elijah and Raven was cuddling Raphael. Balen sat down beside her. He put his arm around her. She looked up at him. He smiled. There was no need for words.

She laid back on the bed and he put Raphael beside her and she fell asleep. He went to sit at the table with Asha and Elaine. Everyone else was outside. They had decided to set a camp and get to know each other.

Balen sat down at the table. Hargreaves had been given the night off to go and speak with the others.

Asha saw that Raven was asleep. "Can we talk? Is she asleep?"

Balen nodded. "I slipped her a sleeping tablet, she needs to rest. It has been an awful time and she's been through so much."

Asha looked at him sincerely. "You both have. I'm proud of you son. I never wanted to keep away but I had no choice."

Balen looked down. "I didn't know you existed. I believed that Michael's father was mine and I hated him. He was a bastard!"

Asha looked down. "I know what he did to Elaine."

Elaine was stony faced. She turned in her seat away from them and undid her blouse. As she dropped the blouse, they could see her ex-husband's initials branded into her back. "I'm glad he's dead."

Asha took her hand. "We got away from him. That was the best we could do. I can't take the pain away."

Elaine smiled. "You made it better. Will Raven be alright? It sounds like she's had it rough. Did Michael do anything to her?"

Balen shook his head. "He wanted to take her to execute her. It wasn't Michael who hurt her, technically it was Nemesis as he made her be the wife of a bastard who treated her so roughly." He looked down.

Asha smiled. "The evil that men do. We must put all of that behind us. You have a choice. It looks like you've made it. I'm glad as it is the right decision as far as I can see. The alternative would be to take over LexCorp. You own all the shares between you. It might be something you have to use later."

Balen got up and walked over to the bed. He picked up Raphael and put him back into his Moses basket without waking him up. He then pulled the covers over Raven. They were all sleeping dressed, just in case.

The miles rolled by as did the days. They made their way down through Spain, seeing very few people. The wide roads were almost empty. There was the odd truck full of produce but other than that they had the road to themselves.

They were almost running on fumes when they got to the first petrol station.

The place looked deserted to start with but as they looked closer, they could see that the shop was barricaded but there was someone inside.

Balen and the military crew left the others and walked over to the shop. They knocked on the piece of thick plywood which was what was now the door and a hatch opened.

Balen smiled. "Do you have any fuel?"

There was a voice inside. "We have, what do you have to trade?"

"What do you need?"

The voice was a little shaky. "We need food. Do you have tinned food?"

Janice ran back to the camper and knocked on the door. Elaine opened the door, and she climbed inside. "Elaine, can we spare food need to trade food for petrol."

Elaine went to the cupboard and took out a few tins. "If we can get everyone full with this, great. We can spare more but try with this."

Janice took the tins back to Balen. He pointed to the tins and smiled. "We need to fill up."

The woman inside shouted. "Put the tins by the door and fill your vehicles and go."

Balen and the others did as they were told and drove off, all vehicles full and enough to get them the rest of the journey.

.

12

The vans and cars pulled off the road onto a dirt track and then through the broken fencing onto a dusty field. There were stumps of what had once been olive trees but no sign of any habitation for miles.

Elaine extended the camper to give more space for everyone to meet. The sides slid out smoothly and she locked it all down so that they could come and go as they wanted. Hargreaves positioned himself in the kitchen and constantly turned-out tea and coffee for any who wanted some.

Archie and Shade had parked their camper a short distance away and the others had put up tents in a circle in the middle.

The dogs were running around to start with, but they soon came to lay together next to the large camper. Pedro had had a go of being with them, but he soon lost interest, he was just too small for their games and they didn't appreciate his nips.

Balen took Raven's hand, and they walked out of camp after indicating to Brad where they were going.

The dust was loose under their feet, but the ground was solid underneath. It was parched and cracked; it had been a long time since it had seen any water. The pipes lay about broken; the watering system destroyed.

There was a pile of large rocks, so they walked towards it in silence. Balen checked around, just in case and they sat on one of the rocks to watch the sun go down. It was still a huge ball in the sky, and they knew they had about an hour. They had stopped early because everyone was fed up with being in the vehicles and after a day of travelling, they needed a break. Sleeping in the cars and keeping on the move was one thing but they were getting closer, and they needed to recoup a little and have time. Space was what everyone craved now, space and time away from the metal boxes.

Balen took Raven's hand, and she leant her head on his shoulder. He kissed her on the head. "Do you miss your holding?"

Raven sat up a little. "Odd thing to ask. Actually, yes, I do. It was much easier there, simpler. Life since has been crazy. I miss just feeding the goats and getting on with things, the milking, making cheese and just enjoying that moment at the end of the day when everyone is quiet as they had what they needed. Since then, everything has involved noise."

Balen smiled, it was a wistful smile. "I know exactly what you mean. I never had the chance for that sort of peace, but I can imagine it. Even being at the compound was a lot easier than being Archangel. Not that I was in control, I can see that now. Nemesis manufactured and manipulated everything, fine-tuned you could say. We didn't stand a chance.

But then I suppose we were either naive or arrogant enough to believe that we were being driven by fate and our own decisions.

I wouldn't change most of it though. I think with hindsight I should have mistrusted Frank a little more when we came to the main complex though. He ran rings around me there and I believed in all his advice.

Looking back most of the rules and laws I put in place were dictated by him. They were not only unreasonable I am surprised they didn't insight rebellion. By the looks of things out there they did. Santander is in ruins. I had heard it was a thriving port and that Transition X was using it to move goods between the UK and Europe. That I can see now is a lie.

I'm beginning to wonder what is left of Europe."

Raven was thinking. "It is all a bit beyond me as I didn't see any of that paperwork but weren't you in touch with the "heads" of the other countries?"

Balen sighed. "When Transition X took over in Europe, we replaced them with our own men. They were far too dangerous to leave in power, or so Frank led me to believe. I am ashamed that I allowed him to deal with that. I can imagine now what he did, and I think we are seeing it first-hand. He fed me fake pictures of thriving towns. I dread to think what we will find."

Raven looked shocked. "So, you are saying that the governments in these countries have been wiped out? Has Transition X replaced them or what is happening?"

Balen looked at his hands. "I don't know. I had enough with running the complex. Frank pretty much took all that over. If things are the same in other places as Santander, then I don't know what we are going to find when we get where we are going."

Raven smiled. "Well, what we are going to find is a fresh start. There are going to be pockets of people and hopefully anyone who is trouble will be long dead. That is the way of things, people who look for trouble usually find it. We will have to rebuild or at least start something then see if we can help set up new ways. I am thinking that all my plans to be able to buy pipework etc may mean more scavenging that shopping."

Balen smiled as well. "You could be right. We will make what we can out of what we have. Do we raise this with the others?"

Raven thought about it. "Well, if we do, we might be able to scavenge some things along the way. It would also alter our thoughts about going near towns. It could be worth finding out if they are still there."

Balen shook his head. "Perhaps better to stay safe, establish a safe area and then reach out. We will be there by tomorrow evening. There isn't much we have seen on the way and likely there won't be. We will have to go out to forage. Look at this land. This could be what we have to work with. Irrigation and delivered water have always been a big part of the "green" here and as we get further south even more. There were enough troubles and problems when the golf courses took the water. A lot of the water came from reservoirs with dams, we must hope that they still hold. There are so many questions, and we are going to have to look for answers. It is better that our place is not on the mains water. It did have its own supply. That came from a well so hopefully it will still be the same. That is if it has been left alone but it is pretty remote, so we do stand a chance."

Raven was watching the sun which was now on its last rays. "When were you last there?"

Balen shook his head. "Me personally when I was about fourteen. Mum and dad, I don't know. I was deemed too much trouble to take with them and I never really wanted to go there much. Oh, how I've changed."

Raven smiled. "By the sounds of it thankfully so. So you spent time there with your father?"

Balen smiled. "No, only with mum. Asha was kept a big secret so that Michael's father didn't find out about him. That was why he thought I was his. They were a hard act to live up to and brother was such a perfect son with all his mental issues that they had to look after that there wasn't much room for the one who didn't need their help. I wasn't going to go into the military, so I was pretty much forgotten about when I started being an embarrassment. It gave me a free hand to do what I wanted though. I don't regret it. I didn't do much wrong, didn't do much right either. I just got on with life."

Raven put her arm around him. "From where I'm looking you have been more than the one to be forgotten about and as to doing much right, you have done more than many people."

Balen was watching the sun go down and they both fell into silence as the last rays faded. They sat there for a while, enjoying the peace before wandering back to the camp.

Hamish was on guard with Brendon and they wandered over. "Nice night."

Balen smiled. "Touch wood nice and peaceful."

Hamish smiled. His face just about visible in the moonlight. "Too peaceful. I was expecting crickets and all minds of night noises."

Raven looked around at the parched earth. "Crickets need food and there isn't much around here for them."

Hamish shook his head. "Could be the truth of it. Everyone is spread all over the place making the most of not being in the cars. It was decided not to light a fire as we don't want to draw attention to ourselves. Shame, it would be a lovely night for one."

Balen smiled. "We will be at the new place by tomorrow night. Hopefully that will be somewhere we can light a fire."

Balen and Raven carried on to the camper van. Oberon left the other dogs and joined them. Beast was already in the camper sitting at Elaine's feet. Elaine, Asha, and Hargreaves were deep in conversation over a couple of glasses of wine.

As they came in Hargreaves got up and got them both a glass. They sat down at the table and Hargreaves joined them.

The night passed without incident as did the journey. There were no vehicles on the road and either side of the road seemed abandoned. They passed the places which had been graffitied as they had been empty for years but as they passed what had been petrol stations they too were empty and had been looted.

There was no need to get any closer as the doors were off the hinges, glass broken and through the open window they could see that any shelves were empty.

Elaine had pulled the camper out in front as she knew the way as they left the main road. The undergrowth was still sparse and dry. Farms were untended and there were no animals they could see immediately. Then Elaine spotted something. Something small and black hanging around what looked like an abandoned shed outside the ruin of a house. There was one black thing and then another. She indicated with her hazard lights that she was going to stop and then pulled the camper to a halt. She jumped out, Asha followed her and Raven and Balen jumped out of their vehicle as well and came over to her.

Elaine put a hand on her arm, and she then pointed. Raven saw what she was pointing at, goats. Raven smiled and looked at her. "How far are we from your place?"

Elaine smiled back. "Under half a mile. I think we may have to come back this way later."

They got back into their vehicles but as they looked back there were black dots on the road, so they stopped. Raven got out and went to the camper. Elaine handed her a bowl of muesli and she walked back past the rest of the vehicles putting her finger to her lips to keep people quiet. She then walked back down the road to where the goats had started following them. Their bells were jingling as they saw her and started running towards her.

She offered the bowl, but they seemed more keen on jumping up and getting a fuss. Raven crouched down and gave the five of them the hugs they wanted. They were small size, local goats. All of them seemed really relieved to see her and as she turned to go, they followed.

It was quite a convoy which made its way up the track to the house near the top. The four jeeps went first, all very aware of everything going on around them and looking for trouble. This was followed by the two camper vans, the car and Raven who was walking, followed by the goats.

The house was a neat white square with a rooved balcony which was integral to the building. It had extensions around the back and outbuildings, all of which seemed quiet.

The windows were shuttered and there was no sign of damage as they came up the track. The jeeps stopped and the military trained crew got out and started to check out the area. They were armed and split up as they went around the main house, checking the shutters. They then checked the outbuildings and took the key that Elaine had given them and checked out the house. Minutes later which seemed like hours they came back out of the house and waved everyone in.

The campers and vehicles pulled up in front of the house. Raven got out of the camper, leaving Oberon and Beast inside. She then went to where Raven was waiting with the goats.

They led them to a shed, there was no straw for a bed, but the goats went inside gratefully and jumped up on the shelving around which was useful as a makeshift bed. Shelving which had once been the chicken laying area but for the night, without any straw it would have to do.

Balen turned up behind them carrying a container of water and he filled the water trough.

They shut the door and left them to it.

Once free of the worry of dog and goat misunderstandings they let the dogs out of the cars and vans and Elaine went into the house.

There was little furniture. The kitchen was basic but modern and had all that they needed. There were three bedrooms, a double and two lots of single beds and a bathroom which had a bath and a toilet.

Elaine looked around and sighed. "Welcome home everyone."

Frantic action followed as supplies were brought in and put in cupboards, the place was tidied and cleaned and eventually everyone had found something to sit on, candles were lit, and they were sitting in the living room.

Balen stood up. "Well, we are here. Tomorrow we can investigate getting the solar power system back up and running and that will hopefully pull water up from the well as well. Tonight, we are going to have to make do with candlelight. I would suggest that for now we keep the shutters closed so that we don't alert the whole valley to our presence. Once we have seen who is around, we will have a better idea of what we can get away with.

By what I remember there is one more farm in the valley below us. This area is remote and the farm we passed was the next nearest neighbour. Mum, what do you know about them?"

Balen sat down. Elaine thought for a moment. "They were an elderly couple, and they kept a few goats for milk. They also had chickens, but I doubt we will find them now. We can assume if the goats are looking for company that the couple have either left or passed on. They were friendly enough, ex pats, been there years and had no intention of leaving. We can go back tomorrow and see if we can find out what happened to them.

The other finca in the area is owned by a young couple with a couple of children. They were farming for self-sufficiency so they may still be there. I would suggest softly, softly as they never did like visitors much before all the trouble. They would be classic hippies if it was the sixties, but I doubt they were even born then.

The rest of this area is farmland, olives, almonds, and the like. Most of it is owned by a large farm and they only turn up when it is time to do things or harvest. They have never been any trouble and indeed they used to process my olives as well and gave me a good price.

The area is pretty self-watering in that the trees don't need more than they can get. I didn't supplement their water much so I hope that in the morning we will find a good crop out there. It is autumn, a bit late but we still might be able to salvage something."

13

The sun rose over the hillside. Raven was sitting out on the patio with a cup of tea and watched it as the first rays clawed their way across the dusty earth. The cactus garden to her right was looking healthy, perhaps a little in need of a top up but the plants had grown large in the Andalucian sunshine.

The looked out over the olive and almond trees, trying to think what they could do with them.

Balen came out of the house and joined her. He had brought a chair from the living room. Everything had been inside the house for safe keeping and as the night before they had turned in without looking around it was for the morning to look about and get a feel for the place.

They had put the tents up the night before and Raven and Balen had stayed in the camper. Elaine and Asha were the only ones who slept in their own room in their own house. They were still asleep as far as they knew as nobody wanted to disturb them. After so many years it was their time, Elaine could finally bring her lover home.

Balen sat down and put his cup on the table. "Well, this is nice. This is more than nice. I never thought I'd see this place again and I absolutely can't believe that I am here. So many happy memories."

Raven was sitting back on her chair and relaxing. "I can see why you would like it. It is as if the rest of the world doesn't matter, it is as if nothing matters, and we will deal with it tomorrow."

Balen smiled. "That is the problem but technically I suppose we don't have to worry. Aside from getting some food growing there isn't anything else to do. No plans for world domination, no Transition X and no Frank constantly on my back to do paperwork. Bliss. Well other than the list of tasks both you and mother will probably come up with. Have you fed the goats."

Raven smiled back. "There wasn't much to feed them with, but I gave them water just before dawn. I've found a feed shed but there isn't much in it. I might take a trip back to the other farm to see what I can find there. There might be some feed locked away. Other than that, there is plenty to forage if we let them out to wander. I want to see what the situation is with the dogs before we do that."

Balen shrugged. "They will have to work it out. The dogs aren't hunting dogs, they are shepherds so hopefully they will see them as "flock". My money is on the chihuahua to cause the most trouble, but Beast could, Cocker Spaniels are sort of hunters. We will have to sort that out later."

They sat in silence enjoying the peace and one by one people emerged from where they had spent the night, found a chair, and joined them.

Elaine appeared from around the side of the building. She was carrying a few rabbits and had obviously been out for a long time. She hung the rabbits on a hook by the door and turned to face everyone. "Good morning. I hope you slept well. Well, here we go!"

Balen stood up and offered her his seat which she graciously took. Balen went and got himself another chair from inside, a dining chair this time. She looked around everyone. "Not a lot to say really. We need to make sure there is no problem with the goats and the dogs, so I suggest we let the goats out first, let them get used to their environment and then see how the dogs react one by one."

Raven left the table and went to the shed and let them out. It was like a rodeo, they skipped out and bounced and danced about.

Oberon was laying outside the camper, and he wandered over for a sniff. The biggest of the goats approached and put her head down, offering a fine rack of horns to the curious dog. Oberon then sniffed her nose; they touched noses, and he went and laid down. Beast had been laying under the camper, she wandered over as well to see what Oberon was looking at but soon got bored, gave them an aloof look and wandered back to lay down in the morning sun.

Pedro on the other hand was in the car throwing himself at the window and barking. The goats looked at him, snorted and wandered off in a line towards the hillside.

Elaine shrugged. "Well, that went well. Of course, now their place here means we will have to put a fence in before we can grow anything. Small price to get milk."

They sat in the morning sun for a few hours just taking in the peace and quiet. There was nothing to do really so they did nothing.

At lunch time Hargreaves rustled up a meal for them, they moved inside to eat it and Hargreaves joined them. They eat in silence but when the meal was done Balen tapped on the table after Hargreaves had cleared the table. "I don't know if we need a plan, but we do need to see what is here, what we can use and I suggest we go on a trip back to see what is at that other farm.

I would suggest that Raven and I go back to the farm and the rest of you look around here. Elaine, can you take a couple of people of your choosing and go and see what is happening with our neighbours?"

Elaine looked about the expectant faces. "That seems like a plan. Take the car and see what you can find out where the goats came from."

Balen and Raven pulled out of the farm. They had left Oberon behind with Beast and they travelled armed but with an empty car. What was in it had already been unloaded into the pantry.

They turned into the drive of the next-door farm and everything seemed quiet. The house seemed intact, so Raven went to the door and knocked. There was no answer. Balen joined her and they cautiously walked around the outbuildings. The animal sheds had their doors open but there were signs that they were inhabited. Goat poo was fresh but also horse poo and what Raven recognised as pig poo in the stone built shed. She was about to mention this to Balen when she felt something push the back of her leg, as it pushed again, she looked down and there was a black pig. The pig was not alone, there were three of them, two sows and a boar. Head sow was by then rubbing her nose on Raven's leg and then looked up so that Raven could scratch her head. When Raven complied the other two rushed her for a fuss themselves.

They didn't look thin or in need of care. They just seemed very keen on some fuss and snorted and grunted.

The grunts alerted two horses which were wandering around the back of the house. They too came over to see what the fuss was all about. Again, they seemed healthy although neither of them was shod.

Raven gave Balen a nervous look. "We may have stolen their goats last night."

Balen shook his head. "I doubt it. All the water troughs are empty and look at that bedding, that hasn't been changed in ages."

They went back to the house, followed by three little piggies. Balen picked the lock this time and they stepped inside, shutting the door as the pigs seemed very keen to follow them.

The house was small, tidy but obviously hadn't been looked after for a very long time. Food in the now turned off fridge was rotten and so was the food in the freezer. They checked the room and found a note on the table.

"Two whom it may concern,

We have lived in this house for many years, and we love our animals very much. We cannot stay and we cannot take the animals with us. We have turned them loose in the hope that they will survive until someone finds them.

We have taken all we need, and we will not be back. What is left you can have. There is feed in the shed, enough for the winter. The deeds to the house are in the drawer, take them. We have gone to live with our family, we are too old to survive here.

We wish you all the luck in the world."

Balen held the note in silence after he had read it out. He then went to the dresser drawer and opened it and took a raft of paperwork out. He looked at the map which went with it. "Their land adjoins my mother's land and seems to be most of this hillside. I think our estate just got a bit bigger."

Most of the house had been cleared of all of the personal effects but the kitchen was intact, as was the tool shed and the outbuildings. The feed shed was well stocked with enough for all the animals for as they said, the winter.

Raven looked around. "If there is trouble it would be hard to defend this much land and two places."

Balen thought about it. "This remote I doubt we are talking trouble. The only trouble will be getting the solar up running and to find enough water. But those animals survived well on their own so there must be water around.

We had better report back if we can get past Pinky and Perky out there.

They took the note and the paperwork and put it in a bag they had found hanging in the door. They left through the back door and despite being nuzzled the pigs were no trouble. Once they were in the car and of no more interest, they mooched off to look for food.

The horses watched them go but before they left, they stopped and went over and stroked them. They seemed calm enough. There was one shed they had not yet opened. It was locked like the others, so Balen picked the lock and inside they found equipment for the horses and two Spanish saddles. Raven looked at Balen. "It is so tempting."

Balen looked at the horses. "An arm or leg break out here would be deadly. Sorry to be a party pooper but we had better be a bit more cautious before jumping on two unknown horses."

They got back into the car and as they were driving away the goats wandered back into the yard. They went to their sheds and then wandered out again. They watched the car leave.

Elaine had taken Archie and Shade with her to visit the neighbours next door. They all went armed but covertly. They also took a jeep in case they had to make a quick getaway.

At first glance the finca looked deserted. The plants were dead from no water and the place looked derelict. The house had its shutters closed and the door was intact.

Elaine looked at Shade who was looking worried. Her dreadlocks hung down over her right shoulder and she was twiddling them in her fingers. Elaine knew this was a sign she was stressed. "We don't know anything yet. Let's just knock."

Shade shook her head. "They are dead, I know they are dead."

Elaine looked at the dilapidated place. She had her doubts and she really wished she had brought the more experienced team with her. This was perhaps too much for Shade. Archie looked worried too. He rarely seemed to show much emotion but there was concern.

Archie walked up to the front door and rapped a couple of times. "Hello, anyone home. We are your new neighbours, here to be friends."

Elaine smiled. It was not a start she would have used but she was quite impressed.

They waited a while, everything seemed quiet and then the door opened. It swung back to reveal what would be a caricature of a hippie. All the clothes, the hair, the glasses. John Lennon on acid. There was a Yoko Ono too, not oriental but similarly dressed and sporting long rainbow hair. Rainbow because of the layers of dye which had obviously now started to grow out.

The wave and waft of weed which hit them made Archie step back. "Woah man, that is a bit serious. Hey, great to meet you. How's life?"

The man tried to hold his hand out to shake hands, but he couldn't quite focus. The woman wasn't much better. "So glad to meet you. Do you want to come in?"

Archie thought on his feet. "Thank you but no, just coming to meet you and we will see you again soon."

The woman waved and nearly fell over. "Yes, really soon, we like visitors."

The couple backed into the house, laughing.

When the door shut Archie smiled. "Well, that is one way to deal with an apocalypse."

Elaine smiled and nodded. They walked away quickly but Elaine signalled that they should stay in the car. She went around the back of the house and found a polytunnel full of weed growing with hydroponics. She had a quick look inside, fascinated by the system and then zipped up the door and returned to the other two. She was grinning. "Well hydroponics works well here."

Both Archie and Shade were laughing their heads off. "Elaine, you look like Miss Marple and have the sense of humour of, well I don't know. Let's get home."

Elaine laughed as well. "We might as well. We already have an aquaponics expert."

They got back in the car and drove back to the finca. By that time Raven and Balen had arrived back. Elaine walked over to their car as they were getting out. "What happened?"

Raven hesitated for a moment. "Well, they have gone, to be with relatives. They left a note and the papers. It seems the crew now includes Pinkey, Purkey and Pepper Pig plus two horses."

Shade was grinning ear to ear. "I always wanted a horse."

Raven laughed. "Great, you can muck out."

Elaine was thinking. "Horses, great, compost. This soil needs improving with fibre which holds water. Compost and manure do that but we have to compensate for water loss. Pigs, horses, goats, all the things we need."

Brad was grinning. "And bacon too."

Everyone glared at him.

Brad looked sheepish. "I was just saying."

Raven smiled. "Two sows and a boar, if we look after them, we'll have a bacon explosion soon enough."

Elaine was quiet and looked like she was thinking. "There is no challenge or problem in this place so far. That is good. That would be the first problem to solve. Now we can focus on looking at the land, sorting out what we can do with it and making sure we have a long-term plan for the animals."

Balen laughed. "We got lucky."

ABOUT THE AUTHOR

Insert author bio text here. Insert author bio text here Insert author bio text here Insert author bio text here Insert author bio text here Insert author bio text here text here Insert author bio text here Insert author bio text here Insert author bio text here Insert author bio text here Insert author bio text here Insert author bio text here Insert author bio text here Insert author bio text here here Insert author bio text here Insert author bio text here Insert author bio text here Insert author bio text here Insert author bio text here Insert author bio text here Insert author bio text here Insert author bio text here Insert author bio text here